AROUSAL

Ray Gordon

BLUE MOON BOOKS
NEW YORK

Published by
Blue Moon Books
An Imprint of Avalon Publishing Group Incorporated
161 William St., 16th Floor
New York, NY 10038

AROUSAL

ISBN 1-56201-231-2

9 8 7 6 5 4 3 2 1

Printed in the United States of America
Distributed by Publishers Group West

Chapter One

Jackie sat by the lounge window watching the snow fall from the heavy, grey sky. It had been snowing when she'd moved into her small flat, almost a year ago to the day. No doubt it will be snowing a year from now, she speculated, following a particularly large flake on its downward journey to the ground.

One winter was much the same as any other – the snow only appeared to be deeper when she was a small child. The summers didn't really change, either. They just seemed hotter and longer in those carefree days.

Contemplating her life and the experiences it had thrown at her, Jackie remembered school, her first day at work, her first boyfriend – her first sexual encounter. Summers and winters had passed bringing nothing more than normality. Years of mundane but probably necessary experiences that, it seemed, had all been part of the growing pains of life.

She smiled as she remembered the day she'd discovered masturbation. Her sheltered upbringing had taught her little of relationships, love – sex. She had just turned twelve when her mother had sent her to bed early for arguing with her. In the warmth of the familiar bed, her wandering hands had settled in the soft, hairless lips between her legs and moved instinctively, slowly and rhythmically round and round her stiffening nodule.

1

Her first ever orgasm had come quickly, like a bolt out of the blue, rocking her young body with frightening waves of unknown ecstasy. The exquisite, marauding sensations had caused her to cry out in pained delight. She'd discarded her dolls to spend guilty nights between the sheets, secretly enticing adult pleasure from her clitoris.

As the first dark curls of womanhood had sprouted and her breasts blossomed, she'd curbed the compulsion to touch herself. It was evil, sinful, she'd been told by a nun at the convent who'd caught her alone in the shower exploring her womanhood. The words had haunted her, destroying the illicit self-love, the delightful rewards her caresses had brought to her young body.

The years had passed and Jackie had met Ian, the first of her only two serious relationships. At eighteen, she'd fallen desperately in love with him and lost her virginity. With no sexual experience, she could only lie back passively and allow Ian's penis to penetrate her.

It had been painful at first, but she had soon learned to make the appropriate noises, even though her satisfaction came only from the closeness of the coupling. She had thought their lovemaking acceptable – nothing wild but warm, secure and wonderfully together.

But, she'd soon discovered, it hadn't been enough. Cruelly, Ian had informed her that her friend, Helen, could give him what he wanted in bed. Unlike Jackie, Helen was a real woman.

The second man, Brian, had sworn her his undying love and pleaded that she prove her love for him by surrendering her body. In her naivety, she'd agreed. One afternoon in a secluded woodland clearing she'd spread herself out under the hot summer sun in readiness for love.

Lowering her panties, Brain had brushed her young

curls aside and used his tongue to explore the intimacy between her soft cushions of flesh. She'd been revolted and pushed him away – it was dirty.

But using his charm, he'd talked her round and slid his tongue into her tight hole. She had cried quietly as he licked and sucked between her legs, murmuring in the form of obscenities what he liked doing to her young body. She'd felt no arousal, no gratification – just disgust.

Jackie had despised Brian for the depraved satisfaction he seemed to gain from sucking on her inner lips and pushing his tongue, rather than his penis, into her body. Was this love? He was abnormal, she'd told herself. But she had despised herself more than him for her abnormality. She should have enjoyed oral sex, a man's hot tongue stirring in her sanctum. From somewhere, deep within her, she knew that.

The inner conflict had raged as the months passed. She'd tortured herself with suspicions that a real woman would have craved Brian's attentions. Maybe her days of childhood masturbation had somehow twisted her mind? Perhaps the nuns had been right and her punishment was the inability to enjoy the delights of her body.

She'd loved Brian and endured his perverse ways in return for his love. But there were boundaries that she wouldn't cross. She'd stopped short of taking his penis in her mouth – protesting wildly at his suggestion, she'd pleaded with him to get psychiatric help. Retaliating, he'd told her that she was frigid – mental.

After eighteen months, Jackie had ended the relationship, not because of the pressure Brian had exerted on her but because she had discovered that he was married with two children. Devastated, she'd turned her disgust inward, towards herself, her body, swearing that she'd never allow another man near her.

For compensation, she'd thrown herself into her job at the bank. It had given her security and paid the rent. But even then, there had been no escaping the sexual intimidation.

Mucky Meg, as they called her, was a nymphomaniac and the bane of Jackie's life. Giving explicit details of her male conquests every morning, she would grin at Jackie and ask how *her* evening had been. Watching TV or reading a book was hardly exciting compared to Meg's outrageous night life.

Secretly, Jackie had envied Meg – the miniskirts, the low-cut tops which left nothing to the imagination, the way she walked, unashamedly displaying her full, rounded breasts. She'd often wondered why some girls seemed so sexually aware and precocious while others, like herself, were shy and reserved. And what it must be like to have several different men every week, all leching after her body.

It wasn't that Meg was more attractive than herself. Jackie wasn't stunning, she knew, but she was by no means plain. At twenty-six, her soft features and fresh complexion – seldom touched by makeup – still radiated youth. And her breasts, though hidden by a baggy jumper or loose blouse, were as ripe and firm as they had been at eighteen. Her long blonde hair was the stuff to drive men wild – when not wound up in a tight bun, begging to be left free to blow in the wind. Her big blue eyes shone with a child-like innocence and yet, to those with deeper vision, mirrored oppressed desires. It seemed that her whole demeanour was subtly designed to hide an imprisoned woman – a sensuous woman. A woman – a stranger within – craving the opportunity to surface and find satisfaction through her body.

Jackie supposed it was a certain charisma Meg had that

pulled in men like a magnet. But she had accepted the differences and resigned herself to her comparatively boring but comfortably safe way of life – until now.

Mesmerised by the swirling snowflakes, she remembered the bitter December morning she'd moved into her flat. One by one, a string of men had appeared, eager to plumb in the washing machine or fix the TV aerial. They were the would-be two-timing husbands of her work colleagues, all making their futile attempts to chat her up. She'd decided then that if she were to remotely consider having another man in her life he'd have to meet her stringent criteria – warm, kind, dependable, loyal and loving. A man who would treat her with respect. A man of her own – not someone else's husband. A man with whom she could build a home and have a family.

The snow was falling heavily as Jackie drew the curtains on the cold winter's scene outside. Another year had passed – nothing changing, forever the same. It was high time to draw the curtains on the winter of her life. She was more than ready for the sunshine, she reflected.

Mucky Meg sparked the final revolt as Jackie sat at her desk working out her mortgage repayments. Meg had had a particularly good night out and was telling everyone how she'd been laid by her latest man. How he'd pulled her knickers down with his teeth before making love to her with his tongue.

Listening to the sordid details and remembering her own disastrous experiences of oral sex, Jackie wondered whether she ought to make some changes – to venture out of her tiny world and discover what other people did during the long, winter evenings. Her thoughts were swayed when Meg asked how 'Prudie' had spent the night. The cold words hit home. Almost six years had passed since Jackie's last sexual encounter. She was certain something was wrong – the delight of a man's tongue buried deep between a girl's legs was, according to Meg, the ultimate sexual experience.

That evening, watching a boring television documentary and wondering what Meg was up to, Jackie decided to wander over the road to the local pub. She'd not been into a pub alone before but she knew that she had to escape the confines of her flat if she were to instigate a change. Not a change that would plunge her into oral sex with every man she met. But a variation that would bring her nearer to the outside world – and, possibly, to herself.

The pub had looked warm and inviting when she'd passed it on her way home from work. A colourfully-lit Christmas tree in the bay window had caught her eye, beckoning her to join in the festivities.

Donning a long skirt, new, white lace blouse and waisted jacket, Jackie took a final look at herself in the full-length mirror. Conservative, as usual, she thought, flattening the pleated skirt with her palms, but practical for a cold night. And, she decided, rather sophisticated. Twisting to one side to catch her profile, she released her hair. Remembering a TV advert she'd seen, she shook her head, allowing the long, golden curls to cascade over her shoulders. She was ready for her debut. Ready to change her life.

Christmas decorations adorned the homely, dimly-lit bar and a huge log fire welcomed her in from the cold as she ventured across the thick red carpet. Soft music played in the background, blending congenially with laughter emanating from another bar through an arched doorway.

Not ready to venture into the far bar, she chose a stool and positioned it where she could see people entering the pub. She hoped to make new friends, to drag herself out of the doom and gloom of her mundane life.

The barman was gay, she decided. Gay, but warm and friendly. His smile greeted her as she perched herself on the stool and placed her handbag on the bar. He didn't flinch an eyelid as she loosened her jacket, unintentionally revealing her long nipples protruding through the thin, silk blouse. Blushing slightly, she adjusted her jacket, nervously tossing her long blonde hair over her shoulder.

Sipping a gin and tonic, she soon began chatting. His name was Tim, he enlightened her, standing with limp wrist in mid-air, admiring her hair as only another woman would. Gold cuff-links sparkled against his crisp white shirt, silk tie held neatly in place with a matching gold pin. A chunky and obviously expensive identity bracelet fell over the back of his hand as he lowered his arm. Clean-shaven and well spoken, he seemed the perfect gentleman. But, sadly, gay.

'Do you work here full-time?' asked Jackie, wondering how he could afford such expensive jewellery.

'Not full-time. I just do a few sessions a week.'

'So where do you work? Your full-time job, I mean?'

'This is it – my only job.' A rich man, Jackie surmised as he launched unexpectedly into his life story.

His lover had left him, Tim confided. It had been awful – a dreadful experience, finding himself alone after two years of bliss. Suicide had been close but now he'd come to terms with it.

Jackie told Tim of her two disastrous relationships and quickly found an affinity with him. They swapped experiences and recalled times of tears and happiness with those they had once thought they'd loved. They laughed and joked about the plebs, as Tim called them – the people with no dress sense who wandered into the bar asking for

weird and wonderful drinks. But Jackie didn't discover
where Tim's money came from. Not from a part-time job
in a pub, she was sure.

Men were all bastards, they agreed, as he refilled her
glass, on the house. She was feeling pleased that she'd
made an effort, at last, to change her life. Tim would
become a good friend, she guessed. Being gay, he
wouldn't pose a threat. He wouldn't be interested in
trying to chat her up as, it seemed, so many men were.
Relaxing and letting her jacket fall open again, she began
to feel she was part of the nightlife, albeit a small part.

'What sort of people do you get in there?' Jackie asked,
looking towards the other bar where the laughter was
growing progressively louder.

'You'll find all sorts in there,' Tim laughed. 'Idiots,
drunkards, builders, solicitors. Go through, I'll introduce
you.'

Although panic stricken, she knew that she had to make
the effort. Handbag in one hand and drink in the other,
she wandered through the archway. Several heads turned
as she made her entrance. One or two mumbled com-
ments slurred from someone's lips followed by several
schoolboyish sniggers. She felt awkward, vulnerable,
wishing that she'd stayed in the top bar, or better still, at
home with a good book. But with an encouraging smile
from Tim, she walked to the bar.

'This is Jackie,' Tim announced, flashing her a wink as
he added, 'a very good friend of mine.' A flurry of
handshakes and offers of bar stools and drinks quickly
followed as she was immediately made to feel at home in
the small regulars' bar.

The crowd consisted only of men who, one by one, took
Jackie aside and tried their utmost to chat her up. She
imagined how Meg would have reacted. She'd be in

her element, she thought, as one man singled himself out from the others and sidled up to her.

The tall, dark stranger introduced himself as David. Handsome, articulate and well dressed in a light grey suit, his sincerely uttered compliments quickly boosted Jackie's confidence. She'd heard all the usual chat-up lines before, of course. But David embroidered them with poignancy. His dark, deep-set eyes intrigued her. He radiated an air of mystery that she hadn't known before. Only too aware of his sexuality, and hers, he was well practised in the art of body language. His movements were slow but power-ful, his voice deep and strong. Jackie soon found herself falling prey to his sensuous charm.

'Do you work locally?' David asked.

'Yes, at a bank. And you?'

'I'm an artist, for my sins.'

Jackie found herself thoroughly enjoying sipping her fourth gin and tonic in the company of a creative, profes-sional man. A mature man in his early forties. A nice change from her friends' lecherous husbands.

Suddenly aware of his gaze focused on her breasts, she tugged on her jacket, wondering why her nipples had become unusually hard. Covering herself, she wished that she'd worn something a little less revealing. Although, mingled with the gin, David's attention sent a quiver through her body. She'd only known that strange and exciting feeling twice before – when she'd been in love.

'What do you paint?' she asked, trying to ignore the butterflies in her stomach.

'Oh, this and that,' David replied nonchalantly, waving a hand in the air as if indicating that he painted anything and everything.

'Landscapes, animals? What, exactly?' Jackie persisted.

David raised his dark eyebrows and grinned.

'Landscapes, yes. But mainly portraits, I suppose,' he conceded, before ordering her another drink.

'Ah, portraits – the eyes, the expression, the feeling. I always wanted to go to art college but could never afford it,' Jackie sighed, suddenly imagining herself running with outstretched arms towards David through the soft hues of meadow grass.

'Not exactly,' he laughed, looking around to see if he could be overheard. 'You see – I paint erotica.'

Jackie sighed with disappointment. Thoughts of Mucky Meg returned, giving her a sinking feeling in her stomach. But she tried to hide her disapproval and show some interest in his work.

'I can't believe it,' she whispered. 'You really paint that stuff?' Surprised by the interest in her voice, she waited in anticipation for his reply. He only managed a smile and nodded, almost as if he was ashamed to talk about it.

Although her image of David as a professional painter had been shattered, Jackie was intrigued. She wanted to know more. Did he paint from photographs or live, nude models? What did he mean, exactly, by erotica? How long had he been painting naked women and when had he started? What had driven him to paint such things?

David was far from forthcoming with his answers. He mumbled something about having clients for sittings and easy money before wandering upstairs to the loo, leaving Jackie none the wiser.

Noticing her alone and somewhat despondent, Tim leaned on the bar and smiled.

'You've made a new friend, then?'

'Yes – David. He's nice, isn't he?'

'Not my type,' Tim laughed, flicking his quiff back. 'But yes, he seems a nice chap. I don't know a great deal about him. Rumour has it that he is an artist.'

'Yes, he was telling me,' said Jackie, wishing that David painted rolling landscapes or galloping horses instead of naked women.

Tim winked and nodded towards the arched doorway. Jackie turned to see David wandering towards her. Casually resting his elbow on the bar, he displayed an enchanting smile.

'I haven't seen you in here before. Is this your local?' he asked, finishing his drink.

Jackie noticed that he'd combed his black hair and straightened his tie. His charisma seemed somehow stronger now, his smile and dark eyes more captivating than before. The intrigue was deepening. She looked at his long fingers and imagined them holding a brush – painting every explicit detail of the naked female form.

'No, I've never been here before,' she eventually replied.

'So where do you go in the evenings?'

'Nowhere, really. I stay in.'

'In where?'

'I've a small flat just round the corner.'

She wished she hadn't used the word small to describe her flat – Meg would probably have described it as a palace. But then Meg had a way with words, and a vivid imagination.

'I live opposite,' David announced. 'Opposite the pub. That's why I'm always in here – no willpower!'

Jackie felt herself surrendering to his powerful magnetism. Thoughts of his work filled her mind. The barriers she'd built up to the male species over the years began to crumble. She'd not experienced sexual arousal for a long time and had thought that she never would again. But her neglected young body was sending out pleading messages for attention, for love – for sex.

'Can I see some of your work?' she asked, wishing that

she hadn't. David glanced at his gold wristwatch and shrugged.

'If you're really that interested, you can come over the road with me now,' he replied. Jackie detected a certain surprise in his tone as if she were the first person ever to take an interest in his work, let alone ask to see it.

The thought suddenly struck her that David must be single. He'd hardly take me home if he had a wife waiting for him, she surmised hopefully. Pushing thoughts of his work to the back of her mind, her stomach somersaulted at the prospect of romance. But she wasn't going to let go of her memories, her experiences with men – the lies and deceit. David had charm, yes. And she couldn't deny that he would make a fine catch. But she was determined to keep her feet firmly on the ground.

Slipping off the bar stool, her jacket fell open showing her ever-hardening nipples straining against her thin blouse. Noticing David's eyes feasting, she buttoned her jacket, wondering if she should go alone to the home of a man who painted naked women.

As she followed David through the arched doorway, Tim flashed her a warm smile and told her to take care. She didn't need Tim's advice. She would take care – too much so to let herself go and enjoy life. She would take care not to fall into the same trap for the third time. But, she knew, if she were to change her life, she would have to relent – just a little. But certainly not to the extent of becoming one of David's models.

The street was cold and uninviting. Snow fell heavily, bringing an uncanny silence to the night. Only a few cars were out, moving cautiously along the white, slippery roads.

As David took Jackie's hand to lead her across the road, instinct told her that she should get to know him a little better before going to his house. Perhaps meet him for a drink again or have a meal together. But, it seemed, it was too late. Her hand still in his, she had already climbed the stone steps to his front door.

Opening the huge door to the Victorian house, David showed her into the large hallway where the welcoming warmth hit her. The house was quiet, apart from a grandfather clock ticking loudly in the corner. David obviously lived alone, she concluded, wishing that she'd worn jeans instead of a skirt.

The lounge abounded with fine antiques, furnishing the peaceful atmosphere with a comfort that only money could buy. Perfectly appropriate for an artist's home, Jackie decided, gazing at the dozens of paintings lining the walls.

Making herself comfortable on the leather Chesterfield, she began to feel at ease in David's presence. Her fears were quickly subsiding, giving way to fairy-tale dreams of becoming his wife and living in his beautiful house instead of her tiny flat. Discarding her fantasy, she swore to keep her head. Although the scene was set for love, she wasn't ready. She'd never be ready, she knew.

'Are these all your own work?' she enquired, scanning the paintings of naked women as David passed her a glass of wine.

'Yes, most of them. Bring your drink, we'll go into my private studio,' he suggested, his dark eyes sparkling in the light. She hesitated, but his reassuring smile quelled her doubts. David was a gentleman – she was safe.

Jackie gazed in amazement as he slid an entire section of book-shelving to one side, revealing a stairway to the basement. 'A secret passage,' she breathed, rising to her feet.

'To my secret world,' David whispered dramatically as

she followed him down the old wooden stairs. The bookshelving had closed automatically by the time they reached the bottom step. The lock clicked loudly, causing Jackie to jump.

'Security,' David proffered. 'If I'm burgled, at least my best work will be safe.'

Jackie found herself in a small den. Soft lighting picked out several oil paintings of naked women in erotic poses set in the Victorian era. His real work, she supposed, admiring a painting of two young women entwined provocatively, tasting the delights between each other's milk-white thighs.

An easel covered with a white sheet stood in the corner of the room. Brushes, rags and paints littered a huge knee-hole desk. A large Chinese tapestry draped on the wall behind the desk caught her eyes.

'This is nice,' she commented, running her hand across the heavy material. David didn't answer. He seemed somehow nervous, as if he were hiding something. Although now instinctively suspicious of his motives, Jackie continued her self-guided tour of the den. An old but expensive couch was set at an angle in the centre of the room giving the appearance of disorder. But, she noticed, it was strategically placed under several spotlights, no doubt to illuminate his naked models. Perhaps he's imagining me on the couch, naked, she thought fearfully as she gazed at David hovering in the corner of the room.

Looking past him, Jackie noticed a small pine door, almost obscured by shadows, hiding ominously in the far corner. She turned her wide eyes back to David.

'I keep my best work in here,' he said nervously, turning a key that seemed far too large for the door.

Cautiously, Jackie followed him into a larger room

where the obvious centre-piece was a huge four-poster bed. More erotic paintings adorned the walls. Background music sounded as if from nowhere as he sat on the bed and beckoned Jackie to join him.

'Well?' he asked as the door clicked shut by itself.

'Well what?' she replied fearfully, turning to look at the door and wondering if it was locked.

'Aren't you going to join me?' he asked, patting the quilt.

Jackie's heart raced as she glanced first at David and then at the paintings. The young, naked women seemed to return her gaze, inviting her to join them in their provocative games. 'Look, I like you, David. But we've only just met,' she spluttered, tentatively moving towards the bed. Her trust failing, she hesitated, waiting for reassurance.

'It's all right, I don't bite,' he laughed, patting the quilt again.

Sitting some distance from David, Jackie pulled her jacket securely over her breasts. He moved in closer and smiled. Taking her glass and placing it on the bedside table, he opened her jacket and gently slipped it over her shoulders. Aware of her erect nipples, she felt her face flush and, smiling nervously, she folded her arms to cover her obvious arousal.

'Your work, David. You said you'd show me your work,' she said firmly.

'You've seen my work. There, on the walls,' he replied, glancing in the direction of the erotic oil paintings.

A strange desire ran over Jackie's trembling flesh as he opened her arms and kissed her full lips. She tried to pull away but she was becoming weak – and he was strong.

Gently pushing her down onto the bed, he kissed her long neck and nibbled her ear. She was enjoying his attention but felt he was going too fast. Thoughts of her

15

previous relationships surfaced and she pushed against his chest. She knew that she was nearing the entrance to the trap – the trap that men set to break the hearts of lonely women who sought love. She thought of Meg and how she would have made passionate love to David and then delighted in telling her story in all its sordid glory.

'I'd better be going now,' she stammered as he began to unbutton her blouse. Silently, he continued his task. 'I really must go, David!' she asserted as he released the last button and parted the soft silk, exposing her lace bra to his appreciative gaze.

'Are you going to take your clothes off?' he almost ordered, abruptly lifting her bra clear of her firm breasts.

'Where's your charm gone?' Jackie yelled, trying to ease herself back into her bra and escape his grip. 'Or do you only use that to lure women here?'

'I didn't lure you, Jackie,' he countered, taking her hands. 'You came here by choice, remember?'

'I came here to see your work!' she retorted. 'I'm not one of your bloody models!'

Gently but firmly, David pinned her to the bed. His deep eyes sparkled again, giving her an unfamiliar feeling of excitement in her stomach. Again, he kissed her neck and slowly worked his way down to her pointed breasts.

Fear and sexual arousal combined to blur Jackie's thinking. As he took her long nipple between his lips and gently sucked, her mind ran wild with emotion. Her breathing deepened as he milked her throbbing nipple until it ached – until *she* ached for sexual relief. Never before had she known such arousal. She fought it, but her long-dormant sexual drive was up and rising at an alarming rate.

David moved down and began to kiss her smooth, flat

stomach. Jackie quivered as his tongue found its way into her navel. Her muscles spasmed. But still she fought her innermost desire – the stranger within.

Taking David's head in her hands Jackie tried to wrench him away but he moved further down to the top of her skirt. Easing the elastic waist band down he teased the white flesh just above her mound with his warm mouth. His hands working with the subtle skill of a magician's, he removed her shoes as he held her attention on her trembling abdomen. Moving back to her breasts, he spread her arms, holding her wrists high above her head as he kissed and gently sucked each nipple in turn.

Jackie had almost given in to the waves of desire coursing through her body when she suddenly realised that something was very wrong.

'What's this?' she screamed. Raising herself on her elbows, she gazed in terror at the leather straps binding her wrists. She tried to climb from the bed only to find that her ankles were also shackled. David had worked quickly and unnoticed while expertly distracting her.

Standing up, he moved to the end of the bed and grinned wickedly. Struggling to free herself as she cursed him, Jackie found that her hands and feet were moving mysteriously apart. Horrified, she looked down to see David heaving on a rope controlling the straps. He continued to pull until her limbs stretched out to the four corners of the bed, leaving her body open and completely defenceless.

'Let me go, you bastard! Let me go!' she screamed hysterically as she continued her futile struggle to break free. Ignoring her pleas for mercy, David lifted her skirt and pulled it up over her stomach. Her red panties clung tightly to her body, faithfully following the contour of her swollen lips and dividing groove.

'There's a wet patch on your knickers,' David observed gleefully, stroking the warm, soft material with the back of his finger.

Vivid memories of grey, convent knickers suddenly flashed through Jackie's mind. How many times had she rubbed through them, beneath them? Hiding them from her mother, she would wait for an opportunity to sneak into the bathroom and wash the white stains from the crotch.

'I'd better take them off,' David announced unashamedly, pulling them down over her mound as she pleaded in one breath, screaming obscenities in the next.

'What a shame you wear tights. Stockings would have made things so much easier,' he mocked crudely, slipping a finger under the elasticated waistband.

'You're a filthy pervert!' Jackie screamed. 'Touch me and I'll kill you!'

Although she twisted and gyrated her hips violently, David managed to tear the flimsy panties and pull them free. Thrashing her head from side to side, she hurled more obscenities at him as her tights gave way to expose her soft, flattened pubic hairs. Given their freedom, the short curls sprang to attention, bringing life to the dark, triangular bush.

Moving between her thighs, David sucked and kissed the dark, musky hair. 'You're going to like this,' he breathed, holding her hips firmly as he buried his face in her warm, damp nest.

'I *don't* like it. I want you to stop,' she whimpered as his tongue parted her outer lips and began to explore the soft, intimate flesh within. She felt broken – violated. She'd spent the best part of her life hiding the most intimate part of her body with lovingly chosen shrouds – panties, bikinis, skirts, even jeans. Now her own sacred spot – her very nucleus – lay bared, open, before the eyes of a brutal stranger.

'You *will* like it – if you let yourself go,' David assured her, breathing in her aphrodisiacal scent while locating her clitoris with the tip of his tongue.

'I won't! You can't do this to me, you bastard! I'll go to the police! I'll kill you! I'll . . .'

Jackie caught her breath and then sighed deeply as David moved his fingers up and down her slit until he found her entrance. Thrusting two fingers into her open body, he gently massaged her cervix until the fluid flowed in torrents over his hand.

Images of Meg disturbed her racing mind as he stretched her open wider and continued his tantalising massage. Releasing his grip on her hip, he began to stroke and caress her swelling clitoris with his free hand as he kissed and gently bit the soft, white flesh of her inner thigh. She gasped as he ran his finger round and round the bursting bud at the top of her valley, the wondrous sensations inducing more warm fluid to pour from the soft walls of her open vagina, bathing and lubricating the intruding fingers.

Jackie had stopped struggling. Suddenly, to her horror, she became aware of an approaching orgasm. She knew she couldn't fight the inevitable as David pressed his mouth over the stretched, pink flesh between her vaginal lips, his fingers sliding in and out of her body as he teased her clitoris with his tongue.

Whimpering with each breath, she could take no more. It was as if her mind had stepped aside to allow a force far stronger than she to possess and use her body for its own debased pleasures. She became rigid as the sensations continued to well up from her clitoris. Pulling against the leather straps, she cried out as her orgasm swamped her very being.

Wet, breathless and trembling, she watched as David methodically removed his clothes, revealing his strong, firm, tanned body. His long, thick penis stood out threateningly, ready to enter her. She gazed in terror as he positioned himself, his huge rod between her open thighs.

Feeling the hardness of his penis pushing against her tight lips, she cried out again.

'You can't do this! I could have loved you – but now you've made me hate you!' Yet somewhere deep within her mind, a voice told her to relax and enjoy the pleasures she was about to receive.

David's penis slid easily into her warm, slippery hole. She gasped as its length opened and filled her until it pressed gently against the softness of her cervix. Slowly at first, he slid his shaft in and out, his dark eyes watching hers with each progressively harder thrust. There was no love or affection – just the cold union of their genitals, a vagina enveloping an intruding penis.

Ramming Jackie's tethered body with such force that she clung desperately to the leather straps, David sucked and bit on her nipples until they stood hard and erect. The repeated pounding against her mound pushed her up the bed until her shackled ankles strained to hold her in check. Sinking his fingers into her buttocks, he pulled her hips up to meet each hammering thrust of his hard penis.

She felt her second orgasm coming as his body turned rigid and, with several splitting thrusts, filled her with his sperm. Her muscles rhythmically crushed his throbbing penis, massaging every last drop from his body as she cried out in the grips of an excruciating climax. 'I've come! I've come! You bastard! Ah you bastard!'

Finally, David collapsed across her heaving breasts, gasping his appreciation of her young body. Jackie lay trembling, her legs rudely forced open as, slowly, he slid his penis from her hole and climbed from the bed. Adding to her humiliation, he delighted in watching his sperm trickle over her labia to run down between her buttocks. Again, she pulled on her bonds, desperate to cover her defiled body – to end the degradation.

David dressed quickly, barely glancing at Jackie as she pleaded for her freedom and continued her threats of retaliation. Her young naked body shone in the light, exposed to his admiring glance as he turned before moving towards the door.

As she cried out again, he closed the door behind him, turning the key. Left alone with only the soft music for company, she sobbed, knowing that he'd be back for more. And most likely, more and more until . . . Until what, she didn't know.

Desperately, Jackie tried to compose herself. To reason. To find some logic amidst the confusion. She would stay calm, she had to. Preserving her sanity was all she could do until the chance of escape came. Sooner or later it would come, she knew, she hoped . . .

Planning her revenge, she closed her eyes. Lulled by the hypnotic music and heat of the room, she almost slipped into sleep. Opening her eyes suddenly, she thought it had all been a dream. She tried to move – then the reality hit her. She was alone, imprisoned, in her cell.

Had she slept? She didn't know. She had no idea of the time – whether it was night or day. Her fear returned quickly when she raised her head and called out for David – her pleas were met with silence. Flopping back onto the soft pillow she tried to relax. Her limbs ached, stretched by the leather straps. She was hungry, frightened and her body still lay mercilessly open and vulnerable – ready for her abuser.

Tugging on the straps to test their strength, Jackie resumed her plans for revenge. She'd kill him. Blackmail him. Somehow, she swore, she'd get David.

Her thoughts were distracted by the key turning in the lock. The small door slowly opened. David smiled and walked towards the bed with a tray.

'I've made you breakfast,' he said softly, placing the tray on the table before adjusting her pillows.

'You'll have to untie me, then,' she murmured, forcing a laugh and searching for a sign of compassion in his eyes. Better to play along with him and his depraved games than to show fear or fight him, she thought instinctively.

David stroked her dry, matted pubic hair with his fingers and smiled. Jackie shuddered as he bent down to kiss her inner thigh. She suspected, fearfully, that he intended to keep her tied to his bed as his plaything – possibly forever.

'I need to wash,' she announced, knowing that her only chance of escape would be when she was free of her bonds. Then she could retaliate, lash out and flee.

'Later,' he replied quietly, running his tongue up and down the length of her glistening valley.

As David licked and sucked at her inner lips, parting them with his tongue to rediscover her clitoris, Jackie desperately tried to plan.

'You're a filthy, disgusting pervert,' she whispered as the tears ran down her cheeks.

'Call me what you will,' he laughed. 'I know that you've enjoyed yourself as never before. I'm right, aren't I?'

Jackie said nothing as he lowered his head and parted her lips again to taste her warm folds. She was horrified to find herself becoming aroused again as he nibbled and licked the soft, pink flesh. Fighting the powerful stranger within, she finally surrendered and allowed her body the pleasures of his tongue. Moving up to her clitoris, he gently caressed and teased it until she was carried again to the summit of sexual ecstasy. She thrashed her head and shouted obscenities at her jailer as the orgasm ripped through her. Ignoring her cries, David continued to kiss and caress her throbbing clitoris, only stopping when it retreated to its hide, satisfied as never before.

As Jackie rested and allowed her orgasm to subside, David loosened the leather straps and gave her freedom. Imagining that he was planning to play with her, she didn't move. She guessed it was a ploy to chase her defiled body around the room before recapturing her and tying her down again after the exercise.

'The bathroom's upstairs,' he said, placing her clothes on the bed as he turned to leave.

'Is this it?' she yelled. 'You humiliate me, use me. And all you can say is – the bathroom's upstairs!'

'If ever you want more, you know where to find me,' David called as he climbed the stairs. 'And you can't deny that you enjoyed it.'

Fuming, she dressed quickly and fled the house before David had second thoughts. For some reason he'd changed his mind. Pity, perhaps? Or fear of reprisals? She didn't know or care – she was free.

The huge orange sun hung low in the sky. The deep snow lay even, obliterating the divide between the path and the road. Jackie breathed in the cold, refreshing morning air as she hurried the short distance to the safety of her flat.

Slamming the front door behind her, she made straight for the shower and peeled off her clothes. Under the hot jet, she cleansed her young, used body, vigorously lathering her sticky pubic hair until every trace of the cocktail of sperm, juice and saliva had gone. But she couldn't cleanse her mind, her thoughts. Still torn with rage and sexual satisfaction, she could do nothing to dispel the vivid images of her body being used and brought to orgasm by a virtual stranger. She could still feel the sheer size of David's penis rudely pushing its way into the depths of her body.

After the shower, she made a cup of coffee and flopped onto the sofa. She contemplated calling the police. But she knew that she had no cause for complaint. She had gone to David's house of her own accord. She considered blackmail. But who would she tell? Tim? Or the others in the pub? They would never believe her wild and wonderful story.

Suddenly realising it was nine-thirty, she grabbed the phone and rang the bank. Meg answered. She was sorry to hear that Jackie was ill. If she knew what I've been through she'd probably come in her knickers, thought Jackie, replacing the receiver.

Disgusted and yet excited by her uncharacteristic thoughts, she went to her room to rest. Under the warmth of her quilt, she mulled over the night's events. Despising David and yet, at the same time, hoping to see him again, she decided to visit the pub that night. He wouldn't have the audacity to go there again, surely? As she drifted off into a deep sleep, someone inside her hoped he would.

Chapter Two

Jackie woke with a start at mid-day. Nightmares of David and the appalling things he'd done to her had constantly wracked her tormented mind as she'd drifted in and out of sleep. The liberties he'd taken with her defenceless body had been incredible, although her orgasms had brought her tremendous relief, she had to admit. But she couldn't understand why, despite her fear, she'd enjoyed the experience. A stranger within, a powerful possessing force was gradually surfacing and taking control, pushing her aside to fulfil a desperate need for sexual gratification.

Under the warmth of her quilt, she suddenly became acutely aware of her naked body – vulnerable, unguarded against her wandering hands. Running her fingers gently over the soft skin of her stomach sent a quiver of excitement up her spine. Her long-dormant clitoris, crudely awoken, was now calling for more attention. Feeling incredibly sexually alive, she allowed the tips of her fingers to run in circles around her aching nipples causing the brown tissue to harden, but her moistening valley urgently demanded her concentration – her caresses.

Kill him? Possibly, she mused as she located the stiffening bud between her swollen lips. But that would be too good for the bastard. She'd think of something else. Something that would leave him sorry for the rest of his life. Money crossed her mind as her thoughts drifted between David and her now fully erect clitoris. She had precious little and David, obviously, had more than enough. But she'd already decided that blackmail wouldn't work: there had to be another course of action that she could take. What, she didn't know. But no matter how long it took, she knew that she'd make him pay for his crime.

The drug-like sensations emanating from the depths of her pelvis dragged Jackie's thoughts away from David, focusing her attention between her legs. With a vengeance, her clitoris suddenly pulsated and burst into ecstasy under her massaging fingers. As if retaliating for the years of denial, her body convulsed, forcing her to arch her back and breathe out grateful cries of satisfaction.

Her stomach somersaulted as her mind drifted back to David's firm, tanned body towering over her as she lay strapped to his bed. Although she couldn't deny her hatred for him, she found herself desperately longing to be penetrated by his thick penis again. To feel his hardness between her outstretched thighs, relentlessly thrusting into the centre of her very being to fill her full of the fruits of lust.

Remembering her childhood days of masturbation, she eased her soft lips apart and teased another exquisite orgasm from her insatiable bud. Bathed in ecstatic ripples of pleasure, she raised her legs and pushed three fingers deep into her hole, stretching the soft flesh, adding to the ecstasy between her legs. The seemingly endless climax caused her muscles to grip and rhythmically knead her manipulative fingers as she breathed heavily and pictured David's long, thick, intruding shaft violating her body. Her breathing slowing and her heart quietening, she relaxed, calm and satisfied.

Reflecting on the night's events for the hundredth time, she climbed from the warmth of her bed and stepped into the shower. Not for a moment did her clitoris allow her to forget the delights it had to offer, or her memory the image of David's penis hovering menacingly over her mound. Lathering the soft, pink folds between her legs caused her bud to stir and send electrifying sensations over her body. Every nerve ending tingled, accentuated by the tiny water jets playing on her glowing skin like a thousand darting tongues. Although her legs were weak with lust, she managed to repress her desire to masturbate and stepped from the shower, from her fantasy.

Drying her breasts with a soft towel provoked her milk buds to harden, heightening her perception of her nakedness as she stood before the mirror, twisting and turning, admiring her gentle curves, the soft hair below her stomach, her femininity. Covering the temptress between her legs with her panties, again she managed to quell the desire to appease her yearning bud.

Dressed in her knee-length skirt and white blouse, Jackie wandered into her bedroom to dry her hair. But even as she sat at her dressing table she could barely resist the temptation to touch herself through her now wet silk panties. Only when the hunger pains grew in her stomach did she manage to control her inner desire.

Darkness fell at four o'clock – still, the evening seemed so far away. But when it arrived, it would bring with it a slim chance of seeing David in the pub. Should he not turn up, as she was sure he wouldn't, she would call at his house and confront him.

Whether to scream at David or cling to him, Jackie didn't know. Her confusion only increased every time she remembered the orgasms that had surpassed all others in her life. She desperately needed to see him, to study him and try to understand her ever-changing feelings for him. Hatred? Infatuation? Lust? Or possibly a potentially lethal cocktail of all three?

The hours had also been lengthened by wandering aimlessly past his house in the snow, hoping for a fleeting glimpse of the man who had sadistically bared and defiled her tethered body. The man who had taken her morals, her values and ruthlessly cast them aside.

A strange anticlimax came with the evening and she suddenly became overwhelmed with disappointment, as if the last twenty-four hours had been nothing more than a strange but wonderful erotic dream. Rather than pinch herself, she touched herself through her panties to see if she was dreaming. The pleasant twinge between her damp lower lips left her in no doubt that she was, indeed, wide awake. In response to her touch, her clitoris stirred and sent another pleading tingle over her body, but there was no time to feed her ever-growing sexual appetite.

Rummaging through her wardrobe, Jackie triumphantly pulled out her miniskirt. She'd bought it on impulse with a view to changing her life some years before but had never found the courage to wear it. Now her life was changing rapidly, she would wear the skirt defiantly and watch the men's eyes as they gazed at her slender, stockinged legs. But she would deny anyone more than a lecherous gaze. She would wear it only to excite, tease and tantalise. And then, in the warmth of her bed, she would appease her aroused clitoris, bringing herself to one wondrous orgasm after another.

Discarding her bra, she looked down at her nipples and grinned. They were hard, long, and deserved to be shown off. Driven by an inner force, she buttoned her blouse and admired the protrusions provocatively marking the centres of her firm, full breasts. Bending down in front of the mirror to slip her shoes on, she caught sight of a nipple, subtly exposed by her gaping blouse. Grinning wickedly, she imagined herself on a bar stool, leaning forward to pick up her handbag while the men shuffled for a better view.

Not being used to wearing makeup, it took Jackie some time to apply her lipstick and eye-liner. Not too tarty, but sexy, she mused, gazing into the mirror at the breathtaking transformation. Brushing her long blonde hair, she wondered why she'd never bothered to make herself up before, why she'd denied her femininity.

She had it firmly in her mind to get her own back on David, on all men, as she wandered into the pub. Three men had lied, tricked and used her and now all men would pay. Although she couldn't deny the pleasures he'd given her, the humiliation, the degradation that David had put her through demanded retaliation.

Sitting on the bar stool, she lay in wait. With her red miniskirt provocatively high around her thighs, showing a small triangle of white material between her legs, she was ready. Opening her jacket, she looked down and smiled. Free from the confines of a bra, her nipples stood out proudly for all to see.

Tim immediately noticed and commented on the change in Jackie. Not just her physical appearance but, he observed, incorrectly or not, she wasn't sure, that she must be in love.

'I don't think I'd call it love,' she laughed, remembering her mind-blowing climaxes and wondering if it *was* some kind of self-destructive, soul-destroying love that had her in its evil grip.

'What, then?' Tim asked innocently.

'What indeed?' Jackie replied, turning her head as the

door opened. A young man wandered up to the bar and flashed her a tentative smile. While Tim served him, she took a deep breath and leaned forward to fiddle with her shoe. Her blouse hung away from her breasts, displaying her long, brown nipples to the young man's appreciative gaze. As she slowly raised her head, she smiled and caught his eye. Visibly stunned, he turned to Tim as if he'd seen nothing. But he looked back, as she knew he would, and lowered his eyes to her crotch.

Realising the potential of her body, the power she could exert over men, Jackie sat upright and allowed her legs to fall apart slightly. The young man's eyes widened at the sight of her panties, stretched tightly over her bulging nether lips. She decided that she would practise the fine art of body language until she could blatantly display her wares and yet appear totally oblivious, completely innocent.

The door opened again and, to Jackie's amazement, David wandered in. As if deliberately to spoil her fun, he strolled up to the bar and smiled. He wore a dark suit, white shirt striped with blue and a silk tie. He was cool, smooth. And she hated him for it.

'Would you like a drink?' he asked nonchalantly as Jackie watched the young man wander off to find a seat.

'No, thank you,' she replied coldly. She wanted to shout, to scream at him, but the words, the anger, wouldn't come.

Aware of the rising tension, Tim quickly passed David his usual gin and tonic and disappeared into the other bar.

'You've got a bloody nerve,' Jackie spat the minute they were alone.

'And you've got a wonderful body,' he returned with his usual captivating smile.

'You used me last night,' she hissed. 'You forced me.

Tied me down against my will – and raped me!'

'Rape? Oh, come on! Surely, you're not complaining?' he laughed, his deep eyes gazing into hers. 'How can you complain? You loved every minute of it!'

Jackie's stomach somersaulted as he gazed down at her white panties, just visible under her short skirt. His hair, dark, clean-cut and swept back, brought vivid memories of his head between her legs – his tongue, expertly taking her to previously unknown ecstatic heights. He was right, she knew, she had enjoyed every minute of it. Suddenly, she felt weak and vulnerable again as the inner force began to rise.

Aware of her clitoris stiffening and her nipples hardening, she struggled to fight her uncontrollable sexual desires. She rudely declined David's offer to join him for coffee in his studio, although she wished that she had the courage to accept. Why she was denying herself the new-found pleasures she craved, she didn't understand. She still had some control over the powerful stranger within.

'Should you change your mind, you know where to find me,' David quipped, and quickly finished his drink. Jackie said nothing as she watched him leave. It wasn't a case of changing her mind, but simply following her instincts – to follow David. The door closed behind him, leaving her torn, aching – despising him for his flippancy and yet desperately needing to submit to his sexual charm.

Tim was no help. He joked and laughed and talked of the weather but his meaningless words drifted across the bar unnoticed. Jackie could no longer fight the magnetic pull acting on her weakening mind. Her willpower drained, she allowed a finger to find its way up her thigh and slip under her panties to touch the wetness inside. Dreamily, she moved her panties aside and slid her inquisitive finger into the warmth.

Suddenly becoming aware of Tim rambling on about the coming of summer, she smiled. He had no notion that the young woman he was talking to had a finger inside her hole – enticing the soft flesh to produce warm, milky fluid.

Returning to reality, as if waking from a dream, Jackie wondered what on Earth she was doing. What sort of change she was going through. From the prudish bank clerk to what? Something was lurking in the depths of her subconscious, goading her to expose her body, coaxing her to become something that she wasn't. Sitting in a pub fingering herself was so far removed from the old Jackie that she found herself horrified.

'I must go, Tim,' she sighed, slipping her finger out and positioning her panties to cover her bulging labia. Tim smiled and told her to enjoy herself.

'You're only young once,' he said. 'If you don't take what you want while it's on offer, you'll only live to regret it.'

Tim's words echoed through her mind as she rang David's doorbell and waited in the cold night air. There was no reply. Her heart sank. Turning to go, she hesitated. Driven by a strange power, she faced the door once again. Pressing the button, she felt her anger rising. 'I can't do this,' she whispered. 'I can't go in there.'

The cold began to creep through her jacket as she raised her hand to ring the bell yet again. Still there was no answer. In her anger, she banged on the door with her fists. It swung open, inviting her into a land of fantasy. A land of sex and lust that had intoxicated her confused mind.

The familiar sound of the grandfather clock welcomed Jackie as she quietly closed the door behind her and entered a world far removed from the bank, her flat – her mundane life. A magical world that she was drawn to like a lamb to the slaughter.

Although empty, the house was warm and inviting. Cautiously, she made her way to the lounge. The book-shelving was open, revealing the stairway to Jackie's world of humiliation. Her body ached in the confines of her tight clothes as she pictured the bed, the leather straps – David's penis. Biting her lip, she tentatively moved towards the stairs, only too aware of her clitoris stirring expectantly beneath her tight panties. Wondering if David was lying in wait, she slowly descended into the bowels of the house.

The main room accepted Jackie's presence with warmth. The familiar smell of oil paints filled her lungs, enticing vivid memories of wanton lust to surface and send electrifying tingles over her body. She eyed the easel and wondered if she were no more than just a model for another erotic painting. A painting that would only reveal its secrets, her destiny, once she was inside the den and the last stroke finished. How will the painting depict me? she wondered as she pushed open the small door. Strapped to the bed, legs rudely open? Or will he cleverly portray me in one of his lesbian scenes?

The sight of the four-poster bed brought a grin to her face. The leather straps hung ominously, waiting to bind her slender wrists and ankles in readiness for depraved sexual torture. Having no power to resist the ever-persuading stranger within, she could do nothing as her legs took her forward towards the bed.

A note lay on the quilt. Jackie picked it up and read the words. 'I'll be with you shortly'. Cursing her naivety and David's impertinence, she crushed the paper in her hand and flung it to the floor. 'I'll be with you shortly,' she hissed, turning to the door. 'Well, I won't be with you!

I've come to my bloody senses!'

The door wouldn't yield – it had automatically locked, trapping Jackie, once again, in David's den of degradation. She shouted and hammered with her fists until they ached, but there was no response.

Sitting on the bed, she waited. Half-an-hour passed, and then an hour – nothing happened. There was only the soft, hypnotic music drifting through the warm air to quell her anger.

Picking up the note, she read the words again. 'I'll be with you shortly,' she whispered, before throwing the crumpled paper onto the bed. 'So that's it. He's waiting somewhere. Probably watching me through the keyhole and waiting.'

The room suddenly became warmer, coaxing Jackie to remove her jacket. Driven by the warmth and her tremendous sexual arousal, she unbuttoned her blouse. Sure that David was spying on her, she defiantly threw the blouse onto the bed and pushed out her breasts. Free of the tight material, her large, firm breasts ballooned. Sensual messages buzzed around her nervous system the moment the air met her hardening nipples. Her clitoris stirred yet again with expectation.

Wandering around the room, she wondered where her captor was hiding. Behind a wall? Behind one of the erotic paintings? Upstairs gazing through a hole in the ceiling, maybe? Wherever he was, however long it took him to come out of hiding, she had put her plan into action. A plan that she hadn't yet formulated in detail but hoped would fall into place the moment David arrived. Somehow, she would strap him to the bed, use his body, stiffen his penis, bring him near to orgasm and then stop short. She would wait an hour, two, three hours until he had no choice other than to urinate while she watched and laughed. The tables will turn, they always do, she mused – and I'll be his captor.

'I know the bastard's watching me,' she whispered, slipping out of her skirt and wondering what the hell she was doing, what sort of plan was materialising. 'Well, here I am!' she yelled, wriggling her panties down over her thighs. 'I know you're there, watching me. Look! My knickers have a wet patch! Aren't you going to come and see? Or are you afraid? You dirty pervert!'

There was no response to her anger but she was determined not to give up. Completely naked, she lay on the bed and fondled her dark, thick pubic hair while she waited in a state of fear and sexual anticipation. Her juices flowed freely and trickled down her inner lips, inviting her fingers to part the folds and explore the warmth inside her tight hole.

Like a piece of bait, she lay ready to be taken, humiliated, bound and used. But she was ready to attack. Once David had taken the bait, she'd strike, scratch his eyes out and tear the flesh from his face before tying him down. Her plan was forming nicely.

The door suddenly opened and David moved quickly towards the bed. Gazing into her wide eyes, he smiled.

'I'm glad you could make it,' he said, hurriedly slipping the straps around her ankles before she had the chance even to speak. She panicked – she hadn't been ready – he'd taken her by surprise and so ruined her plan. Dazed, she sat up to protest, to fight him, to fight the inner force. Her ankles tethered, David gently but firmly pushed her struggling body down on the bed and grabbed her wrists. Jackie put up a perfunctory fight but soon closed her eyes, allowing the straps to bind her to the bed of lust once again.

All thoughts of retaliation quickly dispersed. David's presence sent a tingle over her defenceless, naked body as her limbs were stretched out to the four posts, opening the flesh between her legs in readiness for his every whim. Trembling, she lay waiting for his tongue to explore her delights, for the thick shaft and bulging knob of his penis to penetrate her and entice a desperately needed orgasm to explode between her vaginal lips and bathe her young body with sex.

Jackie suddenly thought of Mucky Meg and wondered at the change. The sudden change – the rude sexual awakening that David's cruel, cold hunger for her body had brought about. Confusion welled up bringing fear again – but it was too late.

'I don't think I can trust you to return,' David said, stroking her hard nipples. 'So I am going to have to keep you under lock and key – forever, I suppose,' he added quietly, as he left the room.

Opening her eyes, she looked down over the slight curve of her stomach to her dark mound, and then further to her fettered ankles. She was aroused as never in her life before. She yearned to touch herself, to bring herself to orgasm, but a sudden realisation hit her – she was no better than a whore, a tart. She cried, uncontrollably. 'Is this what I've been suppressing?' she asked herself. 'A desire to be tied down and humiliated? Is this the change that I wanted? Is there someone inside me, trying to break out? A stranger, possessing my body, my mind? Or is this the way I am – the real me?'

David returned after some minutes with a small silver tray. As he placed it on the bedside table, Jackie lifted her head and focused her tearful eyes. A razor, a soft brush, a bowl of water and shaving foam stood ominously on the tray.

'No! What are you going to do?' she yelled. 'Anything, but don't do that!'

'I'm going to remove your camouflage and expose the real you. Stop masquerading and let out the true woman in you.'

The true woman, the stranger within, Jackie thought as David lathered her dark curls. Her clitoris throbbed as he worked the thick foam into her slit and over her mound with the soft brush.

'You can't do it!' she screamed. 'I'll take you to court!'

'Take me to *court*?' David laughed. 'And what would you say? That you came to my house alone? Stripped off and allowed me to strap you to the bed? Don't be silly. Besides, you'll look much younger by the time I've finished with you. You'd like that, wouldn't you? You'd like to expose your hairless slit in the pub to strangers, wouldn't you?'

Jackie wriggled her hips in an effort to stop him as he picked up the razor and wielded it threateningly above her foaming bush.

'Don't shave me!' she pleaded as he placed the razor just below her smooth stomach.

'It's extremely sharp so you'd better keep still!' he warned. Jackie couldn't relax but managed to calm her trembling body before David began his depraved act.

Starting at the top of the white triangle of foam, he slowly drew the blade down towards her valley. Leaving soft, smooth, naked flesh in its wake, the razor transformed her young body. Years fell away with the curls, taking the soft mound back to adolescence. And then further, to the time when Jackie had first discovered the delights of masturbation.

Pulling her swollen pussy lips up and apart, he removed the last few remaining curls of womanhood, leaving her valley rudely exposed. Her inner lips protruded invitingly between the soft, appetising flesh like young birds in the nest waiting for food. The most intimate part of her body lay crudely presented before his hungry gaze.

'What a transformation!' David breathed, slipping his trousers down. 'I can't resist such naked beauty.'

'Don't! I don't want you!' Jackie screeched as he climbed between her thighs and stabbed at her valley with his hard knob. Finding the entrance, his thick penis slowly slid into her body, her hairless lips tightly encircling the shaft as its length opened and filled her.

Looking down at her baldness, Jackie sobbed and begged him to stop, but he continued to slide in and out, dragging her inner lips back and forth as they clung to the sticky, bulging surface of his penis.

'You look wonderful,' he complemented her, gazing down at the tight, youthful cushions encompassing his glistening rod. 'And now I'm going to come inside you – give you your reward for being such a good little girl.'

Allowing the hard knob to withdraw clear of her hole between each pounding thrust, he spattered her pubescent-looking flesh with one spurt of hot liquid and bathed her cervix with the next until he collapsed over her warm stomach.

'Why did you do it?' she cried as he slowly slid his penis from her body and crawled from the bed.

'Didn't you like it?' he asked, pulling up his trousers and buckling his belt.

'No, I didn't!'

'You should have let go, let yourself come. You wanted to come, didn't you?'

'I didn't want to! Why did you have to shave me? It will take weeks to grow again!'

'No, it won't grow again,' he smiled, clearing away his instruments of pubic youth. 'You see, Jane doesn't like genital hair. She'll make sure that it doesn't grow again.'

'Jane?' Jackie questioned, lifting her head and straining against her bonds. 'Who the hell's Jane?'

David smiled again, his eyes shining with mischief as he called for the mysterious Jane to join him.

A young blonde appeared in the doorway as David carried the tray from the room. The girl's eyes sparkled wickedly as she gazed at Jackie's body, focusing on the naked, white pads of flesh either side of her long slit. Standing by the bed in a short red miniskirt and white top, she introduced herself.

'I'm Jane, and I've come to play with you,' she whispered like a child who'd been allowed out to play with her new-found friend. Her fresh complexion was pale, her skin tight with youth, her features small. Although she was no more than eighteen, she radiated an air of sexual experience rarely found in one so young.

'David!' Jackie screamed. 'David – what is this? What's going on?' The girl grinned, seemingly gloating over Jackie's predicament, delighting in her humiliation.

Raising her eyebrows, she smiled. 'David's done me proud,' she said, leaning over to lap up the sperm trickling from Jackie's exposed, wrinkled inner lips.

'Who the hell are you?' Jackie screamed hysterically, thrashing her hips from side to side. 'Don't touch me!'

'Oh, you silly thing,' Jane sighed, reaching under the bed. 'I didn't want to have to do this but you leave me no choice.' Hauling a huge leather belt over Jackie's writhing hips, she pulled it tight and made it fast. 'There, now that's better, isn't it?' she said, positioning herself between Jackie's outstretched legs. Her face only inches from Jackie's gaping valley, she carefully peeled back the pink lips and gently pushed a finger inside the warm hole.

'You're nice and tight. And *wonderfully* wet with

David's sperm,' she breathed excitedly, moving her face a little nearer.

'You filthy bitch!' Jackie screamed. 'Filthy, bloody lesbian!'

'I'm not filthy and I'm not a bitch!' Jane retorted. 'But yes, I am a lesbian, darling. And I'm going to enjoy playing with your sweet little pussy. You'll enjoy it, too.' Sliding her finger out, she licked the entrance to Jackie's body, drinking the mixture of warm sperm and cunt milk as it flowed over her glistening skin.

'When I get out of here, I'll find you and . . .'

'And you'll thank me,' Jane interrupted, her eyes peering over Jackie's mound. 'When you've had time to reflect, time to think, you'll come back for more. Only a woman knows what a woman wants. What a woman needs.'

'I don't want or need you!' Jackie spat.

'But my tongue is softer than David's. My mouth fuller. My fingers smoother. My knowledge of the female body far greater. You'll thank me and come back for more, my darling. *If* David decides to let you go, that is.'

Struggle as she did, Jackie couldn't stop the young lesbian from mouthing, sucking and licking between her legs. The more she wriggled her hips, the tighter the leather belt seemed to grip her helpless body. She could do nothing as the girl's fingers opened her pussy lips and pulled back the small, pink hood to expose the clitoris that had never known the caress of another woman.

Swearing that she wouldn't respond to the touch of a lesbian, Jackie closed her eyes and tried to think of the real world, the world outside, the bank, her flat and the pub. The world that had seemed so mundane, so boring, but now so safe and necessary – but so far away.

Desperately, Jackie tried to drag her mind away from

Jane's teasing tongue as it repeatedly licked her valley from the bottom to the top where her clitoris fluttered in response to each stroke.

'I'll kill him – and you,' she breathed as Jane giggled and flicked the tip of her stiffening clitoris with her tongue. She spread Jackie's vaginal lips further apart with her fingers and continued her act of oral masturbation, breathing heavily now and then as if the stimulation was to her own clitoris.

A delightful tingle rose from Jackie's erect bud as the other girl pushed her face hard between her stretched honeypot lips, continuing her rhythmical mouthing and sucking. Her mind reeling, Jackie desperately tried to deny her tremendous sexual arousal.

'I'm not a bloody lesbian!' she shrieked as her clitoris pulsated with the beginnings of her first lesbian-induced orgasm. Lifting her head, she looked down between her breasts and focused her tearful eyes on her swollen labia, stretched open, completely encompassing the girl's young mouth. Jane's eyes rolled with euphoria as she breathed heavily through her nose, feverishly consuming her victim's intimacy.

Jane knew exactly what to do when Jackie's stomach muscles rhythmically tightened and relaxed and her breathing became deep and heavy. Running her tongue around the inflamed clitoris, being careful not to touch the sensitive tip, Jane enticed the most wonderful orgasm Jackie had ever experienced from the appreciative bud. Her mind swirling, Jackie cursed Jane between every gasp of ecstasy. Her heart pounded in time with her pulsating clitoris as Jane's long blonde hair tickled her inner thighs, adding to the exquisite sensations between her legs.

Not satisfied with her spoils, Jane continued to tease

Jackie's aching nodule until it responded again. The subsiding orgasm suddenly exploded, flooding Jackie with wave after wave of debased pleasure. The muscles in her legs twitching violently, she desperately needed to bring her knees up to her heaving breasts to close her quim lips securely over her consummated clitoris – to put an end to the beautiful torture. But with her perspiring body spread and tethered, she could do nothing to stop the girl.

Ignoring Jackie's pleas, Jane peeled the bound girl's inner lips open even further, painfully stretching the skin to its limit, and persisted with her tantalising caress. Sinking her nails into Jackie's slim hips and grinding her hot mouth over her clitoris, she only backed away when Jackie's third climax induced an involuntary cascade of warm orgasmic spend to flow from her body.

Gasping with sexual gratification, Jackie fought against the leather straps as Jane's tongue moved down her valley to find its way deep into the wet hole.

'I'll kill you, you filthy bitch!' she cried as Jane lapped up the warm milky fluid. But the heat of Jane's breath against her stretched, gaping hole, and her tongue buried deep inside her body, caused Jackie to cry out again with pleasure.

'Ah, that's nice. That's nice, don't stop,' she heard herself plead. Shocked by her admission, disgusted by the unbridled pleasure from the corrupt union of a female tongue and her open hole, Jackie managed to halt the advancing orgasm.

Content with her work at last, Jane lifted her head and moved to the side of the bed. Her face wet with Jackie's juice and glowing with sexual delight, she slowly pulled her top over her head, revealing her large but firm young breasts. Her long nipples stood out from the rounded balloons like two small, erect penises waiting to be milked. Her body was youthful, almost childlike, her unblemished skin smooth and tight. Unzipping her skirt and slipping her panties down, she bared her full, shaven vaginal lips to Jackie's gaze. Her clitoris protruded from the top of her slit like a worm. Its amazing length held Jackie's attention. She'd never seen another woman's clitoris before but instinctively she knew that the girl must be deformed.

She watched with bated breath as Jane climbed onto the bed and laid her warm body over hers. Raising herself on her arms, Jane slid her hairless lips back and forth over Jackie's hard mound. She could feel the hardness of the long, intruding clitoris exploring her valley. The two pairs of naked honeypot lips pressed together, kissing, caressing, lubricated with Jane's warm milk. Pussy to pussy, navel to navel, nipple to nipple, the female coitus aroused a sleeping desire deep within Jackie's subconscious. The latent lesbian tendency that possibly all women harbour began to surface.

Gazing into her wide, blue eyes, Jane moved her mouth closer to Jackie's. Their lips gently touched. Breathing in the scent of her seductress, Jackie began to slip into a warm pool of tranquillity as Jane's tongue explored her mouth. Warm and tasting of sex, she instinctively reciprocated.

Their lips parted and Jane swung her legs round to sit astride Jackie's stomach. Sliding her wet slit over her navel, she moved up and over her breasts. As Jackie watched, the threatening young pussy moved ever nearer to her open mouth. But knowing that Jackie wasn't ready for such delights and in fear of retaliation from her teeth, Jane parted her lips and rubbed her elongated clitoris over Jackie's nipple. Warm juice trickled down the captive girl's breast as Jane quickly brought herself to a massive climax against the aching nipple.

Arching her back, Jane rested on her hands, breathing deeply and slowly while her orgasm receded. Jackie gazed at the gaping hole only inches from her face. The thick, swollen outer lips shone in the light while the pink inner lips curled like the petals of a rain-drenched flower. Her clitoris stood invitingly erect and proud from the valley. Jackie trembled with an overwhelming desire to taste the feast spread before her hungry eyes – to suck on the wet, sensitive skin, to take the full length of the miniature phallus in her mouth. But she managed to shake off her fantasy, to suppress her libidinous desires and wake to reality.

'Ah, that was nice, wasn't it?' Jane whispered, climbing from the bed.

'I meant what I said,' Jackie hissed. 'I'll get you for this!'

'You'll change your mind and come back for more,' Jane smiled confidently as she dressed. For a second, Jackie knew that she *would* be back for more. She hoped that she would allow her base instincts to surface so she could enjoy herself, her body. So she could enjoy Jane.

David asked Jackie if she'd been having a nice time in his absence as he crossed the room. She waited until Jane had closed the door behind her before screaming at him.

'Unless you untie me now, you'll be in serious trouble!' she threatened, her wet body indignantly spread open before his gaze.

'Oh, come *on*. Don't tell me you didn't enjoy Jane's attentions. She will be upset. Look at it as a new and exciting experience.'

'I don't want an experience with another woman! A girl!'

'That's a shame because she'll be back a little later to

show you what else she can do. In the meantime, have a nice refreshing sleep.'

'Sleep? You're mad! Schizophrenic! You need help!'

'No, *you* need help, Jackie. Help to discover the real you. And that's what I'm giving you – help. After only one lesson in sex, you went to the pub and delighted in exposing your knickers, didn't you? I saw you teasing that young lad – using your body to excite him.'

Jackie didn't reply. She knew that David was right but didn't understand what was happening to her.

David kissed her sticky outer lips and ran his tongue up the length of her valley before moving away. 'See you later,' he smiled, and quietly closed the door behind him.

Jackie fearfully wondered what else a woman could do to another woman's body. She wondered, too, about her identity, her sexuality. What was she, really? A lesbian? Was it the fact that she'd been tied down and forced to endure a female tongue between her legs that had brought her such pleasure? Or had she simply found pleasure in being brought to orgasm? A tongue is a tongue, after all, she thought. Male or female, they are the same.

Tears flooded her eyes as she lay wondering if she'd ever see her flat or the bank again. Vivid images of Jane's body astride her face with her opening pushed hard against her mouth filled her troubled mind. She'd wanted to suck and drink from the intimacy between Jane's young thighs but it was wrong, she knew. Visions of Jane's deformed clitoris haunted her. Why was it so long? What had she done to it?

Hearing the door open, she closed her eyes and pretended to sleep. David gently kissed her cheek before loosening her bonds and covering her with a quilt. The moment the door closed, Jackie opened one eye. Slipping out of the leather straps, she flung the quilt from the bed and quickly dressed. Her sore pussy ached from the rapturous orgasms she'd been forced to endure. As she pulled up her panties, the soft silk caressed her sensitive, hairless quim lips, inducing a new sexual awareness.

Turning the door handle, she gasped in amazement to find that it wasn't locked. It was a trick, she was sure. But she had a chance to escape and if David was hiding, waiting to pounce and delight in her anguish, she'd at least have the opportunity to fight back.

Cautiously climbing the wooden stairs, she became aware of the conflict raging deep in her mind. She desperately wanted Jane – but at the same time she hated her. She hated herself. She wanted to leave the house, to run, but something was holding her back. Something deep inside stirred every time she thought of Jane – her body.

David suddenly appeared as if from nowhere as Jackie crept across the hall. Her heart pounding, her eyes darted between him and the door to the outside world. To her astonishment, he opened the front door and smiled.

'Will we be seeing you this evening?' he asked, as if inviting her round for drinks.

'No, you bloody won't!' she screamed hysterically, lunging at him with clenched fists. David held her arms, telling her not to be so silly and to calm down. Breaking away, she flew through the open door, shouting obscenities as she turned for one last look at her jailer.

The cold air cut through Jackie like a knife as she fled down the steps to the street. It was still dark. She had no idea of the time. Snow fell steadily as she carefully made her way home – her body aching, her mind whirling.

Chapter Three

In the warmth and security of her flat, Jackie flopped onto the sofa and lifted her skirt to examine her used body. Raising her buttocks and pulling her wet panties down, she gazed at her shaved lips. She felt indecent, dirty, naked. Consoling herself with the thought that her hair would soon grow, she lowered her skirt. Gazing at the white stains in the crotch of her panties, she kicked the flimsy underwear across the floor in disgust. She knew her body would return to normal, but her mind would always bear the scars.

A package dropping through the letter box sent Jackie racing to the front door. It was a video tape with an envelope tucked inside the box. Gazing at her name neatly written in red felt-tip, she instinctively knew who it was from. A gold bracelet fell to the floor as she ripped the envelope open. The small bracelet was heavy and obviously expensive. A reward, she thought, for the part she'd played in David's perverse games.

Wandering back into the lounge, she removed the tape from its box and rammed it into the video machine. Sitting in the armchair, she fastened the bracelet around her tiny wrist and gazed at the television in anticipation.

The first scene flashed onto the screen – Jackie, naked on the bed, fondling her pubic hair as she waited for David – she'd forgotten about that. The camera had been somewhere above the bed, strategically placed to capture every inch of her young, curvaceous body.

The scene cut to David bringing Jackie to orgasm with his tongue. A pang of arousal rose from her clitoris as she watched herself contort with sexual ecstasy. The camera caught every expression of desire and sexual satisfaction running across her reddened face – every grimace of mind-blowing orgasm.

She watched in disgust as he then proceeded to shave her dark curls, transforming her pubis to that of a young girl's. Suddenly, Jane moved onto the bed and positioned her head between Jackie's outstretched legs. She parted her now hairless cunt lips and began to suck and lick at the wetness in her exposed valley.

Cleverly edited, there were several shots showing the obvious sexual pleasure expressed on Jackie's contorted face. Writhing and crying out in ecstasy, the video depicted not only her apparent consent but also her undeniable sexual gratification.

Jane moved her body over Jackie's breast and began to rub her lengthy clitoris against the hard nipple. Jackie caught her breath as she became aware of juice trickling between her own pussy lips while she watched Jane throw her head back to look up at the camera as her young body twisted and writhed in orgasm. She opened her mouth and licked her full lips, obviously knowing that Jackie would later watch the lesbian seduction on her television screen.

'I'm not a lesbian,' Jackie breathed as she watched Jane climb from the bed before the screen went blank. Picturing the girl's open valley only inches from her mouth, she slipped her hand between her legs to appease her yearning clitoris. Flicking the remote control, she rewound the tape to find Jane mouthing and sucking her swollen quim lips again. Running her finger from her wet hole to her clitoris several times, she lubricated the hard bud with her warm, slippery juices and lovingly masturbated her sore pussy. Reaching a wondrous orgasm in unison with her trembling body pictured so vividly on the screen, she lay back, breathless, satisfied, while her juices drained into a small pool on the armchair.

Desperately fighting her desires, Jackie couldn't deny her obsessive craving for David. She found herself longing to be in his den of degradation again – tethered to the bed and used as a sex toy – her body rudely laid open and brought to excruciating climaxes again and again. She longed to be stretched and filled by his huge, thick penis. Resting her legs over the arms of the chair, she fingered her clitoris until she reached a second beautiful climax. Rhythmically pumping out its fluid with each throb of her bud, her pussy cried out for more and more fulfilment. Although sore and inflamed, her insatiable clitoris demanded another climax but she had had enough – for the time being.

The screen went blank as she softly caressed herself and relaxed after her orgasm. Examining her smooth, hairless lips again, she was surprised by their sensitivity. The slightest touch to the soft skin sent a tingle through her body. And as David had said, she looked younger – too young, perhaps. But she would keep her white, intimate cushions shaved, she decided, remembering the days before the first dark curls had sprouted just above her tight valley. Wonderful days of discovery, of secretly slipping her fingers between her legs and masturbating. But those beautiful days had returned and, she swore, would never leave her again.

Jackie wondered what had gone wrong, why she'd denied herself the pleasures her body had to offer. She had so loved masturbating as a child but had stopped in her early teens. Perhaps my clitoris would have grown if I'd kept on masturbating, she pondered. Maybe I'm the one who's deformed and Jane is normal. More than ever, she blamed the nun who'd warned her of 'touching yourself down there.' She'd come to think that her body was only to be given and shared in love. Not used by herself for sexual gratification or given to another in the name of cold lust – especially another woman, a young girl.

Aware of her sticky vagina, Jackie ran a bath and wandered into the kitchen to make some coffee. Daylight was beginning to break, revealing the cold, snow-covered gardens behind the flats. Gazing through the kitchen window, she suddenly realised that she could see the back of David's house. The building stood ominously against the dark pewter-grey sky – like a castle protecting its occupants from the outside world, guarding the secrets within its dungeon far below ground.

'Is Jane his wife?' she whispered, staring at the building. 'Or his girlfriend, perhaps?' She didn't like the idea of sharing David, she wanted him for herself. But, to her sheer horror, she realised that she wanted Jane for herself, too. More than David, more than any man, she longed for Jane.

Sipping her coffee while relaxing in the warm bath, Jackie made her plans. She would return to the house and discover the truth. Find out who Jane was and what she meant to David. She couldn't deny the fact that he, they, had money – and from what she'd seen, far more money than erotic paintings would ever bring. How did they get it? And why had she been given the gold bracelet? Perhaps they sold the video tapes of their victims? Somehow, she would discover all there was to know about the mysterious pair.

After her bath, Jackie dressed and wandered aimlessly around the flat. It was nine-thirty, another day missed at the bank, but that could wait. There were far more important things on her mind than work. Making another cup of coffee, she noticed the holiday postcards from her friends pinned to the wall. She smiled as she read one from Meg. 'Found a Mediterranean hulk! Wow! What a night! You don't know what you're missing!'

'I'm not missing it now,' she breathed, wishing she were more like Meg.

A photograph fell to the floor as she tucked the card back into place. Picking it up, she gazed at herself pictured with Ian. 'You didn't give me what I wanted, either. Poor Ian, all you had to do was teach me and I'd have been far better than Helen, or anyone else.' Dropping the photograph in the bin, she sighed, wondering what the next chapter in her life would bring. Several times she found herself gazing through the kitchen window, spellbound by the sight of David's mysterious home.

On impulse, she grabbed her jacket and made her way to his house. He wouldn't be expecting her until the evening, if at all. She hoped to find him in, to surprise him and catch him off guard. To talk to him over coffee – adult to adult – to ask him a thousand questions.

Perhaps he's asleep, she thought, climbing the steps and wondering what she would say if he opened the door. Her heart thumping, she pressed the door bell and pulled up her collar. Suddenly, she hoped that he wouldn't answer. She couldn't face him – or Jane. She thought she'd gone mad, the idea was ludicrous.

There was no reply. Relieved, she carefully descended the snow-covered steps but hesitated when she noticed a small path leading to the side of the house. Compelled by curiosity, she crept round to the back of the building.

He might be in his den with Jane, she thought, picturing the girl tethered to the bed as David brought her to orgasm with his tongue. Driven by a salacious sexual impulse, Jackie tentatively tried the back door. It opened, all too easily, she thought as she stole inside like a thief. Quietly closing the door, she found herself standing in the kitchen. Everything was neat, clean and tidy – a woman's touch, she decided: Jane's touch. Finding her way to the lounge, she listened to the silence ringing in her ears for a moment before entering.

The book-shelving was partly open. Feeling sure that David was working, either at his easel or on Jane, she gently trod one tentative step at a time until she reached the stairway to the den. Creeping down the stairs, she glanced back, wondering if the shelving would automatically close, locking her in until her body was required for use, but it remained open, giving her an easy escape route should she need one.

The studio was empty and the small door to the den was ajar. Holding her breath, she crept across the thick carpet and spied through the crack in the door. The room was empty. Sure that she was alone in the house, she began to sift through the piles of sketches strewn across the knee-hole desk. Keeping her ears open for any movement upstairs, she gazed at the sketches. In explicit sexual detail, she stared in horror at a sketch of a young woman's naked body – her own naked body. Showing her shaved lips gaping wide open, exposing an oversized clitoris, the sketch left nothing to the imagination. But there were more. A sketch of a naked man. She was sure it was Tim, the resemblance was striking, it had to be him. He was taking a young woman's tethered body from behind. The chained woman was Jackie.

Placing the sketch on the pile, she opened a drawer and

found herself gazing at a string of pearls. Gold rings, wrist watches, brooches, pendants and all manner of expensive jewellery filled the drawer. Running the pearls through her fingers, she jumped when she heard the front door bang shut. Dropping the gems into the drawer, she pushed it closed and frantically looked for somewhere to hide. Turning to the den, she froze, imagining what David would do if he found her alone in there. A filing cabinet stood under the stairs, leaving just enough space for her small frame to squat behind it.

Barely breathing, she remained perfectly still as heavy footsteps thumped down the stairs. From her hide, she saw David and Jane moving towards the desk.

'Who have we got this afternoon?' David asked.

'Er, there's Elizabeth Rhodes at three,' she replied flicking through the pages of a diary.

'And this evening?' he enquired, moving towards the filing cabinet.

'Mrs Blythe-Smith,' Jane replied, closing the diary and placing it on the desk.

'You'll have to deal with her – for obvious reasons,' David laughed, banging the filing cabinet shut.

Without giving Jackie any clues as to their relationship, they climbed the stairs. Able to breath freely again, she crept from her hide and moved back towards the desk.

Opening another drawer, she discovered several video tapes. Evidence, she thought, grabbing two tapes at random. But evidence of what, she had no idea. Clutching the tapes, she took a last glance around the room, wondering if she'd ever see it again – if she'd ever be strapped to the bed again while Jane used her body for her perverted sexual gratification.

Voices emanated from the top of the house as she crept cautiously across the lounge and stole past the grandfather clock. Breathing a sigh of relief, she quietly closed the front door and carefully trod the newly-fallen snow the short distance to the safety of her flat.

'Whatever they're doing, it's got to be illegal,' she told herself, pushing the first video tape into the machine. The screen flashed. Suddenly, the four-poster bed came into view.

Sitting cross-legged on the floor with her big eyes focused on the television, Jackie gasped. Lying on her stomach with her limbs strapped to the four bed posts, a young, shapely woman with long dark hair was being whipped. Her red, glowing buttocks tightened with every terrifying crack of the heavy leather belt.

Jackie couldn't see who was wielding the whip, or who the woman was. Nor could she determine whether she had consented to the beating – probably not, she surmised.

Hurriedly ejecting the tape, she pushed the second one into the machine and gazed, open-mouthed, at the screen. A close-up shot of a vibrator being pushed between a pair of bulging pussy lips. In and out the huge, penis-like vibrator thrust before sliding from the gaping hole and moving up the wet valley. Two fingers stretched the swollen lips apart to reveal a huge clitoris, where the vibrator moved round and round before settling. She could clearly see that the skilful hands belonged to a woman. Jane, perhaps?

A second vibrator was introduced to the gaping hole and slowly pushed deep inside. There was no sound track but Jackie could imagine the moaning and groaning as the vibrator stiffened the clitoris to an incredible size. The camera panned in, filling the screen with the tip of the vibrator against the now elongated clitoris. Its length confirmed Jackie's fears, it was she who was deformed, terribly underdeveloped. Suddenly, the hard nodule pumped and pulsated rhythmically like a penis. She watched in amazement as the swollen skin reddened and the clitoris visibly throbbed, time and time again, with orgasm. Never before had she seen the delights of female orgasm so graphically displayed.

The ringing telephone forced her away from the intensely arousing scenes. Lifting the receiver while aiming the remote control at the video, she whispered hello.

'I wouldn't visit that house again, if I were you,' a woman's voice warned.

'Who is this?' Jackie asked. The dialling tone purred softly in her ear.

Jane? she wondered. No, not Jane. Then who? Replacing the receiver, she glanced at her watch – ten to three. 'Elizabeth Rhodes at three,' she breathed, remembering Jane's words. All thoughts of the phone call quickly faded. Pulling her coat on as she left her flat, she walked as fast as the snow-covered pavement would allow her. The big house came into view as she turned the corner. She needed somewhere to hide to spy on Elizabeth Rhodes when she arrived.

The telephone box gave shelter from the snow as well as providing a perfect view of David's front door. Jackie checked her watch again – almost three. She hoped no-one would want to use the phone while she waited. That would be just my luck, she thought, huddling in the cold, draughty kiosk.

After some minutes, a taxi pulled up and stopped outside the house. The driver opened the rear door and a woman climbed out. She said something to the driver before making her way up the steps to the front door.

It was difficult to judge her age, but Jackie surmised that she was in her late thirties, or possibly early forties. She was well dressed in a dark, fur coat and leather boots.

Her long, dark hair flowed over her shoulders as she swung her head in response to the opening door. David greeted her with a broad smile. Turning, as if to check that the coast was clear, she entered the house.

Although she'd had only a split-second glimpse of her face, Jackie thought that she recognised the woman. 'I've seen her somewhere,' she breathed, opening the phone-box door. 'But where?'

Courage, curiosity and an exciting element of danger drove her to wander across the road and round to the back of the house. She had no plan, no idea of what she was going to do as she pushed the back door open and crept into the kitchen.

Voices emanated from the basement as she edged her way cautiously across the lounge to the partly open book-shelving. The top step creaked as it took her weight. One by one, she lightly trod each step until she'd reached the bottom.

To her surprise, the large Chinese tapestry hanging behind the desk had been drawn back like a curtain, revealing another door. She approached the door and dropped to her knees, levelling her eye with the key-hole. The dark-haired woman, completely naked, was strapped over a large wooden frame. With her slim legs straight and her feet wide apart, her large rounded buttocks were in full view. Jackie followed the dark dividing line between the pale crescents of flesh down to two bulging cushions of pink skin. She was amazed by the extent that the wrinkled inner lips protruded from the valley. Stuck together, they formed one thick mass of pink flesh, dripping with juice like a panting dog's tongue.

Jane suddenly came into view pulling on a pair of rubber gloves. David was nowhere in sight as she began to rub oil into the milky white buttocks, paying special attention to the dark crease.

'Now, what have you to tell me about this week?' Jane asked sternly as she worked vigorously on the woman's buttocks.

'I masturbated last night,' she confessed.

'Oh, that's naughty,' Jane sighed, moving her hands away. 'Now you promised me that you wouldn't do that any more, didn't you? You know only too well that when you need attention, you come *here*, to *me*. I'm afraid you'll have to be severely punished.'

Jane disappeared from view for a second and then returned with a long, thin cane. The first stinging blow landed squarely across the ample buttocks, leaving a thin weal. The second, harder blow, caused the offender to cry out as her buttocks tightened in agony.

'That's enough!' she screamed as the third blow struck.

'I'm sorry, but you are going to have to learn the hard way,' Jane admonished, landing the hardest blow yet.

Jackie's clitoris throbbed with each successive blow until, to her utter amazement, she realised that she was near to orgasm. Breathing heavily, she slipped a hand inside her knickers as she watched Jane administer the sadistic and yet acutely stimulating punishment.

By the tenth blow, Jackie had crumpled to the floor, quietly moaning as her clitoris exploded beneath her trembling fingers. 'What's happening to me?' she whispered, barely able to balance as she rose on her knees to the keyhole once more. 'I've become sex-mad.'

Jane discarded the cane and rubbed more oil into the glowing buttocks before kneeling on the floor to inspect the result of her work.

'I think you're ready,' she said, slipping a finger deep into the woman's trembling body. Which hole she had rudely penetrated, Jackie couldn't see. But the woman quietly moaned with delight as Jane rhythmically worked her fist slowly back and forth, manipulating and massaging the inner flesh.

The sound of footsteps above the ceiling sent Jackie racing to her hiding place behind the filing cabinet. David wandered down the stairs and disappeared into the room where Jane was correcting the offender's wicked ways. Before the door closed, Jackie caught a fleeting glimpse of the woman's bulging vaginal lips. Held firmly in place by a metal clamp, a large pink object protruded from her stretched hole. On David's instruction, Jane wielded the cane over the crimson moons as he closed the door, obliterating Jackie's view.

Fleeing up the stairs and across the hall, Jackie heard the awful cries for mercy emanating from the torture chamber but they were only met with more harsh slaps of the cane, the sound of which made her wince. Desperately trying to clear her mind of the gruesome scene, she covered her ears.

She had never believed the stories she'd read in the Sunday tabloids. Exclusive stories of sex dens with accompanying pictures of whips, handcuffs and leather-clad women. Now, she'd seen it at first hand – in all its terrifying depraved reality. But, still more terrifying, the scenes had sexually excited her beyond belief. She remembered masturbating her clitoris to orgasm while watching herself being attended to by Jane on video tape. Her head reeled in confusion. She was discovering a strange, frightening new side to herself. A side that, now unleashed, could no longer be suppressed. A side that, she had to admit, she didn't *want* to suppress.

Hesitating at the front door, Jackie was in two minds whether to return to the keyhole to watch the woman's gruelling punishment once more. But no. She knew she'd receive the same brutal torture if she was caught. A strange yearning deep within her subconscious goaded her to return and experience the pleasures of humiliation – of the cane in Jane's capable hands. Eventually breaking away from her deplorable fantasy, she made her escape.

Out in the street, the cold breeze against her burning face quickly brought Jackie back to reality, to her normal senses. In their innocence, people wandered past the house, completely unaware of the scenes of degradation inside. Watching their faces, she felt the need to tell them, to expose David and his wicked, debauched ways. But she knew that her terrible secret had to remain locked away, for she had been captured in full, living colour on video tape, strapped to the bed, delighting in debauched scenes of lesbian lust. She was now part of David's depraved world – and his world was part of her.

She wondered how David earned his money as she walked home. She thought about the video tapes again. Is that how he earns his money? she mused. No, even the porn market wouldn't provide the luxuries that David had surrounded himself with. Unless, the terrifying thought suddenly struck her, this is only the tip of the iceberg.

Her thoughts turned to the jewellery stashed in the desk drawer. Where had it come from? What was it doing there? Who did it belong to?

The minute she arrived home she collapsed on her bed hoping to find some solace in sleep, but there was no escape. Dreams wracked her tormented mind, bringing her vivid, colourful pictures of her naked body receiving the painfully beautiful punishment she craved. She saw herself in the swirling mist of her dream, dripping in gold, strapped over the wooden frame while Jane lovingly massaged her buttocks with aromatic oils.

The stinging blows from the cane caused Jackie to wake. Breathing deeply, she was aware that she was about to come. Just in time to catch her climax, she caressed her clitoris appreciatively, inducing it to burst and send its waves of ecstasy over her trembling body to satisfy the stranger within.

Chapter Four

Jackie felt that she had the weight of the world on her shoulders – as if there had been a murder and she knew who the culprit was but couldn't tell without incriminating herself. She wanted to ring the Sunday tabloids and tell the story of David and his den – expose the man he really was. But quite apart from the virtual certainty of exposing herself as a seemingly willing participant, she didn't want to lose her secret world. Her exciting, almost incredible world of fantasy that had reached out and awakened her with its sensual kiss.

She hoped that Tim would be able to fill in some of the gaps in David's mysterious life. If he was involved, a few tentative questions may produce some clues. And David's young, blonde accomplice – did Tim know her? The crowd in the pub, how well did they know David? There must be *someone* who knows him well, she thought.

Arriving at the pub at seven, Jackie found Tim sitting on a bar stool reading a newspaper. Even in his trainers, pressed blue jeans and casual shirt he looked well dressed. Could I be so very wrong about him? she wondered. Could this seemingly kind, warm and friendly man really be a monster who defiles women by forcibly taking them from behind? Is this really the man depicted in David's sketch?

'Night off?' she asked, wandering towards him, her

wide, blue eyes transfixed on the ample bulge in his jeans. Tim looked up in surprise.

'Hi, Jackie. Yes, I'm off out this evening,' he replied, gazing guiltily, she thought, into her eyes.

'Anywhere nice?' she continued, looking down at the heavy gold pendant hanging around his neck.

'Just a friend's house,' he smiled, folding the paper and placing it on the bar. 'Let me get you a drink.'

Digging his hand into his pocket, Tim called to the girl behind the bar. Although Jackie hadn't seen her before, there was something familiar about the young, dark barmaid that worried her.

'Ah, Rosita, a gin and tonic for Jackie, please,' Tim said, placing a crisp, ten-pound note on the bar.

Jackie watched the girl push the glass up to the optic and then carefully slice the lemon. Her movements were slow and methodical. Her long dark hair swung from side to side as she turned to reach for a bottle of tonic.

She had huge, bulbous breasts that strained against her tight blouse. Jackie found herself imagining Rosita lying naked on David's bed, her body strapped and spread in readiness for sex. The thought sent a quiver up her spine – and a delightful tingle through her clitoris.

'You cold?' Tim asked, passing Jackie her drink.

'No, no. Does the name Elizabeth Rhodes mean anything to you?' she enquired, closely watching for a change in expression. The change was obvious, as was Tim's lie.

'No, I don't think so. Rhodes? Rhodes? No, I can't say that I know that one,' he replied, avoiding her accusing gaze.

'How well *do* you know David?' she asked, neatly sliding her buttocks onto a bar stool.

'Your David?'

'Good grief! He's not *my* David!' she returned indignantly. Sipping his drink, Tim raised his eyebrows to the ceiling as if asking some divine power for help.

'Not very well,' he eventually replied. 'Why?'

'No reason,' Jackie said, adjusting her miniskirt to expose the tight, triangular patch of her red panties. Tim lowered his eyes to Jackie's crotch and smiled.

'You're a sweet little thing,' he said. 'Be careful, won't you?'

'Careful?' she repeated, her eyes catching his. 'Careful of what?'

'Is that the time?' Tim asked, glancing at his gold wrist watch and making odd facial expressions as if his very life depended on an appointment. 'I really must be going. Look after yourself, won't you?'

Rolling up his paper, he walked briskly towards the door before Jackie could question him further. As soon as the door closed, she quickly moved to the window and watched him cross the road, sure that he'd go into David's house. Glancing back at the pub, he hesitated, and then walked past the house to disappear down the road.

'Rosita, isn't it?' Jackie asked the barmaid as she slid back onto the stool.

'That's right. And you're Jackie.'

'Yes. I know you from somewhere but I can't quite place your face,' Jackie said, finishing her drink.

The girl denied all knowledge of knowing Jackie. But when she launched into a lengthy story explaining that she'd only recently moved into the area and embroidered it with unnecessary detail, Jackie wondered why she was making so much of the point. The question was simple. In fact, it hadn't been a question at all, more of a passing comment.

Jackie wondered if she was going mad. First, she'd

thought that she'd known Elizabeth Rhodes. She'd even thought Tim to be part of David's web of deception. And now the barmaid. She wondered if, in her desperation to discover more about David and his secret world, she'd become mentally unstable. The crowd in the other bar were ordinary people leading ordinary lives, she told herself. The pub wasn't a front. It wasn't part of David's trap to catch women and then lure them to the house. There was no conspiracy.

She had become crazed in her thinking, certainly sexually crazed, she mused, eyeing Rosita's ballooning breasts and wondering how large and hard her nipples were – how long and erect her clitoris became when aroused. She could be the girl on the video tape, she thought, gazing at Rosita's long, dark hair as she turned to serve another customer. Suddenly, the girl's gold necklace flashed in the light. Jackie couldn't think why she hadn't noticed it before. It was a thick, expensive, gold chain with a small diamond clasped within the gold petals of a flower.

Everyone is dripping with gold, she mused, eyeing the bracelet that David had given her. Her mind wandered again. She knew that there must be a connection. But they can't *all* be involved, she thought, watching Rosita disappear into the other bar at the sound of someone tapping a coin on the counter. Wondering if her weird and wonderful sexual feelings required psychiatric help, Jackie tried to clear her swirling mind of Rosita's beautiful young body. She tried to relax and enjoy her drink, enjoy the evening. But her thoughts drifted back to the warning phone call.

'I wouldn't visit that house again, if I were you'. The woman's words ran through Jackie's mind as Rosita returned to ask if she wanted another drink.

'You don't know David, do you?' Jackie asked, her eyes transfixed on the sparkling diamond nestling in the girl's cleavage.

'Who?' Rosita said innocently.

'It doesn't matter,' she replied. Asking for another gin and tonic, she realised that there were many more pieces to be fitted into the puzzle before she could even hazard a guess at the complete picture. If Rosita was involved, she would find out, eventually. And, she found herself hoping, taste the delights of her young, dark body.

The seventh gin and tonic went straight to her head. Dizzy and confused, she slipped her coat on and wandered across the road to David's house. Standing in front of the huge building brought a sense of danger. But mixed with the gin and sexual arousal, she couldn't resist the powerful temptation to go inside.

'I know Tim's in there,' she whispered angrily, creeping around the back of the building. Her legs were unsteady, her head spinning in the cold, fresh air. She knew that she should go home as she opened the back door. Home to her flat, her job, her mundane but secure life. But a force far greater than she compelled her to enter.

The kitchen light was on as if in readiness for Jackie's arrival. The door to the hall was open. The lounge door was also open and the book-shelving slid back. In the uncanny silence, she made her way down the stairs, wondering if she were walking straight into a trap. She half-hoped it *was* a trap. She *wanted* to be caught and strapped to the bed again. To be sexually abused – by Jane.

The heavy Chinese tapestry was drawn over the door leading to the secret room. The room that had haunted Jackie ever since she'd seen Jane administering the delights of the cane. Curiosity killed the cat, she thought as she pulled the tapestry aside to reveal the door.

Glancing over her shoulder, she turned the knob and inched the door open before cautiously venturing inside. The room was larger than the den. A variety of vibrators lined the shelving along one wall. Several canes stood ominously in an umbrella stand. The clean, tiled floor reminded her of a doctor's surgery. The air hung heavy with the powerful perfume of aromatic oils. But the stench of sex was stronger.

The wooden frame, neatly covered in red velvet, was an ingenious contraption. Shaped as the letter X, the victim's wrists and ankles could be clamped in place, their body forming a star. Jackie turned a large metal handle and watched as the frame revolved, enabling the victim to be turned from the vertical to the horizontal position. Turning another handle, the hinged centre section folded down, bending the victim's body over until the hands reached the toes. Returning the frame to its original position, she looked around the room.

A small hospital trolley with a glass top stood near to the frame. Vaseline, rubber gloves, bottles of oil and cream and an assortment of ominous-looking devices were neatly laid out in readiness for the next victim.

'Clever, isn't it?' a voice bellowed. Jackie's heart leapt with fear as she turned to see David standing in the doorway. 'Would you like to try it out?' he invited, firmly closing the door. The gin blurred Jackie's mind as he moved towards her and removed her jacket. Quickly and skilfully, he unbuttoned her blouse before she had the chance to make for the door.

'I see you've taken to going out without a bra,' he observed as he eased the blouse over her shoulders to reveal her firm breasts. 'You're obviously finding your true sexual identity, at long last.'

'Let me go! You're a pervert!'

'No, I'm not a pervert. I just enjoy the delights of the female form. I enjoy helping young ladies such as yourself to discover their true identities, their sexuality.'

Pushing against his chest, Jackie hurled obscenities at him but had no power to resist. Tugging on her skirt, he managed to pull it down over her thighs, exposing her tight, bulging panties. Holding her from behind, he pushed her struggling body against the upright frame and clamped first her wrists and then her ankles, one to each point of the X. After checking the clamps, he asked her if she were comfortable. She spat her reply in the form of expletives as she struggled hopelessly to free herself. The weight of her body still on her feet, she felt no discomfort – only terror.

'Don't beat me!' she screamed. 'Anything, but don't cane me!'

'I'm afraid I'll have to cut your tights off,' David announced, ignoring her pleas. 'I'd have thought that with your new-found hobby of exposing your knickers to strangers you'd have turned to stockings by now, but not to worry.' Donning a white coat, he took a pair of scissors from a drawer. 'If you'd been sensible, this wouldn't have been necessary,' he said, waving the scissors threateningly in her face.

'You really are mentally ill!' she hissed. 'You won't get away with this, I promise you that!'

'Let me worry about that, you just enjoy yourself.'

'Enjoy myself! You're sick!'

Jackie sobbed as the cold steel ran down between her splayed buttocks, cutting through the thin silk panties and her tights. Following the crease down between the pale crescents, he slit the material under her crotch and up between her lips to her abdomen. Easing the two halves of her panties down her legs, he rolled her severed tights down to her ankles. Before rising to his feet, he gently kissed her inner thigh and touched her warm, swollen lips. Jackie wriggled and cursed but could do nothing to stop him.

'Hello, Jackie,' Jane said cheerfully as she walked into the room. 'I told you that you'd be back, didn't I?' Jackie said nothing. She felt anger, but also arousal; hatred, but a simultaneous strange consuming love for David – and for Jane.

Moving around Jackie's shackled body, Jane looked into her eyes and smiled. She was wearing a crisp white nurse's uniform. The skirt was ridiculously short, exposing her knickerless pussy, and the top far too tight, lifting and forcing her breasts together to accentuate her cleavage. But the uniform gave the impression of child-like innocence, like that of a young girl playing at doctors and nurses. To complete the façade, her long blonde hair was bunched beneath a white cap.

'You're weird! Completely mad, do you know that?' Jackie hissed, aware of her clitoris enlarging slightly as she eyed Jane's stockinged legs and remembered her open body only inches from her face.

'The doctor will be here to examine you in a minute,' Jane announced, positioning the trolley nearer to the frame.

'Doctor?' Jackie questioned uneasily. For the first time, she experienced the sheer horror of cold fear. 'What doctor?'

'A doctor,' Jane said. 'An ordinary doctor – well, his examination techniques *are* rather extraordinary, I suppose.'

'You're all mad! You should be locked up!'

Jackie's heart raced as she watched Jane open a small

drawer. Suddenly, the thought crossed her mind that there was more to this than perverted sex. Doctor? Examination? The awesome surgery scenario was perfect. Apart from the vibrators and the frame, there was no telling the difference between a hospital examination room and David's 'surgery'.

'What are you going to do to me?' Jackie asked shakily, remembering having read somewhere of a man who performed horrendous experiments on his kidnap victims.

'This is necessary, I'm afraid,' Jane replied sympathetically as she slipped a blindfold over Jackie's wide eyes.

'I don't want the cane!' Jackie screamed hysterically.

'You won't get the cane if you're a good little girl,' Jane assured. 'Just be quiet and let the doctor examine you and you won't get the cane.'

In the darkness, Jackie was aware of the door opening and people moving about. She thought of the Sunday tabloids again, imagining they were already on to David. She pictured herself in the papers – strapped to the frame – depicted as an only too willing associate of the sordid scene.

'She's all ready for you, doctor,' Jane said as the door closed. Jackie trembled with fear as someone ran a finger down her spine and gently kissed the nape of her neck before gripping her buttocks in their hands as if to weigh them.

'Who the hell are you?' she yelled as her buttocks were eased apart by the two cold hands. 'What are you going to do to me?'

The doctor said nothing as he released her buttocks and turned the large handle. Jackie felt her body slowly folding over until her hands were near to the floor. Her legs splayed wide apart, her buttocks lay rudely open to reveal the intimacy within her crease.

Terrified, she listened to the awesome sound of stretching rubber as the anonymous doctor donned his gloves in preparation for the examination. She then heard a jar-top being unscrewed. Suddenly, her buttocks were pulled apart again. The coldness of the vaseline caused her heart to leap as it was carefully smeared between her buttocks with special attention paid to the small, private entrance to the depths of her body. Remembering David's sketch, she panicked and screamed.

'No, please don't! Not from behind! I know it's you, Tim. How could you do this?'

The doctor remained silent as he slowly screwed the jar-top down. Jackie winced in anticipation, her muscles tightening as she waited, ready to resist the awful penetration.

A finger disrespectfully found its way into the tight hole and slowly sank inside as she whimpered and swore to get even with Tim. As the intruding finger ran round and round, exploring the darkness within her bowels, she gasped with sexual arousal – and fear. The finger slowly slid out, causing her to quiver with a previously unknown delight. Her clitoris fluttered as the tight hole closed but still she begged in vain for her freedom.

A large, cold object was introduced to the tiny opening, twisting and gently pushing against the resisting muscles. Suddenly, her muscles gave way and the object sank deep inside. Its length violated her body, filling and stretching her as it slid deeper and deeper into her core.

Praying that she wouldn't be beaten, she remembered Jane's words. 'You won't get the cane if you're a good little girl'.

'I am being good, aren't I?' she sobbed pathetically as the solid object was twisted and pushed even further into her body. There was no reply. 'Just don't cane me or do it from behind and I won't tell anyone about you, Tim, I promise!' Her proposal went unheard.

The object began to move, sliding in and out an inch or two, filling and stretching her, producing delightful sensations that caused her clitoris to respond again. Suddenly, the cold invader began to vibrate, sending waves of sexual pleasure deep into her bowels – relaxing her muscles with its soothing rhythm.

Jackie remembered the video tapes and wondered if a camera was positioned somewhere behind her, capturing the vile scene. She suddenly had the terrifying notion that her ordeal might be viewed by hundreds of men all over the country. She'd often heard Meg talking of blue movies. Is this how they're made? she wondered, becoming aware of the doctor's presence again.

Working silently, he clamped the vibrator in place and moved his attention to Jackie's larger entrance. Three fingers pushed their way through the dampness, parting the soft walls as if gauging the girth and length of her passage. Pushing further, they reached her cervix and massaged the hard roundness of the entrance to her womb, enticing a flow of warm liquid to fill the bloated canal. Jackie knew that she couldn't take much more as the fingers stretched and kneaded the soft flesh. She breathed heavily as the hood of her clitoris caressed the erect bud with the doctor's every trespassing move.

Removing his hand, the unseen abuser selected a suitably sized vibrator from the shelf. Flicking the switch, he pushed the buzzing phallus between Jackie's gaping lips and carefully clamped it in place. The vibrations flowed through her pelvis as the hard, pink rubber swelled her canal to its limits. Gasping as the sensations began to flood her mind, she fell limp and relaxed. She'd given in to her desires – to the inner force.

The doctor carefully positioned a third vibrator at the top of her savagely opened slit and clamped it to the frame so that it rested gently against her clitoris. Her body immediately became rigid. Every muscle spasmed as the torturing sensations from the vibrators flowed in wondrous harmony.

Her first orgasm erupted within seconds, ripping through her entire body, stimulating every tiny nerve. Catching her breath between each wave of ecstasy, she felt that her body would split open from her abdomen to the base of her spine. She suddenly became conscious of a frightening instinct awakening within the depths of her soul. As if possessed, she breathed obscenities, mouthing her sordid delight at the doctor's unorthodox examination procedures. The stranger within had risen, yet again, to use Jackie's body for its perverse pleasures.

The gripping climax finally receded, allowing her to recover from an orgasm of a strength and duration that she had never thought possible. But her recovery was to be short-lived. The vibrators resonated like a piano chord, sending their hypnotic music through her pelvis to the depths of her body, combining to achieve another mind-blowing peak.

Gasping for breath, Jackie gritted her teeth as she felt the birth of an orgasm deep within her womb. It came suddenly, gushing up from the root of her clitoris to erupt like a volcano over the pulsating tip. Incessantly, the music of the vibrators played on to the beat of her throbbing clitoris until she could take no more.

The beautiful, sexual pain eventually subsided, leaving her quivering flesh drenched in perspiration. Her long, blonde hair, matted and darker in colour, trailed in a pool of sweat on the floor.

'No more,' she murmured. 'Please, no more,' as the

vibrators continued to play on her aching body, transmitting their reverberating caresses the length and breadth of her yawning furrow.

The third climax took longer to come. Jackie couldn't save herself from the rapturous torture as her ripening bud began to blossom again. Warm juice ran down her inner thigh as her body twitched and convulsed uncontrollably. As the sensations strengthened and centred on her flowering bud, her muscles relaxed to allow a stream of hot urine to flow freely down her legs. Then it came. Her clitoris discharged its most powerful orgasm yet, rendering her semiconscious with its intoxicating blasts of euphoria. Her heart banged hard against her heaving chest, filling her ears with pulsating blood. Gasping for breath, she thought she was about to die.

Jackie cried as the doctor switched off his instruments of sexual delight and slowly extracted them from her exhausted body. The frame moved, bringing her back to a vertical position where she hung, limp and drained, from her shackles.

The blindfold still in place, the doctor released her and carried her to a couch. She lay naked and panting for breath as he covered her with a quilt. Twisting and turning as the aftermath declined, she couldn't even think of removing the blindfold to discover the identity of the doctor – the man who had brought her the most exquisite orgasms any living soul could ever dream of experiencing. She could think of nothing other than her stretched aching holes, still throbbing and burning with satisfaction.

Eventually coming to her senses, Jackie sat up and lifted the blindfold from her stinging eyes. Wincing in the bright light, she gazed around the room – the 'surgery.' Her clothes lay in a neat pile by her feet. The door was open, offering freedom.

Discarding the quilt, she parted her legs and looked down at her inflamed quim lips. They were distended and sore – the soft skin still glowing from the recent bizarre fornication. Her bright red inner lips protruded, stuck together like the folded wings of a butterfly. She felt dirty, violated. Her clitoris tingled as she folded the delicate pads of flesh together to protect the sensitive membranes within. It was over, at last. The doctor had obviously made a hasty retreat. She was free.

Barely able to stand, she managed to drag her skirt up her legs and over her hips. Removing her rolled-up tights from her ankles, she quietly slipped her shoes on, listening for signs of life between each breath. Sitting on the couch again, she stared at the wooden frame and imagined the doctor kneeling on the floor gazing at her indignantly opened body. The severed halves of her panties lay in a pool of sweat and sex juices, heightening her disgust and yet sending an electrifying thrill through the tingling nerve endings between her thighs. Pulling her blouse over her shoulders, she grabbed her jacket and made for the door.

There was no sign of life but she was in no doubt that the doctor, David and Jane were hiding somewhere. Staggering up the stairs and across the lounge, she buttoned her blouse over her hard, brown nipples as she neared the hall. She half expected David to be waiting by the front door, ready to bid her farewell and invite her back for another session of lust. But there were no goodbyes. Having played her part, she was expected to leave the stage with no acclaim for her role.

Slipping her jacket over her shoulders, she wandered down the stone steps to the street. Turning to look at the house, she smiled, and then cried. She cried for David and Jane and all they stood for. She cried for herself, for what she once was – and the stranger she had become.

The night was cold. Slipping her hands into her jacket pockets, she pulled out a thick, gold ring studded with diamonds. A million thoughts raced through her mind as she wandered home, clutching her spoils. The ring, she knew, was payment. Her remittance, her settlement – the wages of sin.

Jackie sank into a hot bath and cleansed her defiled body, paying special attention to the sticky, delicate folds between her legs. She felt strangely content with her new, unruly life and the shameless pleasures it was bringing her. Pleasures that never in her wildest dreams had she thought possible.

Gazing at her naked mound reminded her again of her early days of masturbation and the terrific satisfaction her orgasms had brought her. Now, in her wickedness, she felt more than sexual satisfaction. Like a naughty schoolgirl caught with her soiled knickers around her ankles, she delighted in her delinquency.

Shaving the stubble from her soft skin, she wondered what the future would bring. Although disgusted with herself, she looked forward eagerly to her next sexual encounter.

Chapter Five

While having breakfast, Jackie suddenly remembered where she'd seen Elizabeth Rhodes. Rummaging through a pile of magazines, she triumphantly pulled out an old copy of the local newspaper.

On the front page, pictured outside her country house, was the mysterious Elizabeth Rhodes. The wealthy widow, in her late thirties, had been burgled while she'd been out one evening. Fifteen thousand pounds' worth of cash and jewellery had been taken in the raid on her home. Mrs Rhodes was under suspicion of attempting to defraud the insurance company as there were no signs of forced entry. The thief, it was alleged, must have had a key to the front door and the alarm system. As a result, the insurance company wouldn't pay up.

Jackie quickly put the puzzle together – the drawer full of jewellery, David's wealth, and Elizabeth Rhodes. 'He robs them,' she murmured, gazing in disbelief at the paper. 'While they're tied up and being caned by Jane, he robs them!'

It wasn't difficult for her to find Mrs Rhodes's phone number. But as she dialled, she wondered what on earth she was going to say. She couldn't give her identity away. Nor could she mention David's sex den without incriminating herself.

A well-spoken woman eventually answered the phone.

Jackie hesitated and was about to hang up but she quickly managed to formulate a plan.

'You don't know me, Mrs Rhodes. But if you'll tell me exactly what was stolen from your house, I may be able to return it.'

'Who is this?' came the cautious reply.

'What was stolen?'

Obviously taking the chance to have her jewellery returned, the woman read out a list of the stolen items. Having written everything down, Jackie ignored her questions and hung up.

She wasn't sure why she wanted to return the stolen goods. Pity, maybe? she mused. The thought suddenly struck her that she could blackmail the woman and earn herself a small fortune. *And* keep the jewellery, if she were able to take it from David's drawer without being caught. But she wanted to meet Elizabeth Rhodes and discover what sort of woman she was. She wanted to meet a woman who paid to be humiliated and beaten with a cane.

Forgetting about her job at the bank, Jackie quickly showered and dressed in jeans and a jumper in preparation for burgling David's house. She could only think of making money, a reward, as she stuffed the list of jewellery into her pocket and opened the front door.

The ringing telephone halted her. Closing the door, she walked into the lounge and picked up the receiver.

'Hello.'

'I told you not to go to that house, didn't I?'

'Who is this?'

'I'm warning you again, young lady – keep away!'

'Who the hell are you?'

'Don't get involved – you're way out of your depth!'

'Unless you tell me . . . Hello, hello?'

Replacing the receiver, thoughts of Rosita flooded her mind. 'It can't be her,' she mumbled, wandering towards the front door.

Forcing thoughts of the call to the back of her mind, she decided that she'd accept cash in return for the gems as she walked to David's house. Although the call had worried her, she knew that there was far too much at stake to let it spoil her plans.

'This is it,' she whispered excitedly as she stole round the back of David's house. Elizabeth Rhodes would part with a couple of thousand in return for her jewellery, she was sure.

Reaching the back door, she was delighted to find it unlocked. 'They're asking for trouble,' she breathed, stealing through the kitchen to the hall. Her heart thumped hard against her chest as she reached the lounge and paused. Again, she wondered if she was walking into a trap.

To Jackie's relief, the book-shelving was open. Although she thought it odd that David should leave the house unlocked with the jewellery in the drawer and the sex den open to intruders, she didn't give it a second thought.

The silence was almost deafening as she crept down the stairs. Her heart pumping adrenalin through her veins, she reached the bottom step and moved towards the desk. The danger aroused her. She half-hoped that she would be caught, strapped to the wooden frame and brutally punished for her crime. But the thought of money played on her mind, suppressing the desires of the stranger within.

Quickly opening the desk drawer, she made her inventory. There were only five easily identifiable items on her list, but among the mass of jewellery it took her some time to find them. She was tempted to stuff a gold watch into her pocket as she grabbed the last item on the list but no, that would be pushing her luck just a little too far.

The front door opened as she fled through the kitchen and out into the garden. Breathing easily again, she crept round the side of the house and out into the safety of the street. 'I've done it! My first-ever jewellery raid has been successful.'

It took exactly half-an-hour to drive to Elizabeth Rhodes's house. Jackie imagined David making the same journey, checking his watch every five minutes, wondering how Jane was coping with their victim.

Parking her car out of sight, she wandered up to the huge house. Two ugly stone lions standing either side of the steps to the front door greeted her as she gazed up at the old building. Raising the heavy brass door knocker, she let it fall and waited.

Dressed in a knee-length skirt and loose jumper, the timid Elizabeth Rhodes opened the front door and invited Jackie in without asking who she was.

'I don't have many callers,' she said in a soft voice as she closed the door and showed her visitor into the lounge. 'Have you got my jewellery?'

'It's quite safe,' Jackie replied. 'But there's the question of the reward first.'

'I realised that you'd want something. How much?' she asked tonelessly, moving towards the drinks cabinet.

After all her rehearsing and planning, Jackie couldn't find the courage to ask for two thousand pounds. She gazed around the expensively furnished room. Obviously Elizabeth Rhodes was well off, if not rich. She can easily afford it, Jackie convinced herself. And besides, the jewellery's worth far more. Suddenly, she had an idea.

'What's it worth, Mrs Rhodes?' she said coolly, neatly putting the ball into her court.

'A couple of hundred for your trouble, I suppose. And do call me Liz,' came the unexpected reply.

Suddenly fired with anger, Jackie found the strength and courage to speak her mind and talk business.

'Two thousand or forget it!' she stormed.

'Two thousand pounds is a lot of money. But I want my jewellery back and if that's your price, then I will pay it. Wait here while I make a phone call to my bank.'

She returned after some minutes and offered Jackie a drink. Her smile was almost a grin, as if she was about to play the winning shot.

'I can give you the cash within the hour or so,' she said, pouring herself a neat vodka. Jackie declined a drink, she wanted to keep a clear head. But Mrs Rhodes poured her a vodka anyway and placed it on a small table. Suddenly, Jackie sensed that something was wrong – very wrong. Why phone the bank? she wondered. Surely, there's no need for that?

'Your phone call. I hope for your sake that it wasn't to the police,' she said.

Mrs Rhodes hesitated and glanced at the window as if she was expecting someone. Without answering, she wandered around the room – playing for time, Jackie surmised.

'You didn't phone the police, did you?' she persisted.

'Do you think that I'm going to let a stupid young girl like you walk off with two thousand pounds?' Mrs Rhodes asked in a sarcastic tone. 'Of course I've called the police! They'll be here any minute.'

'I think you'd better ring them back and tell them that you've made a mistake,' Jackie returned.

'A mistake? You're probably the one who broke into my home in the first place. Either that, or you're in league with whoever did. You've made the mistake, not me!'

Jackie sipped her drink and sat in an armchair. Holding all the aces, she was enjoying every minute of the game.

'Where were you when your house was broken into?' she asked coolly, flicking her hair over her shoulder.

'Out, why?'

'Out where, exactly?'

'That's none of your business!'

'But it is. You see, I know where you were.'

'You can't possibly know! Anyway, I was at a friend's.'

Jackie paused for a moment, allowing Mrs Rhodes a little time to think. Rolling her glass between her palms, she smiled sweetly and glanced at her watch. 'They're taking their time, aren't they?' she remarked, allowing her smile to turn into a smirk. Mrs Rhodes paced the floor nervously, glancing at the window every few seconds.

'They'll be here any minute,' she eventually said, pulling the net curtains aside.

'Good, I haven't got all day,' Jackie returned, sinking back into the armchair to show her obvious unconcern.

'I was at a friend's,' Mrs Rhodes repeated hesitantly.

'So you said.'

'But I was! Why don't you believe me?'

'Is that what you told the police when they questioned you?'

'Yes, yes. Of course it is, why?'

'I don't think it is, because they would have checked your story, wouldn't they?'

'Why check my story? I was the victim of the crime!'

'Did the insurance company pay up?'

'Why do you ask?'

'I just wondered,' Jackie smiled.

'Wondered what?'

'What it costs these days to be stripped naked, tied

down and have your body sexually abused – whipped with a cane?'

The woman's mouth fell open. She was visibly stunned. Knocking back her vodka, she refilled her glass and collapsed on the sofa. Her big brown eyes gazed at Jackie.

'How do you . . . Who are you?' she asked fearfully.

'Don't worry, Liz. Your secret's safe with me. Pay up and you'll never see me again, I promise you that.'

'But I don't have that sort of money in the house. The most I could raise is a thousand and that's at a push. Is there nothing else you want?'

Jackie's heart raced. She suddenly pictured Liz strapped over the wooden frame, her buttocks splayed, her thick pussy lips protruding. She gazed into her eyes as her clitoris stirred. Liz was an extremely attractive woman, fresh complexion, slim – and very wealthy. Fired by the inner force, Jackie carefully contemplated her next move.

'You'd better call the police and tell them that you've made a mistake,' she said triumphantly. Without a word, Liz hurriedly left the room to make her call. When she returned, she sat down and waited to hear Jackie's terms. Her face was pale, her hands shaking.

'I'll take a thousand and . . .' Jackie began, but she couldn't say it. Liz looked at her expectantly before refilling her glass with a large measure of vodka.

'And what?' Liz repeated with a smile, as if she knew exactly what Jackie had in mind.

The tables had turned, it seemed. Jackie cursed herself for her uncontrollable sexual desires – the irrepressible force constantly rising within her subconscious to take control. Her plan was rapidly falling apart, she had to think quickly, act before it was too late.

'A thousand pounds and . . .'

'And this,' Liz interrupted, lifting her skirt up over her stomach as she lay back on the sofa. Jackie eyed her naked, tanned thighs, the tight, white panties, faithfully following the contour of the soft swelling between her legs. Dark pubic curls fringed the edges of the alluring silky material.

Making no conscious decision, Jackie automatically moved towards the sofa and fell to her knees, gazing wide-eyed at the offering. 'And this,' she breathed, pulling the tight panties off and slowly moving her face towards the thick, dark bush. Her heart thumped wildly at the prospect of sucking another woman's clitoris, bringing another woman to orgasm with her mouth, her tongue. Pressing her face against the curls, she breathed in the heady scent of the warm, moist dividing groove.

'Not yet,' Liz said, covering herself with her hands. 'We haven't settled the deal yet, have we?'

'But I thought . . .'

'If you want my body in way of payment, then I agree. But nothing else. You'll get your pound of flesh, but no more.'

Jackie desperately wanted to taste the delights before her, to push her tongue through the soft hair and explore the female form, her own form, in a way never before possible. But she needed money. She knew that she could never return to the bank, not now. Torn between the chance of experiencing a hard clitoris pulsating with orgasm against her tongue, or money, she decided to call Liz's bluff.

'All right, just give me the money and we'll forget about that,' she said, nodding towards Liz's clasped hands.

'Are you sure?' Liz smiled, opening her hands and peeling her quim lips apart to display her extended bud. Jackie gasped as Liz pressed the pink skin surrounding the growth, drawing out its full length. It visibly hardened to the size of a large nipple as Jackie gazed with bated breath.

'No, forget it,' she forced herself to say, dragging her eyes away from the inch-long protrusion, desperately trying to suppress the urging voice in her mind. Liz ran a finger slowly up and down the length of her glans, breathing deeply with each stroke. It grew in girth and length as she caressed the tip, but Jackie wasn't going to be beaten. As much as she wanted to take the miniature penis-like shaft in her mouth, she was determined not to back down.

'You win,' Liz eventually conceded, bringing herself near to orgasm with her slender fingers. 'I know you want me as much as I want you – but you win.'

Moving her open mouth towards her reward, Jackie closed her lips over the long, hard bud and gently sucked. Liz let out a deep moan as Jackie's hot saliva swirled around the bud and her tongue flicked the tip, stiffening the miniature phallus to bursting point. Like a babe at the breast, she mouthed and sucked, delighting in the sensations that she was giving another woman. Confusion reigned in Jackie's mind as Liz pulled her nether lips further apart and breathed deeply. But soon, her mind settled – she gave in to the stranger within. Inhaling the aromatic bouquet and savouring the bitter-sweet flavour of sex, she pressed her mouth against the open flesh. Moving Liz's fingers, she allowed the swollen lips to close over her face. Right or wrong, it didn't matter anymore. Jackie's change, her possession, was complete.

Moving down towards the wet hole, Jackie felt her own clitoris tremble as she sipped her first ever drop of female sex fluid. It was warm and slippery. Fervently, she drank the aphrodisiacal nectar as it trickled from the magical cavern until, diluted, the flavour diminished.

'Make more!' she demanded, sucking at the dry well. Liz pulled her reddened skin up and apart to reveal her urethral opening.

'Lick me just there and you'll have more,' she gasped. Jackie followed her instructions and teased the small, red slit with her tongue. As promised, the nectar flowed freely again as Liz caught her breath and grimaced as if in pain.

'Now put your fingers inside,' Liz ordered as she pulled Jackie's head up to position her mouth over her clitoris once more. Jackie managed to slip first two, then three and four fingers deep inside the hungry cavern. As she licked and sucked on the little phallus, the muscles deep within the hole tightly gripped her hand and she found it increasingly difficult to move her fingers. Like a vice, the cavern suddenly closed over her intruding fingers as Liz cried out. Her clit pumped and throbbed incessantly against Jackie's caressing tongue, making it difficult for her to breathe as Liz crushed Jackie's head between her thighs. Liz let out another long, soft moan of pleasure and then crumpled in a trembling heap on the sofa. Her face covered in the warm, milky fluid of orgasm, Jackie lifted her head.

'You came in my mouth,' she gasped appreciatively, wiping her face with her hand. 'I made you come in my mouth.' Liz opened her eyes and smiled.

'That was nice, but you've a lot to learn about oral sex. I suppose you'd better come in my mouth now, as you so aptly put it,' she whispered, lowering her skirt and moving onto the floor. Without a word, Jackie slipped her jeans and panties off and relaxed on the sofa with Liz between her open thighs. Closing her eyes as Liz parted her lips and began to lick the drenched crease, Jackie breathed deeply and relaxed.

'Your clitoris is rather small, isn't it?' Liz murmured. 'Mine used to be like that until . . .'

'Until what?' Jackie gasped.

'Never mind. It's something I can't talk about.'

Running a finger round the hard little bud, she opened Jackie's lips further and engulfed the pink flesh with her mouth. Jackie felt her mind leaving her body, blowing away on a wind of lust as she opened herself completely and let go.

Liz worked expertly with her tongue until Jackie began to tremble. Gripping Liz's head and forcing her mouth hard against her open slit, she cried out as the stranger within took control. 'Fuck me with your tongue. Put it in me!'

Electrifying waves of pleasure coursed their way through Jackie's shaking body as Liz pushed her tongue deep into the expectant hole and tasted the soft inner walls. Her timing perfect, she moved along the open slit and sucked an orgasm from Jackie's ballooning clitoris. Grabbing her feet, Liz pushed them high up in the air, revealing the entire length of the wet, swollen groove. She licked from the bottom to the top of the fissure time and time again, drinking the fluid as it spewed from the gaping hole. At last, she felt Jackie relax and gently lowered her trembling legs to the ground.

'Well?' she said. 'Was that nice?'

Jackie nodded, her eyes still closed, her body still quivering.

'Yes, that was nice,' she eventually managed to gasp.

'Wait there, I'll get your money for you,' Liz said, jumping to her feet and wiping her mouth on the back of her hand.

Jackie dressed quickly while Liz was out of the room. She was surprised that she was going to pay up. She'd thought that she'd have to settle for sex without the money – although that would have been more than enough, she had to admit. She thought of Liz's words while she waited. 'You've a lot to learn about oral sex.' She wondered at the sexually experienced lesbian hiding behind such a timid-looking woman and hoped that they'd meet again.

'One thousand,' Liz said, handing Jackie a wad of notes. 'And now, my jewellery, please.'

'It's in the car. Come with me and I'll give it to you,' Jackie said, stuffing the notes into her jeans as she walked unsteadily towards the door.

Passing Liz the jewellery, Jackie gazed longingly into her eyes as she started the engine. There was no emotion, no mention of seeing each other again, much to her disappointment. Liz hadn't even asked her her name. Perhaps that's it, Jackie mused as she smiled and pulled away. The payoff is complete, and that's it.

She stopped in the town on her way home and treated herself to a shopping spree. She spent three hundred pounds on clothes – miniskirts, tops, shoes, a new winter coat and several pairs of stockings and lace panties – but no bras.

Back at her flat, she counted out the thirty-five remaining twenty-pound notes. 'I'm rich!' she squealed. 'Or I will be when I return more of the jewellery to its rightful owners.'

The phone rang as she was stuffing the notes behind the wardrobe. She paused for a moment, thinking that it must be the bank. She'd tell them that her resignation was in the post, she decided as she picked up the receiver.

'Jackie?' David's deep voice asked.

'Yes,' she replied hesitantly, wondering how on earth he knew her number.

'Can you call round to see me? I have a proposition for you.'

The line went dead before she had a chance to question him.

'A proposition?' she muttered, changing into her skirt. 'Now what sort of proposition would that be? I wonder. To join them in their little business venture, I expect.'

The front door was open when Jackie arrived at David's house. She felt sophisticated in her new clothes, professional, as if she was going to an interview with a view to becoming a partner in the business. Bounding down the stairs to the den, she called out for David but he was nowhere in sight. Making herself comfortable on the four-poster bed, she waited, wondering what David would offer her.

'Ah, Jackie,' he said as he entered the room. Catching his gaze, her heart leaped. His smile was warm and inviting. Even after all that had happened, she still felt an electric charge run through her body when she was near to him.

'Hello,' she said softly, wondering if he'd noticed her sexy new skirt and top.

'Follow me. I want to show you around and talk to you about my little proposition.'

Walking through the studio, Jackie felt confident, important. Far better than a bank clerk, she mused as David pulled the tapestry back and opened the door to the surgery. She followed – like a lamb to the slaughter. The door closed behind them and she turned to see Jane removing the key from the lock.

'What is this?' she asked fearfully.

'This,' David began. 'This is a difficult situation, Jackie. You see, I had a telephone call from one of my clients. It seems that a young lady called at her house to return some stolen property. She was delighted, of course. But I, we, are far from delighted.'

'*Far* from delighted,' Jane echoed, moving towards the frame.

'You see, we work hard for our money and we don't take kindly to other people stealing it from us. Especially as we've already given you some very expensive jewellery.'

David took Jackie's arms and held them up to the frame while Jane secured her wrists. She struggled as if her life depended on it, which, she thought, it probably did. But David's strong arms held her fast – there was no escaping his grip. Grabbing her kicking feet, he held them tight while Jane finished her job of bondage.

'That's better,' he said, a little out of breath as he brushed his dark hair back with his fingers. 'You put up quite a fight, don't you?'

'Let me go!' Jackie screamed, knowing that this time she was in serious trouble. 'Please let me go! It wasn't me. I don't know anything about any stolen jewellery. That Rhodes woman is lying . . .'

Realising her fatal mistake, she gazed in terror at Jane. 'Who said anything about Rhodes?' Jane asked, taking a cane from the umbrella stand and slapping it across the palm of her hand. 'I didn't mention that name. Did you mention that name, David?'

'No. All I said was, a client of mine.'

Jackie froze as David moved behind her and lifted her skirt. Pulling on her panties, he managed to slip them down to her splayed thighs. 'Scissors, please,' he said, turning to Jane. She passed the scissors and stood in front of Jackie, gazing into her terror-stricken eyes as David cut every last shred of her new clothing from her trembling body.

'Will you do the honours?' David asked. 'I've got some business to attend to.'

'With pleasure,' Jane breathed, her eyes lighting up like a child's as she flexed the cane under Jane's nose.

'Please, no!' Jackie yelled as Jane turned the frame's handle, slowly bending her body over until her head was near to the floor. 'I'll do anything, anything!' she sobbed as Jane gently tapped her pale buttocks with the cane.

'Just here, I think,' she said, tapping a little harder. 'What do you think, Jackie? Is that the right place?'

'No, no. Please don't!'

'No? What about here, then?' she said, tapping harder still.

The cane suddenly swished through the air and landed squarely across Jackie's splayed buttocks. She screamed as the cane landed for the second time and then the third.

'Please stop. Please stop!' she screeched, but Jane continued the punishment. Ten, fifteen, twenty times the cane landed on the red-raw flesh until, her arm aching, Jane stopped. Dropping the cane into the stand, she sat on the floor to gaze at Jackie's upturned face.

'Well, did you like that?' she asked. Jackie could only sob but, somewhere deep inside, she had to admit to herself that, amid the stinging pain, she *had* been strangely aroused. Jane rose to her feet and began to rub some cold, soothing cream into Jackie's burning flesh. The coolness and the touch of Jane's fingers between her buttocks excited her. She became aware of her clitoris enlarging a little every time Jane neared her small hole with her sensuous, cooling touch.

'All done?' David asked, closing the door behind him.

'The first stage of the punishment is over,' Jane replied, wiping her hands on a towel. Jackie opened her eyes on hearing Jane's words.

'No more, please. No more!' she begged.

'I found this in your flat,' David said, bending his knees and waving the wad of notes in Jackie's face. 'It's better than nothing, I suppose, but the jewellery was worth ten times more. And we have another problem – what are we to do with you?'

'Let me go!' Jackie pleaded. 'I won't say anything to anyone, I promise. Please let me go!'

'We can't do that, I'm afraid. You see, there's too much at stake, isn't there, Jane?'

'Yes, too much at stake. So what are we going to do, David?'

Turning the large handle, he sighed. 'I don't know. I really don't know.'

Jackie knew that she'd provoked him by returning the jewellery, but it had all been an exciting game. The sex den, the caning, just a game. But now she was beginning to realise that he was extremely serious – she really did present a big problem.

The frame moved, slowly bringing Jackie back to the upright position. Her face flushed and streaked with tears, she looked to Jane for sympathy. But her gaze was only met with a salacious grin.

'I think I'll call the doctor. Perhaps he can come up with an idea,' David said, turning the other handle to move Jackie to the horizontal position. Lying on her stomach, she felt a little more comfortable, although her buttocks were still stinging. To her horror, she found herself almost looking forward to the doctor's perverted sexual examination.

'Why not let me join you?' she suggested. 'I can help you both with whatever it is you're doing.'

'It wouldn't work,' David replied. 'You see, we don't need anybody else. You'd just be a burden – a risk.'

'I wouldn't. Please give me a chance,' she begged.

Without answering, Jackie's jailers left the room and closed the door. She could hear them talking about her, about the doctor. Suddenly, she realised that there was only one way to deal with the problem, with her, permanently. 'They can't kill me,' she breathed. 'God, they wouldn't do that, would they?'

'The doctor's on his way,' Jane announced, entering the room. 'He'll only be a few minutes.'

'People know I'm here,' Jackie said, groping for a last chance for her freedom. 'Several friends of mine know all about you, David, and this place. They'll come looking for me.'

'Oh, that just makes matters worse,' Jane sighed disappointedly as she ran her hand between Jackie's legs and pushed two fingers into her hole. 'You see, I've been trying to get David to let me keep you for myself. Keep you locked up here as my plaything. But now, well, I don't know. He won't agree if your friends are going to come looking for you.'

'No, they won't. No one knows, honestly,' Jackie cried. 'I was just trying to . . .'

'The doctor's here,' David called through the open door. Jane blindfolded their victim before asking the doctor in. That's a good sign, Jackie thought. If they were going to kill me, they wouldn't bother to blindfold me.

'This is our problem,' David said sternly.

'And quite a nice little problem it is,' a male voice replied. Jackie didn't recognise the doctor's voice. It wasn't Tim, she was sure. So who was it?

'You'll have to turn her over. I can't possibly work with her on her stomach,' he instructed.

David quickly brought the frame back to the upright position and released the clamps. Although she fought furiously, Jackie stood no chance of breaking free as he turned her round and held her in place while Jane clamped her limbs. The frame moved quickly, tipping her onto her back, her legs splayed, her body open – ready for the doctor.

'I want her dealt with, permanently,' David instructed. 'No playing around this time.'

'I understand,' the doctor replied solemnly.

Jackie froze as two hands stretched open her hole and rubbed cold cream into the soft flesh. A large object was introduced to the entrance and slowly pushed home, deep into her body. Someone pinched her nipples. Jane, she suspected, as she sobbed.

'I'm sure I can get two in there,' the doctor mumbled, moving the object to one side.

'No! Please, you can't, I'm not big enough!' Jackie screamed.

'Yes, you are,' came the muttered reply as her labia were eased apart a little further.

A loud bell suddenly rang out. 'Who the hell's that?' David stormed.

'She said something about her friends knowing where she is, knowing about us,' Jane yelled frantically.

'Why didn't you tell me?'

'I thought she was bluffing!'

'Well, they'll never find her – they'll never see her again. Quickly, get upstairs.'

Jackie was aware of hurried movements before the door slammed shut. She heard the key turning in the lock and then footsteps bounding up the stairs. Left alone, she squeezed her muscles and ejected the intruder from her hole. It fell to the floor with a thud. Hoping she'd be heard by whoever had come to the house, she screamed for help for all she was worth. But her cries went unheard.

Chapter Six

Jackie struggled desperately to break free but she knew it was pointless; she couldn't even shake the blindfold from her eyes. Minutes dragged by like hours as she waited, panic-stricken, to discover her fate. Eventually, the key turned in the lock and the door opened. Holding her breath, she listened to the footsteps walking slowly across the tiled floor towards her.

'It's me,' Jane whispered, leaning over and sucking hard on her nipple. 'David and the doctor have had to go out so you'll just have to wait, I'm afraid.'

'Wait for what?' sobbed Jackie.

'Wait until they return, I suppose. They'll be a few hours, though. Business, you see. Apparently . . . Well, you've no need to worry yourself about that.'

Removing the blindfold, Jane pressed her mouth to Jackie's, kissing her passionately, probing with her tongue, savouring the warm saliva. Alone with Jane, Jackie knew her chances of escape would never be better. Returning the kiss, she moaned through her nose, as if aroused.

'I'm uncomfortable,' she sighed. 'My arm has gone dead. Can't we go to the other room? I want to be with you on the bed. I want to make love to you.'

'And I want you, too,' Jane breathed, moving her face down to Jackie's stomach and pushing her tongue into her navel before licking the soft skin down to her mound to settle in her moist slit. Pushing her mouth between the warm, pink lips, she slipped her tongue into the creamy hole and ran it round and round, exploring the intimate hotness of Jackie's violated body. Jackie writhed and moaned a little as Jane's tongue darted in and out, lapping up the freely flowing juices.

'Let's go into the other room,' Jackie pleaded. 'I want you on the bed. I want to taste you, too.'

Standing up, Jane smiled. Jackie knew the young lesbian was more than tempted. She couldn't resist having her lips stretched wide open, her clitoris sucked and her hole licked.

'I want to taste you, down there, between your lips,' Jackie persisted, gazing at the girl's short skirt. 'I want you to squat over my mouth so I can love you with my tongue.'

'You won't try anything silly, will you?' Jane asked, her eyes wide with anticipation as she released the clamps to give Jackie her freedom. 'There's no escape, the book-shelving can't be opened without a special key, and David's taken it with him,' she added, helping her captive to the floor.

Jackie slowly found her feet and stretched her limbs. Freedom was so close now and she grabbed her chance. As a woman possessed, she turned and lifted Jane off the floor, landing her heavily over the frame with a dull thud. Mustering up an uncanny strength, Jackie leapt on top of her and pinned her down with her weight as she quickly fastened the clamps.

'So, the tables have turned,' she laughed triumphantly, tearing Jane's short skirt from her trembling body.

'David will be back any minute so you'd better let me go!' Jane warned fearfully as she wiggled to free herself.

'But you said that he'd be a few hours,' Jackie laughed,

ripping Jane's panties from her pale, vulnerable buttocks.

'I lied. Look, let me go and I'll help you to escape. I can open the book-shelving. Let me go and I'll help you, I promise!'

'Help me? To do what – get back on the frame? Or help to violate my body – to cane me?'

'No, no, help you to get out of here!'

'Oh, I'm getting out anyway, but there's something that I want to do before I leave – something that I'm going to enjoy very much!'

Selecting a cane, Jackie slapped it across the palm of her hand as Jane looked on in terror. Tapping it lightly across her buttocks, she asked if she'd found the right spot. Jane didn't answer – she knew that she deserved all that was coming to her.

Jackie punctuated the strokes that fell gently across the unblemished skin of the girl's tightening buttocks with hard cracks of the cane that made Jane wince. Progressively swishing the thin bamboo faster through the air, her anger rose as the stranger within began to take control.

'How sweet revenge!' she laughed wickedly, landing the first really hard, stinging blow to the twitching crescents. Her youthful body quivering, Jane yelped and pleaded for mercy as a second, harder blow struck home. Again and again, Jackie thrashed the girl's young buttocks until they glowed a warm crimson, criss-crossing them with thin, red weals until Jane screamed hysterically for mercy.

'And now for your filthy little cunt!' Jackie bellowed, shocked but somehow aroused by her choice of words. Flinging the cane across the room, she ran her fingers along the shelf of vibrators and selected the largest – a long, thick, cylindrical object, far too large even for a multiparous woman, let alone a young girl like Jane. Grinning wickedly, she wielded it threateningly under

Jane's eyes, brushing the tip against her nose. 'How do you like the idea of having your tight little cunt stretched open by this? Being some kind of perverted nymphomaniac, you'd like that, wouldn't you? Well, I'm going to make sure that you *don't* like it! This is going to open your cunt so much that it will probably tear the delicate skin, and if it doesn't, then I'll force another one alongside it!' The alien words fell from her lips with ease. They weren't her words, she knew – they came from a stranger within. But the idea of stretching a girl to the limits aroused her clitoris as never before and it throbbed, calling for attention.

'The tables have turned,' she repeated gleefully, moving between Jane's open legs. Roughly stretching her buttocks apart, she dug her fingernails into the soft flesh, pulling them up to expose the lower end of the pink fissure where the soft lips fuse together. The hole lay invitingly open between the rubbery flesh, oozing with cream, waiting to be stretched and filled to capacity. Presenting the massive phallus to the open slit, she slowly pushed and twisted until the tip slipped inside. Jane gasped as inch by inch her canal was opened until her cervix halted the intruder and her young body was completely impaled. Jackie grinned at the pink, stretched flesh as she carefully clamped the vibrator in place.

Jane moaned with pleasure as Jackie flicked the switch, her soft, inner flesh responding immediately by gripping and bathing the phallus with more warm, creamy liquid. 'I'll bet you've never had anything that big in your cunt before,' Jackie laughed, wiping a generous helping of vaseline around the entrance to her smaller hole. Jane could only whimper as a second vibrator pushed its way past the tight ring to sink gently into her bowels.

'Is that nice?' Jackie asked, switching it on and tightening the clamp.

'Ah, yes, that's nice! But don't cane me again – just let me relax and come, I desperately need to come!'

'You're going to come all right!' Jackie promised excitedly, grabbing a third vibrator from the shelf and clamping it against the girl's hard, protruding clitoris. She gazed in awe at the tight flesh, stretched to splitting point by the mammoth vibrator, as the young body shook and trembled violently. Jane quivered and moaned quietly as her orgasm neared. Milky juice ran down the pink shaft of the vibrator, glistening in the light as it dripped to the floor. Jackie's clitoris began to stir again and throb between her swollen lips, but she wasn't interested in her own sexual satisfaction yet. For now, she wanted only to savour her revenge.

Jane continued her low moans of pleasure and gasped with delight as the vibrators buzzed in unison within the warm depths of her slim, young body. Her muscles twitching spasmodically, she began to move her hips as if meeting the thrusts of a hard penis as it opened her body and rammed her cervix.

'You're enjoying it, aren't you?' Jackie asked, desperately trying to fight off her own rising arousal as her clitoris tingled and ached for caress.

'Ah, yes! Yes!' Jane breathed appreciatively as another wave of ecstasy enveloped her.

'Well, that's not the idea!'

Retrieving the cane, Jackie gently tapped Jane's buttocks again, somehow intoxicated with the power she had over the defenceless young girl.

'No, don't cane me! Please, not again!' Jane cried. 'Just let me come! My cunt aches to come, just let me come!'

Merciless, Jackie thrashed Jane's buttocks with all her

might. One stinging blow after another caused the girl to cry out. Jackie wasn't sure if her victim screamed in orgasm or pain but she didn't care. She was delighting in her long-awaited revenge. On and on she beat the girl's crescents, stiffening her own clitoris with every blow until she was forced to massage her bud and bring relief. With her fingers between her puffy lips, she brought herself to a massive orgasm as she continued to thrash Jane's buttocks. Her legs almost giving way, she rubbed her clitoris until it retreated under its hood, satisfied – for a while, at least.

Eventually returning to her senses, Jackie surmised that if David returned early, he'd probably allow Jane to give her the beating of her life. Landing one last blow across the crimson buttocks, she flung the cane on the couch and opened the door.

'You can't get out,' Jane panted. 'You'll never escape!'

'I'll get out! And you'll never see me again!'

'Don't leave me like this! I can't take much more,' Jane whimpered as another orgasm welled up from her womb to erupt through her aching, rock-hard clitoris.

'You can take it,' Jackie assured her as the girl's young body again convulsed and writhed uncontrollably. 'You'll have to take it! Besides, that's what you've grown up to believe your dirty little cunt is for, isn't it? Being abused, fucked by vibrators, stretched and treated as if it's just some debased, vile hole between your legs?'

Leaving Jane whimpering, she made her way up the stairs to find the book-shelving closed. 'I'll smash my way out if I bloody well have to!' she swore. But, to her surprise, it opened with ease as she put her weight against it. Running through the lounge, she heard Jane cry out as another tormenting climax coursed its way through her tethered body. 'That'll teach the filthy bitch,' she sniggered, wondering how many orgasms it was possible for a woman to have as she ran across the hall and opened the front door to make her escape.

The flat was cold. David had turned the heating off, obviously not expecting Jackie to return for some time, if at all. But he'd be round before long, she knew, to drag her back to the dungeon where he'd tie her down and beat her – kill her. She felt cornered. She had nowhere else to go, nowhere to hide. And why should she hide? Why should she run? She'd done nothing to deserve the situation, she told herself, collapsing onto the bed.

The telephone rang. She knew who it was as she walked into the lounge and picked up the receiver.

'You'd better get yourself round here, the police are on their way to your flat.' There was an unusual tone of urgency in David's deep voice.

'Good!' Jackie screamed. 'I'll tell them all about you when they arrive! You've saved me the call!'

'It's not quite that simple, Jackie. You see, there have been several robberies recently, all by my own good hand, of course, and the police suspect you.'

'Why me? They'll believe me when I tell them everything.'

'No, no, they won't. You see, Mrs Rhodes rang me. She's put two and two together and come up with five, I'm afraid. She doesn't suspect me at all, that's the beauty of it! Don't ask me how, but she knows your name and address.'

'She can't possibly know. You're bluffing.'

'Think what you like, but she's told the police that she gave you money in return for her stolen jewellery – how are you going to explain that?'

'I don't believe you! You're just trying to get me back to your house so you can . . .'

'Oh well, have it your way. Don't say that I didn't warn you.'

'But she *can't* know who I am. Not unless you told her.'

'Did you go by car to her house?'

'Yes.'

'Well, there you are, then. She probably took your car number. All the police had to do was enter the number into their computer and . . . Well, if I were you, I'd think seriously.'

Liz wouldn't have called the police, surely? Not after . . . But she couldn't be sure. Perhaps David really was trying to help her, or save himself – or both.

'Are you still there, Jackie?'

'Yes, yes. And I still say that you're bluffing!'

'You spent three hundred pounds, didn't you?'

'Yes, I bought some clothes. Why?'

'What will the police think? You haven't turned up at your job for some time. You spend three hundred in cash. They'll soon find out where you went and what you bought and . . .'

'All right, all right, I believe you. So what shall I do?'

'Come and stay with us. You'll be quite safe, I promise you.'

'Safe! How can I be safe with you and that perverted doctor friend of yours? You're all bloody perverts, the lot of you!'

'It's entirely up to you. Stay there and get yourself arrested, or come here. We'll protect you – hide you.'

'Yes, hide me in the surgery and torture me!'

'No, we won't. Anyway, as I said, it's up to you.'

Replacing the receiver, Jackie flopped onto the sofa in despair. David was right, she knew. Elizabeth Rhodes, it seemed, was out to get her. And she could hardly let on about David and Jane. There was no way anyone would believe her fantastic story of the sex-den, the surgery, vibrators and wealthy clients paying to be beaten – and besides, she was a part of the set-up. Once they had her for stealing Liz's jewellery, which wouldn't be too diffi-cult, they'd probably pin the other robberies on her.

Dusk had fallen rapidly and the flat was still cold. Jackie pulled the net curtains aside and looked out onto the icy street to see several cars driving by, cautiously making their way along the snow-covered road. One stopped opposite her flat. Without waiting to find out who it was, she fled through the back door and ran into the garden.

The freezing air hit her. Snow was falling in huge flakes from the dark sky. In her panic, she'd forgotten her jacket, but she knew that she daren't go back for it. Climbing over the wall she grazed her leg, cursing as she ran through the neighbouring gardens and out into the street. Without looking back, she turned the corner and stopped to catch her breath. 'God, what am I doing?' She shivered as the wind whipped up the snow around her ankles.

Walking slowly to David's house, the horrifying truth suddenly hit her – she was a criminal on the run. But there was little or no choice – trust David and Jane, or face possible imprisonment. 'The devil and the deep blue sea,' she murmured, climbing the steps to the house.

David opened the door and quickly ushered her into the hall as he looked out into the street before slamming it shut. Leading her into the lounge, he seated her by the fire and poured her a brandy.

'You saw sense, then?' he asked, passing her the glass.

'I had no bloody choice!' she replied angrily, rubbing her badly grazed leg. 'This is all your fault! I thought that you were going to kill me!'

'Kill you? Don't be stupid! We were simply trying to

frighten you, that's all. That Rhodes stunt of yours nearly had us all locked up!'

'Well, you made a bloody good job of frightening me! Who is this perverted doctor, anyway?'

David said nothing as he sat in an armchair and sipped his drink. She didn't repeat her question. She was safe, for the time being at least, and that was all that mattered. Relieved that David had only been trying to frighten her, she relaxed in the warmth of the fire and finished her drink.

The door bell rang. Standing behind the lounge door, Jackie listened intently as David invited someone into the hall. She thought it was the doctor – but then she froze.

'I'm sorry to trouble you, sir. We're calling at all the houses in the immediate locality making enquiries about a woman who lives just around the corner in Graves Road – Jackie Wilson. I don't suppose you know her, do you?'

'No, officer, I don't. What's she done?'

'I can't say too much, sir, but we need to speak to her in connection with a burglary, amongst other things.'

'Well, I'm only sorry I can't help.'

'No need to worry, sir. Her picture in the local paper will spark someone's memory, it usually does. Her car's still outside her flat so she can't have gone far. We'll find her. As I said, I'm sorry to have troubled you. Good night.'

Jackie's face paled and her legs buckled as David wandered back into the lounge.

'Well, that was interesting,' he said nonchalantly, taking her empty glass.

'Interesting! You know what this means, don't you? I can't leave this place! I'm a bloody prisoner!'

'That's true,' he smiled. 'If you so much as take one step outside, someone will see you and . . .'

'And I'm done for! What a mess, what a bloody mess!'

'Don't worry, you can stay with us, I've told you that. Here, drink this.'

'I can't go to the pub, my flat – I'm a prisoner!'

David sat in the armchair and folded his arms. His expression took on a serious tone as he looked at Jackie and nodded towards the sofa for her to sit down. What's his game? she wondered. What the hell does he want from me?

'You said that you wanted to help us with whatever it is we're doing, remember?' he began.

She nodded as she made herself comfortable, ready to hear the worst.

'As you will appreciate, you've made things extremely difficult for us. You'll have to stay here until . . . Well, until God only knows when. You've no money, you can't go out.'

'What are you saying?' Jackie asked hesitantly.

'I'm saying that you'll have to pay for your keep. You wanted to work with us anyway, so that shouldn't be a problem.'

'Pay? How, exactly?'

'Helping with the clients. Just being available, that sort of thing, I suppose.'

'Available for what?'

'We'll talk about it tomorrow, I've got some work to do.'

'How's Jane?' Jackie enquired, remembering that she'd left her in a compromising position.

'Sore. Extremely sore,' David replied. 'She's downstairs if you want to go and see her. Oh, by the way, you'll have to sleep downstairs, in the four-poster bed. Just to be on the safe side.'

'I don't suppose she's very happy with me at the moment.'

'Go and see her. She's all right, she'll be pleased to see you.'

Slowly, Jackie made her way down the stairs to the den to find Jane resting under the quilt on the four-poster bed.

'Oh,' Jane murmured, peeping over the quilt. 'I wondered when you'd be back.'

'Sorry about . . . Well, an eye for an eye, I suppose,' Jackie smiled, sitting on the edge of the bed. 'How are you?'

'The debased, vile hole between my legs aches like hell!'

'And so does my bum!'

'All's fair in love and war, as they say,' Jane whispered. 'I must get up and have a shower, we've got a client coming this evening. An extremely rich client.'

'Not Mrs Rhodes?'

'No. This one's far richer than she is. A Lady someone or other. You'd better stay in here while I deal with her.'

'How do you get all these rich clients? I mean, do they really answer adverts or something and come here to pay for . . .'

'Adverts! Good God, no! David uses his charm – and reads the obituary columns, of course. They're all wealthy women whose late husbands have left them their fortunes. I shouldn't be telling you all this. Anyway, I've got to talk to David. You stay here out of harm's way.'

'But why do wealthy women want to be caned and abused?'

'Because they're lonely.'

'That doesn't make sense. When my father died, my mother didn't turn to a place like this for . . . Well, to be abused, sexually.'

'Ah, but these women can't have men friends as most can. They're women of standing in the community, many are in the public eye and they need, as we all do, some sexual comfort – some attention, I suppose. Anyway, I'm going to get ready,' Jane said, closing the door behind her.

Intrigued, Jackie waited for a couple of minutes before creeping up the stairs. She still couldn't imagine why women paid to be caned, although, hiding behind the book-shelving caressing the weals across her buttocks, something inside her understood only too well. Slipping her hands down her panties, she stroked the soft skin either side of her crease as she listened intently to the conversation.

'Usual procedure,' David said. 'Make sure that she leaves her bag in the studio and give me three-quarters of an hour. Preferably an hour, if you can.'

'It's all right, I *have* done this before,' Jane sighed. 'Besides, she's been here three times now, she knows how long it takes.'

'Yes, yes, I know. But things seem to be going wrong lately. I don't want this messed up, do you understand?'

'Yes, I understand.'

'And keep Jackie well out of the way. Make sure that she stays in your room. Tell her that we're having a visitor or something and that she mustn't come down. She mustn't know anything about Lady Stockwell. I don't want her to see her, hear her, or anything. The last thing I want is that damn girl returning thirty thousand pounds in cash to Stockwell!'

'I hope you're right and she does have that much in the safe.'

'She's probably got a damn sight more than that stashed away. I've done my homework, don't worry. Anyway, have you ever known me to be wrong?'

'No, but . . .'

'Well, then. You just make sure that you do your job here.'

Hastily making her way down the stairs, Jackie flung herself onto the bed. 'Thirty thousand!' she breathed, her hand now down the front of her wet panties. 'That poor woman's lost her husband and . . . Still, she shouldn't be coming here for sex. It's her own fault – it serves her right.'

Jane swanned into the room and smiled. 'We've got half an hour before she arrives,' she said. 'You'd better go to my room – up the stairs, first door on the right. There's a television, *en suite* bathroom and plenty of clothes in the wardrobe. And don't mention anything to David, will you?'

'About what?'

'About you knowing that a client's coming here this evening. He gets a bit funny at times.'

'Don't I know it!'

The luxurious surroundings of the bedroom quite took her breath away. The huge room was straight out of a glossy magazine, she surmised – everything pink, from the Chesterfield and the bed, to the walls and ceiling. The carpet was so thick that she looked down, thinking that she was walking on air. Not wanting to miss Lady Stockwell, she quickly went into the large, *en suite* bathroom where she found more expensive matching furniture. Gold trimmings abounded – the shower, the television mounted in the wall above the bath, even the telephone. 'God, they've got some money,' Jackie breathed, slipping her clothes off. 'Crime *does* pay!'

After her shower, she rummaged through Jane's wardrobe and selected a red miniskirt and a tight T-shirt. Applying Jane's makeup at the dressing table, she gazed at herself in the mirror. She was attractive, she knew – far more so now that her body had been awakened, her clitoris used to bring her pleasure, as it should. Her complexion glowed with life, her eyes sparkled. The stranger within was rising fast, coaxing her, driving her on to become a stranger to her old self. But she was pleased by the transformation, so far. 'As long as I don't end up totally perverted, I don't mind,' she smiled at her reflection. Brushing her long hair and admiring herself in the mirror, she heard the front door open.

'Lady Stockwell,' echoed David's charming voice. 'It's so good to see you again! Do come through.'

Jackie finished her hair and slipped quietly to the top of the stairs in time to see David go through the front door. She must be tied up by now, she speculated, creeping down the stairs to the lounge where she found the book-shelving partly open. Listening to the murmur of voices, she made her way to the studio. The tapestry was drawn back, but the small door was closed. Dropping to her knees, she spied through the keyhole.

Jane was standing to one side of the young woman who was lying naked on her back on the frame. Judging by her slender body and firm, well rounded breasts, Jackie surmised that she must be in her early thirties. No caning then? she mused, gazing between the woman's open legs at the inviting groove running down her mound as a river down a mountain. Somehow aware of her observer, Jane placed the blindfold over the woman's eyes and quietly opened the door. Motioning Jackie to come in, she smiled and held a finger to her lips.

'So, Lady Stockwell, we'll start with the aromatic oils, shall we?' she suggested, carefully positioning the trolley by the frame.

'I've been so tense recently,' Lady Stockwell replied.

'You do whatever you think best.'

'Just leave it to me, I'll have all that tension washed away in no time, you'll see.'

Soft background music mingled with the sweet fragrance of the oils, creating a relaxing atmosphere as Jane massaged the client's curvaceous, tanned body. They didn't speak as she worked on the smooth plateau of her stomach, moving ever nearer to her hard breasts. Eventually, Jane ran her hands beneath the woman's full breasts, causing her to breathe deeply in anticipation. Working in ever-decreasing circles, she finally touched the hardening nipples, squeezing and manipulating them until they grew long and pointed.

Lady Stockwell released a long sigh as Jane moved down and worked on her inner thighs, slowly inching her way towards the mousy bush between the aristocratic legs. Finally, her tiny hands caressing the mound, she took a hairbrush and sensuously stroked the soft hair aside to expose the gaping groove. Jackie watched closely as the lips visibly swelled and parted even more to reveal a trickle of creamy fluid oozing from the little pink hole.

Happy that she'd aroused the woman sufficiently, Jane parted her pussy lips, stretching the shiny, pink skin, and gently caressed the soft, exposed flesh within. The woman let her head fall to one side and moaned again as Jane pushed two fingers between the fleshy folds, deep inside her body, to massage the warm passage. The thick, creamy fluid began to flow, a little at first, but then in torrents over Jane's hand.

'Do you think you're ready to try it this week?' Jane asked quietly as she pulled the woman's lips up and apart and began to stroke around the base of her stiffening clitoris.

'Yes, I think so,' breathed the Lady.

Slipping her fingers from the drenched and gaping hole, Jane took a vibrator from the trolley and switched it on. It buzzed softly as she again peeled back Lady Stockwell's lips and introduced the tip to the pink hood of her clitoris. The woman breathed a cry of delight as Jane moved the tip over the hood and then pulled it back and ran it round and round the exposed, erect bud, causing it to throb and grow. Glancing at Jackie, Jane motioned for her to push her fingers into the vacant hole. Jackie grinned as she gently slipped first two and then three fingers into the wet warmth and began moving them, rhythmically round and round and in and out.

'I'm coming, I'm coming – don't stop!' the woman cried within minutes of the girls starting to work expertly between her legs, her stomach tightening and relaxing rhythmically. And then it came, exploding between her outstretched lips, waves of orgasm rocking her body, bathing every nerve ending with sensual pleasure. On and on her climax seemed to last, her cream pumping over Jackie's fingers, her clitoris visibly pulsating until, gasping for breath, she fell limp and relaxed. 'I thought I was with my husband for a moment!' she gasped. 'That was wonderful – absolutely wonderful!'

Checking her watch, Jane asked Lady Stockwell if she would like to come again, but she declined. 'I must get back,' she whispered. 'I don't want to be out too late. It will take me some time to drive back to Grantham Wood, what with the snow and everything.'

'Just one more time,' Jane insisted, switching the vibrator on again. 'Just one more time, and you'll feel all the better for it, I promise you.'

'Will you do it yourself this time? My husband used to . . . Well, you know what I mean,' she breathed as

Jane placed the vibrator on the trolley and smiled.

'Of course I will. I thought that you'd be ready for that by now,' she replied, wriggling her tongue at Jackie and pointing to the woman's milky slit. Jackie frowned and vigorously shook her head, but Jane pulled her nearer and pointed between the woman's legs again.

Resting on her knees, Jackie parted the crimson lips and allowed the tip of her tongue to touch a globule of milky fluid. Creamy, sticky, warm, the taste of female nectar excited her. Breathing heavily, she lapped up every last drop before stretching the soft, protective cushions of flesh open and moving her attention up to the hard clitoris. The woman moaned delightedly as Jackie sucked and licked until the climax approached.

'Don't stop, don't stop!' she gasped as she twitched and convulsed and wriggled with delight. Pressing down on the pink skin with her fingertips, Jackie eased out the full length of the blossoming bud and continued to suck until the tip ballooned and throbbed and reached its goal. 'Enough, that's enough!' the woman cried as her slim body shook and trembled with ecstasy. As if possessed, Jackie fervently lapped up the fresh cream as it flowed over the pink skin. 'Please stop!' the woman begged. 'I can't take any more!' Relinquishing her prey, Jackie stood up and wiped her mouth, all too aware of her own clitoris throbbing and the juices flowing down her inner thighs from her aching hole.

The girls watched as the woman's bud slowly receded under its hood, leaving her quivering body flushed and drenched in perspiration. Quickly motioning for Jackie to leave, Jane released the clamps and helped Lady Stockwell to the floor. 'I thought I was with Terry, my late husband!' she cried. 'I miss him so much.'

'I know,' Jane comforted. 'You've got me, though. You

can come here whenever you feel the need. You know that, don't you?'

'Yes, thank you. What you did to me somehow brought me closer to him. It reminded me of our times together – I do miss him.'

Leaving the woman to dress, Jane slipped out of the room and found Jackie sitting on the four-poster bed.

'Well, that's another two hundred,' she smiled.

'Two hundred!'

'Shush, she'll hear you. Yes, two hundred. Where's David?'

'I don't know, I haven't seen him.'

'God, I hope he's back. He's had time enough,' Jane whispered, rushing out of the room.

Jackie gazed through the crack in the door as she heard David bounding down the stairs. 'Everything all right?' he asked, quickly dropping a bunch of keys into the woman's handbag as she emerged from the surgery.

'Yes, everything's fine. I feel so much better now, thank you. Thank you both,' she said, slipping her coat on.

'I think we'll start you on the CDC on your next visit,' Jane smiled sweetly.

'Oh, yes, I'd like that,' she replied, picking up her bag.

Taking a bundle of twenty-pound notes, she passed them to David before following him up the stairs. Grinning, Jane flopped onto the sofa and sighed with relief.

'Well, she's gone. Did everything go all right?' David asked as he sauntered down the stairs counting out the money.

'She wanted to leave early.'

'Sorry, but it took me longer than I thought it would. There were some people milling about in the lane outside her place. I had to wait until they'd gone.'

'Did you get the money?'

'Yes, twenty thousand.'

'But you said . . .'

'Yes, I know, I know. Where's Jackie?'

'In there.'

'What? I told you to make sure that she stayed in your room.'

He opened the door to find Jackie resting on the bed.

'You've been in here all the time?' he asked. Jane stood behind him nodding her head and making odd facial expressions.

'Er . . . yes. I've been sleeping, you woke me up,' Jackie lied.

'That's good, I mean, you must have been tired, what with the police and everything on your mind,' he smiled. 'I'm going upstairs. Any chance of something to eat, Jane?'

'Yes, I'll be up in a minute.'

Jane waited until David had gone before closing the door. 'You don't know anything about Lady Stockwell, all right?'

'You've got ten thousand each! Plus another hundred!'

'No, it's David's money, not mine. He pays me more than enough, of course. It's his business, you see, I just work for him.'

'Work for him? But I thought . . .'

'Don't think. Just keep quiet and everything will be all right. Now, are you going to come and help me make something to eat?'

'Yes, OK. Do you sleep with him?'

'God, no! Sleep with . . .'

'What's CDC?'

'Look, don't keep asking questions. Think yourself lucky that David is allowing you to stay here. If he gets upset and kicks you out, then you'll go to prison for sure.'

Jackie followed Jane to the kitchen, wondering how she'd got herself into such a situation. She wished that she'd never met David but, she had to admit, her life had been far from mundane since that fateful meeting. And she couldn't deny that part of her had found a niche. An inner voice was telling her to let go and relax and enjoy her new life. At long last, the stranger within was finding contentment and satisfaction through her body.

Chapter Seven

Jane was a superb cook. Even though she'd only knocked up a cheese and mushroom omelette, it was the best that Jackie had ever tasted.

'You're good at everything,' she sighed, gazing longingly at Jane across the table.

'I try my best,' smiled Jane. 'Do you like it, David?'

'Yes, it's very good,' he answered indifferently. 'What are we going to do about your clothes and things, Jackie?'

'I don't know. I can't go back to my flat to get them, can I?'

'I've got more than enough clothes for both of us,' Jane volunteered happily.

'But there must be things that you need.' David persisted. 'I'll go round there tonight and get whatever you want. I'm sure that the police won't be watching the place twenty-four hours a day.'

Gazing into David's deep eyes, Jackie's stomach somersaulted. She was torn between the odd couple, between male and female. Both, she knew, could take her to the extremes of sexual pleasure but, given the choice, she didn't know which one she'd choose. Remembering her previous sexual encounters and how they'd left her cold, she contemplated David's methods, his strange, weird but wonderful approach to sex, to the female body. Confused, she desperately wanted to know more about David, about

Jane. When, how and why they'd turned from normal to what was usually considered to be abnormal – perverted? Somewhere, sometime, they had changed. Or, Jackie pondered, had they always been so different?

After the meal, Jackie made a list of some essential items for David to collect. He left saying that he'd be calling into the pub for a drink on his way back to catch up on the local gossip. 'It's a shame I can't come with you,' Jackie sighed despondently.

'It is,' he agreed, catching her gaze and returning her smile as he closed the door.

'Right, I'm off to bed, I'm tired,' Jane yawned after she'd cleared the table and loaded the dishwasher.

'And me,' Jackie said, eyeing the young girl's nipples pressing through the tight material of her top. 'David told me to sleep downstairs, in the four-poster, so . . .'

'You can't sleep down there! You can sleep with me in my bed, it's big enough,' Jane suggested. 'If that's what you want, of course?'

'Yes, that's definitely what I want,' Jackie replied, aware of her inner voice, but now torn more than ever before between the man and the woman.

Jackie wanted to ask a thousand questions as she undressed. Who was the doctor? What was CDC? What was the relationship between David and Jane? She was sure that there was far more to it than simply employer and employee. Had they once had a sexual relationship? A wave of jealousy enveloping her, she hoped not – she wanted them both, but didn't want them to have each other. And there was the question that had been nagging her mind for some time – why had David chosen to seduce her? A dowdy bank clerk, she had no money to speak of, nothing to offer, apart from her body of course, which, far from being offered, had been greedily taken. But, it seemed, David had a never-ending supply of female bodies at his disposal, so what was the fascination with hers? Jane wouldn't answer her questions, she knew. She'd have to discover the answers herself.

The girls climbed into Jane's bed and huddled their warm, naked bodies together. For the first time, Jackie felt safe, secure, and sexually aroused as never before as she allowed her hands to wander over the young girl's firm, fresh body. Unable to restrain herself any longer, she asked just one question. 'Why me? Why did David choose me?'

'Because you have that look in your eyes, as if you're hiding or suppressing something. As if the real you is crying out for freedom. David seems to have the knack of recognising that look – the look of a distant stranger within, as he puts it. And he chose you because he thought that I'd like you. And I do!'

Jackie knew what was coming and closed her eyes in readiness as, twisting her body around, Jane slipped beneath the warmth of the quilt. Positioning herself over the older woman's body, she gently kissed the naked groove between the splayed legs. Presented with Jane's young slit hovering invitingly above her face, Jackie returned the pleasure. Licking and sucking in unison, they induced warm creamy fluid to flow from each other's open holes, their buds swelling and hardening as their bodies writhed, entwined in the magical union of two females. 'Do as I do,' Jane instructed, pushing her tongue between the swollen lips and deep into the wet hole. Jackie complied, tentatively exploring the hot, intimate flesh with her tongue, tasting, drinking the intoxicating nectar from Jane's body. Imitating her young lover, she moved to her clitoris, sucking and nibbling at the hard nodule to stiffen it even more and entice it from its soft, protective hide. Insidiously, Jane began to lick the entire length of Jackie's slit, lapping up the warm milk as Jackie, too, drank, until, following silent instructions, she moved back to once more engulf Jane's yearning young bud. Writhing and beginning to convulse, Jane moaned softly in appreciation. Jackie continued her caresses, sucking on Jane's long bud until both girls melted into the warm dampness of their quivering bodies, into a sea of ecstasy. Mouth to clitoris, clitoris to mouth, they sucked the orgasms from each other until their wet and drained bodies fell limp, satisfied with the spoils of lust.

Rolling from Jackie's exhausted body, Jane nuzzled her mouth to the warm nest between her legs and fell asleep. Reciprocating, sucking at her friend's wet flesh as a babe at the breast, Jackie too drifted into sleep.

The sun had already risen. Finding herself alone in the huge bed, Jackie lay for a while, contemplating her new way of life, her new home – her prison. She was comfortable – in body *and* mind, she reflected, remembering the early mornings in her own bed when she'd been virtually unaware of her clitoris, with only another long dreary day at the bank to look forward to.

Showering and dressing, she wandered downstairs, but there was no-one around. As she settled on the sofa in the lounge with a cup of coffee, wondering what the day would bring, the telephone rang. Hesitantly, she picked up the receiver and listened.

'Hello,' said a female voice shakily.

'Hello.'

'Jane, is that you?'

'Er, yes. Who is this?' she replied, wishing she hadn't.

'It's Lady Stockwell. Is David there?'

'No, he's out, Lady Stockwell. Can I take a message?'

'Oh, I don't know. I was just ringing to tell him, both of you, that I was burgled last night.'

'Oh, no. How awful!'

'Yes. You see, I can't tell the police exactly where I was. I don't really know what to tell them.'

'What have you said so far?'

'Just that I was out for a drive, but what with the snow, well, I think they found it rather difficult to believe. I just wondered whether David had any ideas.'

'I'll ask him to ring you the minute he comes in, Lady Stockwell. In the meantime, try not to worry too much. I'm sure everything will be all right.'

'Oh, thank you. I don't understand how they got in, I mean, there were no broken windows or anything. I simply can't believe that this has happened to me. I only wish that Terry was here, he'd know what to do. Anyway, I'll wait to hear from David.'

Jackie replaced the receiver as David strolled in and stared at her.

'Who was that?' he asked sternly, moving slowly towards her.

'It kept ringing and ringing so I . . .'

'Who was it?'

'Lady Stockwell, she's been burgled.'

'How do you know her?'

'I don't know her, she just gave me her name and said that she'd been burgled – she must have thought that I was Jane.'

Jane stood in the doorway motioning for Jackie to join her as David picked up the phone.

'You shouldn't have answered it,' she whispered angrily, taking Jackie by the arm and leading her into the kitchen.

'It kept ringing and ringing . . .'

'I hope everything's all right. If he gets upset . . . Well . . .'

Much to Jackie's relief, David wandered into the kitchen without mentioning the incident. All must be well, she thought, returning Jane's reassuring smile. David pointed to a bag on the floor before turning to leave the room. 'Your things,' he smiled. 'From your flat.'

Jackie looked at the bag and then at David, wondering why he hadn't made any advances towards her recently, and wishing that he would. Perhaps he's leaving me to Jane, for her pleasure, her sole use, she mused as he left the room. Lugging the bag upstairs, her mind whirling, she decided to confront Jane.

'I've been thinking,' she said as Jane followed her into the bedroom and closed the door. 'I reckon that you and David have set me up. Or, at least, he has.'

'What *are* you talking about?'

'Well, put yourself in my position. One minute the two of you are tying me down, raping and beating me – and the next, you're both as nice as pie, saying that I can live here and that you'll protect me. I mean, I'm not stupid, something's going on, isn't it?'

'No, no. Well, David has told you that you'll have to earn your keep, as I do, hasn't he?'

'Oh, yes, but how? That's what I want to know.'

'You know how! Like I did last night with Lady Stockwell. Attend the clients, as David puts it, while he . . . Well . . .'

'Robs them?'

'Yes, I suppose so.'

'And you don't mind being a part of that?'

'I did at first. But I suppose I've got used to the money now.'

'I haven't got a penny!'

'You will have. David will probably start you off on a thousand a week, just until you get to know the ropes, and then . . .'

'One thousand pounds every week?'

'For starters, yes.'

'It's a lot of money, but compared to what he must pocket . . .'

'Yes, but he takes all the risks, doesn't he?'

David's knock on the door interrupted the girls' conversation. They watched as he wandered into the room and sat in the armchair by the window. Rubbing his forehead absentmindedly and frowning, he appeared to be strained, worried.

'There's a problem,' he began despondently.

'Problem?' Jane enquired, her big eyes widening as she flashed Jackie a glance.

'Yes, I've just had Elizabeth Rhodes on the telephone – again. It seems that she's been thinking.'

'Thinking about what?' Jane asked anxiously.

'It doesn't take a great deal of brain power to work out that Jackie either stole the jewellery herself, or knows who the thief is. And it doesn't take a lot to realise that Jackie wouldn't steal the goodies herself, and then return them at a fraction of their true value, does it?'

'I suppose not,' Jane replied cautiously. 'But that doesn't matter, does it? I mean, Jackie's here now so there's nothing to worry about, is there?'

'True, but you went a step further, didn't you, Jackie?'

Jackie hung her head in shame as her hands began to tremble.

'You see, she told Mrs Rhodes that she knew all about her, and I quote, kinky ways, unquote. And to make matters worse, she then asked how much it costs these days to be tied down and sexually abused, whipped with a cane.'

'Oh dear,' Jane sighed.

'Yes, oh dear, indeed! It doesn't take a mathematician to work out the common denominator – i.e. me! You see, Jackie, our golden rule has always been absolute confidentiality. And that rule has been blatantly broken.'

'What are you going to do?' Jane asked, moving towards Jackie protectively.

'Use our insurance, I suppose.'

'Insurance?' Jackie enquired fearfully.

'Yes, you see, we take out what I call an insurance policy with every new client whereby we record them on video tape removing their clothes of their own accord and enjoying the session. Should Mrs Rhodes decide to take the matter further, then I will have to send her a copy of her tape. The tapes are an ideal blackmail deterrent.'

'But she's got her jewellery back,' Jackie said positively.

'Yes, financially, she's only down by a thousand pounds. I can make that up, if I have to, but I don't like a mess. It upsets me when things go wrong and, you must agree, this is a bloody mess.'

The girls said nothing as David stood up and walked towards the door. Frowning, he suddenly turned and looked at Jane.

'Will you go into town? I need a dozen or so blank video tapes, we're running low and I've got several new clients in the pipeline. It's twelve o'clock now, I want you back by one because Mrs Blythe-Smith is due then.'

'Yes, I'll go now,' Jane replied, taking her coat from the wardrobe. 'I'll, er, see you both later, then.'

Alone with David, Jackie became fearful for her safety. He stood in the doorway, intimidating, staring, as if wondering what to do with her. Beckoning her with a finger, he turned and went downstairs. She hesitated before following, wondering if he had decided on her punishment. But he called out, loudly, giving her little choice other than to follow him.

'Right!' he said sternly as he led the way through the studio and into the surgery. 'I have a job for you, my girl.'

'Job?' she asked uneasily, her wide eyes following his every move.

Pressing a button, David opened a concealed door in the far wall of the surgery. With no frame to outline the door, Jackie hadn't noticed it before. Venturing inside, she found herself in yet another large room which housed several video recorders and a long bench covered with tools and what she thought to be several vibrators, all in pieces.

'The basement runs under the entire house,' David explained proudly. 'I sectioned off the rooms some years ago, when I first started the business.'

'It's a huge room,' Jackie observed, wandering towards the bench. 'What are all these?'

'Prototypes. I manufacture sex-aids to order. Most of my ladies are bored with the standard vibrators on the market, so I sell them tailor-made vibrators, amongst other things. And that's where you come in, your work, so to speak.'

'My work?'

'Yes, to pay for your keep you have to work.'

'Doing what, exactly?'

'Testing the prototypes. It's fun, you'll love it.'

Eyeing the assortment of awesome moulded plastic shapes, Jackie's heart missed several beats. She contemplated running, but where to, she didn't know.

'This is my latest,' David said proudly, picking up a long, cylindrical-shaped object. 'It doesn't look much but . . . Well, you'll be trying it out later.'

'No, I think not!' she returned anxiously, backing towards the door. 'There's no way I'm going to test any of your bloody weird gadgets!'

'Take your skirt and panties off and we'll give this one a go,' he continued, oblivious to her protests as he selected a long, pink object with a bulbous end and folded rubber wings.

'No, no! I said that I'm not testing . . .'

'Come on, Jackie, I haven't got the time to play around. Skirt and panties off and get on the trolley – or go home, to your flat.'

'You can't blackmail me into . . .'

'Can't? But I *am* blackmailing you, aren't I? Now, get on the trolley, please. Don't worry, I'm not going to test any of these on you,' he assured, waving a hand at the vibrators.

'What, then?'

'You'll see. I've been working on this project for some time, it's for a rather unusual client of mine.'

Jackie followed David's eyes to the trolley – a small bed on wheels.

'I'm not getting on that!' she stormed.

'Suit yourself. If you don't like the work, then leave. Close the front door on your way out, will you?'

Slipping out of her skirt, she complained and moaned as she pulled her knickers down to her ankles and climbed on the trolley. David grinned, telling her to relax with her legs out straight and her arms by her sides. Closing her eyes and expecting the worst, she suddenly realised that she was lying completely naked, her body shamefully exposed before an older man as if it was nothing more than an object. Suddenly, the trolley hummed and her legs began to rise, bringing her knees up to her chest. Her ankles held in two stirrups, she couldn't move as her swollen lips bulged between her thighs as if ready for an internal examination. Desperately trying to sit up, to escape the awesome device, she realised that her wrists had been automatically clamped by two soft rubber grips either side of the trolley. Her stomach churned with fear, something she was fast becoming used to – but it was fear, all the same.

'It's ingenious, isn't it?' David laughed like a mad professor. 'The whole thing is electrically operated. It's quite safe, of course.'

'Let me go! What sort of person would buy this?'

'Ah, this is for a rather strange young couple who want to . . . Well, as they put it, play doctors and nurses. I have all sorts of weird and wonderful requests from just as many weird and wonderful clients!'

'You're bloody weird,' Jackie hissed as he moved to the end of the trolley and gazed between her thighs.

'You look so much better without all that ugly hair, don't you agree? It's nice to see a woman clean shaven, her femininity displayed rather than hidden away.'

Jackie felt her embarrassment rising as he lowered his head for a better view of her swollen lips, bulging more now between her smooth thighs. 'Why don't you take an interest in my face, my looks, my hair? My personality, my character – me? This isn't what a woman's body is for,' she shouted. 'This is cold sex – perverted, debased sex. Have you never been in love? Have you never shared your body with a woman in the name of love? Or have you always been a dirty pervert?'

'I am *not* a dirty pervert, Jackie. And I *am* taking an interest in your personality. You see, most women don't understand their bodies, many have never even experienced orgasm, would you believe? All I am doing is bringing out the best in women, bringing out their true identities. Teaching them how to get the best from their bodies.'

'What, by caning them, stuffing vibrators up them?'

'You've changed, haven't you? Since we first met, you've had more pleasure from your body than you ever thought possible. That's true, isn't it?'

Jackie didn't answer. She knew that he was right, but she had trouble admitting it to herself, let alone anyone else. 'I don't suppose I could sell these trolleys to the hospitals. Shame, really,' he commented, lifting his head and moving towards the bench. Selecting the long, pink object with the bulbous end and folded rubber wings, he squatted on the floor level with her indignantly exposed slit as if he were doing nothing more than repairing a machine.

'What the hell are you doing?' she yelled as he peeled open her inner lips to expose her wet hole.

'Trying this out, that's all,' he said innocently. 'I think we'll start you on the CDC soon.'

'What the hell's that?' she asked fearfully.

'Just relax,' he ordered, opening her lips a little further.

Jackie gasped as the long, cold object sank deep into her body and gently pressed against her cervix. David made one or two adjustments and stood up. 'Right, I've got some things to get on with so I'll leave you to it,' he said, grinning as he walked towards the door.

'What's it supposed to do?' Jackie asked nervously.

'You'll see. It's a surprise,' he laughed, closing the door behind him.

Closing her eyes, Jackie sighed, wondering how she'd allowed herself to be trapped, yet again, by David. But then she wondered just who had trapped who. She was enjoying every minute of her sexual awakening and the money would be an added bonus – far better than working at the bank. But in reality, she knew that she was the prisoner, she was on the run from the police. Gazing at her knees pressed hard against her breasts, she imagined David's view of what had once been the most intimate, private part of her body. Now it was nothing more than a pleasure centre to be used – shared with other people. Again, she remembered squatting over a mirror in puberty, gazing at her smooth, hairless lips. Now, she appeared the same as she did then, as a schoolgirl with no signs of womanhood, other than the protrusion of her inner lips, hanging between her thighs, wet and glistening.

The object deep within her body did nothing as she waited in fear and yet anticipation of sexual excitement. But suddenly, the pink intruder moved slightly, like a monster stirring from the deep. Gripping the phallus with her muscles, she felt it stir again, only this time the movement was stronger.

Realising that she had some control over the object, she squeezed her vaginal muscles harder. It responded by sending an electrifying tingle through her pelvis and deep into her womb. Breathing heavily now, she squeezed her muscles tightly again. The thing slowly expanded, stretching her passage slightly as it throbbed and wriggled inside her.

'There must be a knack to this,' she murmured as the phallus rewarded her with another wonderful pulsating quiver. Her clitoris stirred in response to the intruder each time she squeezed, taking her a little nearer to her orgasmic heaven each time. Her excitement was rising fast but she couldn't discover how to make the thing do anything other than send delightful twinges through her pelvis.

As she raised her hips slightly to make herself more

131

comfortable, the rubber wings spread out, opening her lips to expose her little pink nodule. A small rubber tentacle sprouted between the wings and slid up her valley, vibrating slightly as it gently pressed against her stiffening bud. The sensations caused her to gasp and squeeze her muscles harder around the object. Again, it responded by expanding with pulsating throbs, opening her canal further still. Gradually, the wondrous vibrations increased in strength, bringing her ever nearer to orgasm.

In full flow, the vicious yet tantalisingly wonderful circle ran on and on. A quiver tightened her muscles causing the phallus to induce another, stronger quiver. Her clitoris hardened, the vibrations grew in response. She found herself becoming increasingly closer to the summit with every breath and yet, just before she was about to explode into ecstasy, the device seemed to keep her hovering on the threshold. Her body desperately needed the release, the satisfaction that climax brings, but no matter how hard she tried, she was unable to reach the point of no return.

Now, her muscles squeezed the enlarging phallus in involuntary spasms. The rubber tentacle teased her bud with intermittent bursts of vibration as the wings opened her swollen lips further. 'I'm coming, I'm coming,' she murmured feverishly as her orgasm desperately tried to erupt, but the device seemed to sense the contractions, the hardening of her bud, the beginnings of sexual relief. Slowly, cruelly, the vibrations subsided and the wings folded, denying Jackie her desperately needed climax.

Yet the moment her bud began to shrink, the vibrations increased again to entice it from its hide. The wings opened fully, stretching the soft, pink flesh in readiness to fly her up to her personal heaven as the shaft expanded, filling her body with its awesome girth.

Again, Jackie felt the birth of an orgasm welling up

from her womb. This time, she was allowed her just reward. Like a thousand caressing fingers, the device touched every nerve-ending between her splayed legs until she moaned a long breath of satisfaction. The rubber tentacle tickled and teased her throbbing bud until it had sent its last wave of pleasure rippling over her entire body, bringing pleasure and a satisfaction that left her calm and serene as never before.

Slowly, the vibrations decayed and the wings folded, gently bringing Jackie down to earth. As her breathing eased and her heart slowed, she relaxed in the wake of one of the most beautiful climaxes she'd ever known. Her body glowing with the tingle of lust, her mind drifting in a deep pool of tranquillity, the stranger within had once again found satisfaction.

But the inner voice begged for more, goading her to tighten her muscles again in search of a response from the delectable intruder. Desperately, she fought her desire to grip the monster and waken it once more. But overwhelmed by some strange force, she crushed it within her hole. It jumped slightly in answer to her call, the wings twitching, unfolding gradually as the tentacle snaked its way along the opening groove. The shaft expanded in response to the gripping muscles, gently swelling and filling her cavern again as the tentacle reached its goal and buzzed gently against the soft, protective hood of her stirring clitoris.

Jackie breathed heavily as her second trip to heaven neared, praying that the invader would show some compassion and grant her another wondrous climax. Replying to her messages of sexual desire, the monster raised its head and expanded inside her hot body until she thought that she'd split open. Like huge fins, the rubber wings swept apart again, dividing her full, inflamed lips. The wet cushions lay open, allowing the tentacle access to her swollen pleasure centre. Answering her prayers, the device brought her a wonderful multiple orgasm that seemed to go on forever, wave after wave of rapturous spasms crashing over her drenched body, drowning her very being in a sea of wanton lust.

Crying out with the pleasure between her legs, she gently floated to the surface of the pool of warmth that had engulfed her mind. Returning to her body, she breathed slowly, deeply, as the monster receded, releasing its beautiful grip as it slid from her hole and lay motionless against her buttocks. She had enjoyed the sensations, but she knew that it was false, nothing more than an electronic device designed to bring women unknown sexual pleasure without intervention from themselves, their fingers, let alone a partner. She began to wonder whether sex, her body, should only be given in love. Did it really matter that she could experience the delights between her legs alone? Her thinking became confused and she tried to clear her mind of a world without men, where vibrators served woman equally, if not better.

'Well?' David said, wandering over to Jackie's consumed body, bringing her back to reality. 'What do you think of my perceptive penis, as I call it?'

'It's . . . It's incredible! God, it's beautiful!' she breathed, admitting to herself, at last, that she was finding more than sexual pleasure in her now massive orgasms – more from her body than she had ever imagined possible.

'I said you'd find the work fun,' he grinned triumphantly. 'And now, I've something else for you – my little guinea pig.'

'No, no more! I can't take any more – I'm not a bloody sex-machine!'

Picking up his sodden creation, David carefully wiped its glistening surface and placed it on the bench, ignoring Jackie's protests. Jane wandered in carrying a pile of video tapes as David moved towards Jackie with another horrendous-looking device.

'Oh, I thought you'd get Jackie in here,' she said, stacking the tapes on a shelf over the video recorders. 'What's he done to you?'

'Tried out one of his gruesome inventions.'

'Oh – was it nice?'

'Yes, it was. But I don't want any more.'

'It was more than nice judging by the amount of juice your pretty little cunette has produced,' she observed, lowering herself to inspect Jackie's drenched slit.

'Three's a crowd,' David observed as Jane began to lick the length of Jackie's open groove, lapping up the beautiful products of her vagina. 'I'll try this out later,' he added, returning a large rubber ball to the bench.

'Don't go,' Jane pleaded, turning to David. 'It would be a shame to leave the poor girl in this position without giving her a little more pleasure.'

David eyed the trolley and smiled. 'I suppose you're right,' he agreed. 'What do you think, Jackie? Would you like to come again, to feel your clitoris tremble with orgasm?'

'I don't want any more of your gadgets inside me . . .'

'Gadgets? Oh, no. It's time you were rewarded with the real thing,' he grinned, taking out his already stiff penis.

'You'll let me help, won't you?' Jane begged, her hand now down the front of her knickers.

'It's all yours,' he replied, standing at the end of the trolley with his hard rod only inches from Jackie's gaping hole.

'No, no! Not that! I've done my work, I'm not having

you do that to me whenever you feel like it! What the hell do you think I am? Tell him, Jane. Tell him about us,' she cried.

'He knows about us, darling,' Jane replied, peeling back Jackie's inner lips. 'This is something that I can't give you, so think of it as an extra treat – an added bonus.'

Taking his penis in his hand, David pulled the skin back to expose the hard, purple knob before introducing it to the pinken folds surrounding Jackie's open hole.

'No, no,' Jackie breathed as David guided his prick in. 'It's not fair to use me like this!' But confusingly, she was thankful that, at last, she was to be rewarded with the real thing, as David had put it.

'Not fair! Think yourself lucky, darling. You have David and me to please you – not many girls have both genders at their beck and call,' Jane comforted as David pushed his length slowly into the warmth of Jackie's body. David slid his huge member in and out of the tightening hole, covering his shaft with her milky fluid. Jackie sighed and allowed her mind to run free as her bud responded to his urgent thrusts, enticing the beginning of yet another eruption from the sensitive tip.

'Tell me when you're about to come, David,' Jane instructed. 'I want to watch it spurt all over her lovely, bald cunette.' He grinned at Jackie, promising that he would bathe her naked quim lips in his sperm rather than fill her womb – just for Jane's sake. As he rammed his hard knob repeatedly against the smooth roundness of her young cervix, Jackie half smiled, wishing that things were different, that they were a normal couple enjoying meals, the theatre together. But no, this was her new life now, and, for a moment, she accepted the change, allowing herself the debased pleasures her body was bringing her.

Slipping back and forth between the stretched inner lips, David's glistening shaft swelled to even more gigantic proportions as his climax neared.

'No, no, in her mouth,' he gasped, catching Jackie's eye again, gripping her thighs and spreading her outer lips with his thumbs. 'I don't want to waste it – I'll fill her pretty little virginal mouth!'

'No way!' Jackie screamed. 'I won't do that!'

'But you will, darling,' Jane ordered. 'If you don't, we'll leave you here all day and all night – all week, if necessary, until you agree.'

His eyes rolling, David slid his length from Jackie's body and moved around the trolley to present the swollen knob to her hot mouth. Cursing him, she turned her head away from the wet, threatening member and struggled to free her fettered body. Now, she couldn't accept her new life.

'Come on,' Jane breathed. 'Be a good little girl and take your medicine.' Taking two handfuls of Jackie's long blonde hair, she gently lifted her head from the pillow to face her destiny. Gripping his throbbing rod in his hand, David pushed the glans against her tightly closed lips.

'Open wide,' Jane instructed angrily. 'You'll stay here until you do it, so why not get it over with?'

Unable to hold back any longer, David moved the skin back and forth over his purple knob and breathed a deep moan.

'Do it!' Jane yelled, squeezing Jackie's nostrils between her fingers as she watched a drop of clear fluid dribble from the bulging head. As Jackie opened her mouth to gasp for air, David pushed his rod home to fill her cheeks with hot sperm.

'Drink it, darling,' Jane coaxed softly. 'Drink it all up like a good little girl. It's only sperm, lovely, hot sperm.'

As he withdrew his penis, Jackie choked and gasped. 'I hate you both!' she spluttered, still swallowing the remnants of his fruits. Jane smiled. 'Wasn't that wonderful?' she asked. 'Can you manage to fill her down there now, David?'

'I can try,' he replied, stabbing his flaccid penis between Jackie's open inner lips.

'I hate you – you perverts!' Jackie screamed as David's growing penis slipped deep into her body once more, stretching her with its girth, filling her with its length.

'Do it to her hard, David,' Jane ordered excitedly as she watched his glistening length slip in and out. 'Fuck her really hard and take it out when you are about to come. Promise to take it out, I want to see it.'

'I will, I will,' he gasped as he thrust harder, missing her hole and sliding his knob up her sodden valley.

Guiding his knob to Jackie's clitoris, David rubbed the two hard buds together as he gasped and grimaced, allowing the sperm to flow over the bursting clit as it swelled to an incredible size with orgasm.

Jackie raised her head to see the liquid gushing out over her stomach, her swollen lips, her thighs.

'Don't stop, don't stop!' she pleaded suddenly as David rubbed his flagging knob against her sensitive bud. Her body trembled as the sperm ran over her inflamed lips and down between her buttocks, but she wasn't happy. 'Put it in again!' she screamed in the grips of her climax. 'I haven't finished!' Summoning his last reserves of sexual control, David stiffened his shrinking penis for a few more seconds by sheer willpower, ramming it to its hilt into Jackie's quim and bringing her to a shuddering orgasm that left her perspiring body tingling with gratification.

'Sorry I didn't last very long,' David said regretfully.

'You did very well,' Jane assured. 'Didn't he do well, Jackie?'

'Yes, yes, he did. Now, let me go. I've had more than enough!'

'Oh, by the way, Jane. We'll start her on the CDC soon,' David said nonchalantly, zipping up his trousers as he moved towards the door.

'Good idea,' she replied. 'She certainly needs it!'

'What's CDC?' Jackie asked, struggling to free herself.

'It's just something that the doctor does, you'll see. Don't worry about it now.'

'The doctor!' Jackie yelled. 'I've had enough of all this!'

'It's all right, he won't be here until later. Now just relax.'

'But I don't want to see that perverted doctor! He wants to tear me open!'

Jane ignored Jackie's ranting. 'I have to clean you properly,' she breathed, moving down to the wet slit where she wiped her teasingly with a tissue until she was dry. Peeling back her inner lips, Jane began to rub Jackie's clitoris with her fingers. Jackie quivered slightly and then sighed despondently.

'I can't come again,' she whispered. 'It's too soon.'

'That's where the CDC will help you,' Jane laughed as she stood up. 'And don't ask me what it is because it's a surprise,' she added, releasing Jackie from the trolley.

'Now, tell me what you thought about David coming in your mouth. Did you like it? Do you want him to do it again?'

'It wasn't as bad as I thought it would be. I suppose I quite liked it. But I couldn't breathe!'

'Next time, I won't have to pinch your nose, I hope, so you'll enjoy it more.'

'Next time? I don't know about that,' Jackie replied, grabbing her skirt and panties to bring some dignity to her inflamed and used slit.

'We'll see,' Jane laughed. 'Go and have a nice hot shower and I'll see you a little later.'

Allowing the warm water to gush over her young body, Jackie cleansed her sore mound and wondered how many orgasms she'd had since meeting David and Jane. She wondered, too, how many more she would have and where it would all end. Although she couldn't stop worrying about the doctor, and the police, she was happy enough living in the house. But she knew that it couldn't go on indefinitely. She would have to start planning for the future before long.

Slipping into a short dress she'd found in Jane's wardrobe, she began to think of her flat, her own clothes and everything she'd left behind. Rummaging through the bag David had brought from her flat, she found her diary and flicked through the pages. The entries brought a tear to her eye. Meg and the other girls at the bank. What were they all thinking? They were bound to have heard about the robbery, be asking questions . . . Her thoughts in a turmoil, Jackie wrote a letter of resignation to the bank and sealed it in an envelope, wondering if she'd ever post it.

The sound of the front door bell almost stopped her heart. 'The doctor!' she gasped, rushing to the top of the stairs. Peering over the banister, she watched David open the front door and ask someone in. Her heart in her mouth, she held her breath until the visitor came into view.

His hands in the pockets of his cashmere coat, Tim wiped the snow from his feet on the doormat and followed David into the privacy of the lounge. Jackie feared the worst as she returned to the bedroom. 'Tim's the doctor, I know it!' she breathed as she sat on the bed. 'And he's come to tear me open!'

Chapter Eight

Clutching her handbag, Jackie took one last look around Jane's bedroom before closing the door. Creeping downstairs, she could hear the low drone of David and Tim talking in the lounge – but thankfully, not what they were saying. She didn't want to know what terrible fate Tim – the doctor – was devising for her, what awesome devices he planned to employ to plunder her holes. She'd had more than enough, she decided, as she quietly closed the front door on her debauched world to slip into the cold reality of the street.

Gazing at the pub, she wasn't sure what to do or where to go. She'd made no plans, other than to escape and leave David, Jane and the doctor to their perversions. 'I'm a wanted criminal,' she whispered to herself as she wandered along the snow-covered pavement, pulling the collar of Jane's fur coat over her face.

A bus pulled up alongside her, distracting her thoughts. As the doors opened, she impulsively leaped aboard. The driver gave her a blank look as she pulled a five-pound note from her bag and held it out to him.

'Where to, love?' he eventually asked.

Spontaneously, she didn't know why, the words tumbled from her mouth. 'Grantham Wood, please.'

'I don't go there. The nearest stop is a mile or so away, if you don't mind the walk.'

'No, I don't mind,' she smiled as he took the note.

Taking her seat, she suddenly remembered the origin of her unknown destination. 'Lady Stockwell!' she gasped, gazing at the pale, vacant faces of her fellow travellers and wondering if they'd recognise her as a woman on the run.

The bus stopped alongside a common and the driver called out to her. 'This is as far as I can take you, love – walk straight across the common and you'll come to Grantham Wood.'

Thanking him as she stepped out into the cold country air, Jackie gazed across the snow-covered landscape stretched out before her. 'A mile or so,' she sighed as she began to tread her way through the deep snow, wondering why on earth she was going to Grantham Wood. Following several pairs of footprints, the walk took far less time than she'd imagined, bringing her into a small lane where the only sign of civilisation was a post office.

'And what would you be wanting with Lady Stockwell?' the old woman behind the counter asked suspiciously.

'Lord Stockwell – Terry, her late husband – is . . . was, my uncle,' she lied unconvincingly. But the woman smiled sweetly, pointing in the direction of Stockwell Manor.

The wind had got up, chilling her already cold, unstockinged legs as she walked up the lane, huddling in Jane's short fur coat. The small village seemed to be deserted – a ghost town, she thought, as she passed an old church. If the nuns could see me now, she reflected, they'd probably cast me into the fires of hell as the devil's daughter!

A large pair of wrought iron gates came into view as she rounded a draughty corner. Reading the words 'Stockwell Manor' carved into a slice of old oak hanging from two rusty chains, she smiled and made her way up the winding driveway to the huge building.

Feeling confident now, she climbed the worn stone

steps and knocked on the front door.'

'Who is it?' a familiar female voice eventually called out.

'I've come to talk to you about the robbery,' Jackie replied.

'Are you from the police?'

'No, no, David sent me – David and Jane.'

Opening the door, Lady Stockwell frowned as she looked Jackie up and down.

'Who are you?' she asked cautiously.

'A friend,' Jackie replied, pushing the door open and walking past her into the hallway. 'Shall we go in here?'

Following her visitor into the drawing room, Lady Stockwell angrily repeated her question.

'My name is irrelevant. I've come to help you, if you'll help me, that is,' Jackie replied coldly.

'Help? I don't need any help, thank you.'

'If you say so, but I do. Now, I'm not really into blackmail, but I need money – I have to go abroad, you see. Five thousand should be enough.'

'Five thousand pounds! Blackmail? What *are* you talking about?'

'About me not telling the world of your clandestine visits to David's house.'

Stunned, Lady Stockwell sat down, nervously running her hands through her short, mousy hair as she stared at Jackie in disbelief. 'I don't know what you're talking about,' she said hesitantly. Jackie suddenly became annoyed, cold and callous as she returned the older woman's glazed stare.

'You do know what I'm talking about! Now get the money!'

She experienced a pang of pity as Lady Stockwell took a handkerchief from her cardigan sleeve and wiped a tear from her eye. In a dull, knee-length woollen skirt and flat shoes, she looked nothing like a woman who paid for lesbian sex – a woman who had cried out in ecstasy as Jackie had brought her throbbing clitoris to orgasm with her hot tongue.

'Come on, you've got plenty of money. I'm not asking for much, not by your standards, anyway,' Jackie persisted, mystified by the sad excuse of a woman cowering before her.

'But I've just been robbed of twenty thousand pounds! That was virtually all I had. My husband's dead and I have no way of running the Manor now.'

'Yes, yes, I know all about the robbery. And I also know who took your money,' she blurted out.

'You know? Then tell me!'

'I can't – not just yet. But I may be able to get it back for you, if you co-operate, that is. And if you don't, then I'll have to reveal your dirty little secret to the world! The Sunday papers would pay me nicely for a story like that, don't you agree?'

'But I haven't any secrets.'

'Being strapped down, naked, while some young lesbian licks and vibrates your . . . I think that's a big enough secret, don't you?'

Lady Stockwell sighed as she wiped another tear from her eye. 'May I explain?' she began, raising her head.

'Explain what?'

'Why I . . . You see, my husband and I had a wonderful . . .'

'You don't have to explain anything to me, I'm not interested,' Jackie interrupted. 'Look, all I need is a few thousand pounds, just to get me out of the country – so I can start a new life.'

'You're in trouble, aren't you?'

'You're the one in trouble, not me!'

'Supposing I called the police. I wonder which one of us would come out worse?'

An interesting point, Jackie mused, remembering her almost bungled attempt to blackmail Elizabeth Rhodes. Gazing at Lady Stockwell, she suddenly saw the opportunity not only to get rich, but to appease her ever demanding clitoris once again.

'It would ruin you to have the world know what you get up to. Imagine what the local vicar would think if he knew that you paid to be licked and sucked between your legs. You're obviously a woman of high standing in the community and . . .'

'You can't prove a thing!'

'Video tape, Lady Stockwell. David's insurance, as he calls it. All his clients are on tape – enjoying their perverted little sessions. David is so clever, don't you agree? He has it all worked out, you see – no loopholes, completely safe from threats of blackmail. The tapes are an education, they really are. Perhaps the vicar would like to show them to his congregation?'

'I've got two thousand pounds in cash, that's all I have in the world. Take it or leave it.'

'I'll take it,' Jackie conceded, becoming increasingly aware of the growing need between her legs as Lady Stockwell took a bunch of keys from her bag. Jackie gazed at the slender legs as she walked to the door, remembering the slim, tanned body delightfully spread across the wooden frame, the gaping valley rudely exposed and running with creamy fluid. Wondering how to word her second demand, she raised her buttocks and slid her moist panties down over her ankles. Stuffing them into her handbag, she looked up as the door opened to see Lady Stockwell smiling slightly.

'I can't open the safe. I've had trouble with the lock ever since I was burgled.'

'Really? Let me try,' Jackie returned suspiciously as she grabbed the keys.

'It's up the stairs, second door on the right, behind the Constable . . .'

'I'll find it,' Jackie interrupted as she bounded up the huge staircase.

Grappling with one key after another, she realised that none of them fitted the lock. Lady Stockwell appeared in the doorway and sauntered over to the safe.

'Not playing for time, are we?' Jackie asked, remembering Elizabeth Rhodes's phone call to the police.

'Time? How do you mean?'

'Yes, time. Keeping me here until the police arrive.'

'You know that I can't involve the police. We've been through that already,' she said, taking the keys from Jackie's hand and fiddling with the lock.

Feeling easier, Jackie sat in an armchair, hoisting her short dress a little to reveal her smooth, hairless lips.

'It's no good, I can't open it,' Lady Stockwell announced, turning to face Jackie.

'Then what do you suggest we do?' Jackie asked, parting her legs further. Her eyes transfixed between the youthful thighs, Lady Stockwell raised her eyebrows and then frowned.

'Aren't you cold, dressed like that in the middle of winter?' she asked.

'You could warm me up,' Jackie replied, opening her legs as wide as she could to part her swollen lips. Moving nearer to Jackie, Lady Stockwell dropped to her knees and smiled.

'What is it you want me to do?' she asked, gazing at the open valley.

'Whatever it is that you like doing to other women.'

'I've never done anything to another woman. I've only . . .'

'Then isn't it time you did? You might even enjoy it. In fact, I'm sure that you'll love it.'

Cautiously moving her head between Jackie's thighs, the titled lady hesitantly licked between the naked, puffy lips. Pulling them up and apart, Jackie popped out her stiffening clitoris, presenting it invitingly to her timid lesbian student. Slowly engulfing the bud, the woman breathed heavily through her nose and began to run her tongue round the hard nodule. Gasping now, Jackie hung her legs over the arms of the chair and closed her eyes as a climax stirred deep within her womb in readiness to erupt. As the front door slammed shut, Jackie let out a long, low moan of pleasure and flooded the woman's chin with her sticky cream. 'God, keep going!' she pleaded as the hot tongue ran round and round her pulsating centre and her hole squeezed out its liquid offering. 'Don't stop, I'm coming! Ah, that's lovely! I'm coming now! Yes, yes . . .'

'I'll deal with her!' a deep voice suddenly bellowed. Turning her head, Jackie gasped in amazement to see David standing in the doorway. Lady Stockwell rose to her feet, her face red with embarrassment, hurriedly leaving the room as he grabbed Jackie by the arm and dragged her to the waiting car.

'You're hurting me!' she screamed as he flung her in the back and ordered Jane to drive. Ignoring her complaints, he strengthened his grip as Jane swung the car out onto the country lane and put her foot to the floor.

No one spoke throughout the journey. David sat next to Jackie, holding her arm tightly as he silently fumed. She knew that she'd gone too far this time and could think of nothing other than the inevitable gruelling punishment that awaited her in the surgery.

'What are you going to do to me?' she asked apprehensively as David dragged her up the steps and pushed her through the front door onto the hall floor.

'Two things!' he stormed as he picked her up and frog-marched her across the lounge, half carrying her downstairs to the studio.

'What?' she cried. 'Please don't hurt me!'

Kicking the surgery door open, he flung her against the frame and quickly clamped her limbs as she sobbed and pleaded for mercy.

'First of all, I'm going to give you the beating of your life!' he yelled, turning the handle to bend her shaking young body over.

'No, please don't! Please, David, don't!'

'And then I'll take you to the police station and make sure that you end up in Holloway Prison!'

Ripping the short dress from her trembling body, he cast it aside and selected a long thin cane from the umbrella stand. Jackie screamed as he lightly tapped each taut buttock in turn before landing the first stinging blow. Again and again he thrashed each buttock in turn until they burned scarlet and she promised to do anything.

'I think that's enough, David!' Jane shouted as she rushed into the room and grabbed his arm.

'Do you? You think that's enough punishment for all the damage she's done, do you?' he stormed, pushing her aside and thrashing Jackie again.

'Stop, David! Punish her, yes. But not that way!'

Dropping the cane to the floor, David sat on the couch in despair.

'I've a damn good mind to kill the bitch here and now!' he raged. 'So, how do you suggest we punish her, then?'

'I don't know, yet. I'll think of something. The point is,

what has she told Lady Stockwell?'

'Nothing! Nothing!' Jackie sobbed.

'You told her everything!' David shouted, leaping to his feet and retrieving the cane.

'I didn't! I said nothing about the money. All I asked was that she pay me to keep quiet about her visits here.'

'The doctor!' Jane yelled in desperation to calm David as he swished the cane through the air to administer yet another stinging blow. 'He'll deal with her.'

'Don't be stupid, I'm not in the mood for playing bloody silly games!'

'No, really. He'll deal with her,' Jane persisted. 'I'll phone him now.'

'Go on, then, and tell him to bring his special bag! I want her cunt stretched open so wide that it tears!'

Jane ran upstairs, leaving Jackie shaking and sobbing pathetically for mercy. Bringing her body to the horizontal position, David pulled her head up and stared into her big, terrified blue eyes.

'You'll just love the doctor. The things he can do to a woman's body are truly amazing,' he hissed through a wicked grin. 'Did you know that it's possible for a man to get his entire clenched fist into your tight pussy hole? And did you know that your other little hole can be stretched open to an incredible size? Oh, yes, you're going to love the doctor! And when it's all over, if you're still alive, that is, you'll end up in Holloway Prison with all those lovely lesbians to keep you company through the long, dark nights.'

Releasing Jackie's struggling body, David threw her onto her back and quickly re-fastened the clamps. She thought that the end had come as he placed a blindfold over her tear-streaked face and began to stroke her breast, running his finger in circles around her nipple.

'What a shame,' he sighed disappointedly. 'You're such a lovely young thing, too – what a terrible waste.'

'Please, David – I'll do anything, anything!'

'You've already done far too much! Do you really think that I'd trust you again?'

'He's here!' Jane yelled, bounding down the stairs.

'That was quick – bring him in, we're all ready,' David called.

Terror-stricken, Jackie lay in the darkness of her blindfold listening to the movements around her.

'Hello, David,' came an unfamiliar voice.

'Hello again. This is our problem – in fact, she's become a recurrent problem. She needs her brains tearing out if you ask me, and her womb! Anyway, I'll leave her fate to you. Do your best.'

'Don't I always?' the doctor laughed, banging what Jackie imagined to be his bag down on the trolley.

The door closed and the key turned in the lock. Jackie pleaded but the doctor only hummed quietly to himself as he opened his bag and pulled on a pair of rubber gloves. Aware of some sort of clamp being fastened to each thick, outer lip in turn, her heart pounded as she recalled David's awesome words: "It's possible for a man to get his entire clenched fist into your tight pussy hole". The clamps moved slowly apart, pulling and stretching her lips open until she thought that the delicate skin would rip. Between her screams, she heard a soft buzzing sound as something was placed over her exposed clitoris, pulling and gently sucking its length from the surrounding flesh. Feeling no pain, she relaxed a little as her clitoris tingled and throbbed pleasantly. Strangely aroused, she gasped, but as the suction increased, her fear returned and she winced and again begged for mercy.

Still humming to himself, the doctor proceeded to push

something into her gaping hole. Stretching the glistening, pink flesh to splitting point, he slowly forced the massive object deeper into her body, painfully filling and stretching her cavern until it reached the end of her tube and rested gently against her cervix.

Jackie could only pray as another cold, solid object was forced between her splayed buttocks into her smaller hole, stretching the tight muscles until she yelped. Happy that both her bowels and vagina were filled to bursting point, the doctor moved up to her breasts and fixed a clip connected to a small chain to each nipple. Reaching above her body, he fastened the chains to a cord connected to a system of small pulleys which were fixed to the low ceiling. Hooking a weight on the free end of the cord, he watched as her nipples were pulled up, painfully stretching the brown, elongated tissue. With every trembling breath, her heaving breasts pulled on the clips, pinching and stretching her aching milk buds.

Suddenly, the door opened and then closed – she knew she was alone. But the doctor's horrendous devices continued to painfully suck and pull on her lengthening clitoris as her nipples were pulled, squeezed and pinched. Her fear suddenly rising as she wondered what else the doctor had in store for her, she began to cry again and pray for her freedom – her life.

Closing the door quietly behind her, Jane moved towards Jackie and lifted the blindfold clear of her bloodshot eyes.

'Are you all right?' she asked, almost sympathetically. Opening her eyes, Jackie gazed at her distended nipples, following the chains and cord up to the ceiling. Raising her head, she focused on the small rubber tube sucking on her bud. Her lips, stretched open by two metal clamps, were red and sore.

'Would *you* be all right?' she sobbed.

'You're not in too much pain, are you?'

'Yes, I am!'

'Well, this is CDC, you did want to know what it was, didn't you? It will transform you, you'll see.'

'I don't want to be transformed!'

'But it will make your orgasms so much better. The CDC – the Clitoris Development Course – is where that little pipe gently sucks on your clitoris to extend it. Over a period of time, it will become permanently longer, as mine is.'

'I don't want a long clitoris!' Jackie cried, suddenly realising that the doctor obviously had no intention of killing her.

'But it will become more sensitive. Mine rubs on my knickers as I walk, when I bother to wear any, that is. It took me an hour a day for three weeks, that's all. It's well worth it,' Jane reassured.

'And what about my nipples? I suppose they will be two inches long after this?'

'Well, not quite that long, but longer and far more sensitive, yes.'

At the sound of heavy footsteps above the ceiling, Jane hurriedly replaced the blindfold and fled. Within minutes, the doctor entered the surgery to check his equipment. Making an adjustment, he increased the suction in the rubber pipe, causing Jackie to grimace and let out a whimper as her bud was drawn even further into the soft rubber tube, forcing it to distend to twice its length. Suddenly, the clips pulled harder on her aching nipples as the doctor added a second weight to the cord. Her heavy breasts hung painfully from the tight, pinching clips, elongating her hard, sore milk buds.

The doctor patted her stomach before leaving her alone

again to endure her pain-wracked body. For what seemed like hours she lay quietly whimpering, hardly daring to breathe for the cruel tightness of the clips biting into her nipples. Then, in response to her cries, David returned and freed her from the doctor's torturing devices, removing the blindfold. Gazing at her gaping hole, he unzipped his trousers and pulled out his long, hard penis. 'No, no! Haven't you done enough to me?' she cried as he stabbed between her inflamed lips.

'Yes, but I intend to have a little pleasure, too. It's only fair, don't you agree?' he grinned, pushing his full, hard length deep into her creamy passage. Jackie grimaced and bit her lip as he pounded her cervix with his rock-hard knob and pushed a finger into her bottom-hole to heighten his debased pleasure. Suddenly, his eyes rolled and he gasped as he filled her with his hot sperm. Pumping on and on, he rammed her tethered body until she cried out in orgasm and he'd emptied his balls into her spasming sheath. Slowly withdrawing his glistening shaft, he watched as her crimson lips gently folded over, covering her full cavern, but leaving a small slit for the juices to flow from her exhausted body.

Releasing her from the frame, he helped to steady her as she wavered, almost delirious with pain – and pleasure. Though shocked by her thoughts, her crude needs, she realised that she desperately craved another climax – David's fingers deep in her hole, exploring the hot darkness, his tongue, licking round her bud, swelling it until it exploded and pleasured her entire body with lust. But clinging to the frame, she gazed down in horror at her nipples, extending almost an inch from the dark, surrounding skin. Lowering her eyes, she stared at her clitoris, protruding between her inflamed and sagging lips like a small penis.

'That looks much better,' David commented, helping her through the studio to the four-poster bed. 'In a few weeks, you'll have the longest clitoris and nipples in the land!'

'Leave me, just leave me, will you?' she sobbed, collapsing onto the bed and pulling the soft quilt over her aching body. Curled in a ball, she waited until David had gone before closing her eyes to make her escape plans. She would escape, somehow, she had to. She would find reality, away from David's dream-world of lust and evil, addictive pleasures. But drifting into sleep, she wondered at the reality she'd left behind – that outside world, so far removed from the prison where her body was used purely for physical pleasure, with no room for her feelings as a woman.

She was woken from a deep sleep by something pulling on her leg. Lifting the quilt, she looked down to see a steel clamp around her ankle, connecting to a heavy chain. She gazed at her nipples, still incredibly long and swollen, and then at her clitoris, too long to be concealed and protected by its pink hood. Her womanhood had gone. She felt like a lump of flesh, chained in readiness to be consumed by whosoever desired her defenceless body. Climbing off the bed, she discovered that the chain allowed her to move only a few feet away from the bottom bedpost. 'There's no escape now,' she whispered sadly, lifting the chain and allowing it to fall noisily to the floor.

'Ah, you're awake,' David observed, closing the door. 'Sorry about that,' he smiled, pointing to the chain. 'As I said, I can't trust you.'

'How long are you going to keep me here like this?' she asked.

'For as long as it takes,' he replied, carefully straightening one of the oil paintings before standing back to admire it.

'For as long as what takes?'

'For as long as it takes you to repay the money you owe me.'

'What money?'

'The twenty thousand that I've just had to return anonymously to Lady Stockwell.'

'How can I do that if I'm chained up like an animal?'

'Simple! I have a few clients who will be only too pleased to pay me for the use of your young body. It shouldn't take you too long to repay me – about five years or so, I'd say. And then, of course, you'll have your stay at Holloway Prison to look forward to.'

Jackie sat wearily on the edge of the bed. He meant it, she knew. Looking again at her nipples, she wondered what sort of person would pay to use a girl's chained and sexually deformed body – only a pervert, she decided.

'Your first client will be here in precisely one hour,' David informed her, glancing at his watch. 'And after that, you have another appointment with the doctor – it's all go, isn't it?'

'I'll escape, David!' Jackie promised, standing naked before him. 'One day, I'll escape – and I'll kill you!'

'That's as may be – but in the meantime, have a rest, you've a busy night ahead of you.'

Tears wouldn't come as Jackie sat gazing at the floor. She desperately needed to cry, to release her emotions, but she could only sit there, motionless, her mind wild with fear, and yet at the same time, empty, drained.

Jane placed a tray of food on the bedside table. As the girls looked at each other, Jackie was sure that she could detect some sympathy, a little compassion deep within Jane's eyes, but she said nothing. Jane didn't speak, either, merely smiling slightly as she left the room to return with a large pot and a box of tissues. This time, she couldn't bring herself to catch Jackie's eyes. Quickly pushing the pot under the bed, she turned to leave.

'A hunger strike!' Jackie cried, eyeing the food. 'And I won't use that pot, either. I won't wash, eat, or use that bloody pot!'

'You'll have to – be sensible, Jackie.'

'I don't *have* to do anything, because they'll be here soon.'

She didn't know how she'd thought so quickly, but it was the best idea that she'd had yet.

'Who?' Jane asked, moving a little nearer. 'Who will be here?'

'On my excursion to Lady Stockwell's, I took out some insurance, as David would call it. Just in case something went wrong and I couldn't leave the country, I wrote several letters and sent them to various friends of mine. Oh, and I also sent one to the police explaining everything. All first class stamps, of course, so they'll arrive in tomorrow's post.'

Yelling for David, Jane rushed from the room and up the stairs, leaving Jackie wearing a huge smile. He didn't immediately come bounding into the room wielding a cane, as she'd expected, but entered some half an hour later, wandering slowly towards her, half grinning.

'So, you took out some insurance, did you? I don't believe you, of course, because you would have mentioned it earlier. But I have to be on the safe side. If the police do pay me a visit in the morning, then I'm in serious trouble. If they don't, then you will have signed your death certificate.'

'They'll be here,' Jackie laughed triumphantly.

'The morning is a long way off. How do you like the idea of being whipped for, say, three solid hours, before your appointment with the doctor?'

Jackie bit her lip and silently cursed herself for not formulating her plan properly. But it had come so quickly, flashed into her head without thought. He was right, she knew, there was plenty of time to administer his gruelling punishment and still be miles away by daybreak. And then, he'd only return to find that she'd lied. But it was too late, she'd played her trump card and had to take the consequences.

'I can't prove it to you, David, but I did the obvious thing to protect myself, as you do with your clients. I learned from you, can't you see that? You gave me the idea.'

'Get her dressed, Jane, will you? Suitably dressed, I mean,' he ordered as he left the room. Jane sighed and gazed at Jackie.

'Why did you have to spoil everything? Our set up here was perfect until . . . I thought that you and I had something special, but now . . .'

'Don't blame me! You and David spoilt it all, not me. Look at my body – shaved, abused, ruined! Look at my nipples, they'll never be the same again!'

'Of course they will, you've only had one session. Anyway, you won't be bothered about your nipples where you're going! I'll get the clothes.'

'Where am I going?'

'You'll see.'

Returning with a pile of clothes, Jane fixed a studded leather collar around Jackie's neck and chained her to the bedpost like a dog before releasing the ankle clamp. 'There is one way out of this, you know,' she whispered as she helped Jackie slip into a tight, red leather microskirt that barely covered her naked pussy.

'How?'

'David didn't want all this any more than you or I. He's

157

very upset and seriously considering selling you to a man
he knows in London who trades in . . . Well, he buys
young women and . . .'

'What do I have to do, then?'

'For the time being, just do as you're told to keep him
as calm as possible. If he says jump, then jump. If he says
crawl, then crawl – no arguments or trouble, understand?'

'If you say so, but . . .'

'Is she ready?' David grunted, dumping a small leather
bag on the floor.

'Just about,' Jane replied, buttoning a matching leather
waistcoat over Jackie's breasts which left a wide band of
naked flesh around her middle. 'Just the boots, and that's
it.'

'Nice, very nice! She should fetch a good price,' David
remarked, running upstairs to answer the telephone. He
yelled down the stairs for Jane to join him.

'What is it?' she asked, running into the lounge.

'Lady Stockwell – she says there's someone trying to
break into her house.'

'So, why doesn't she call the police?'

'She's convinced that it's Jackie, come back to steal
some money or something. I told her that after we'd left
her place Jackie had run off and escaped.'

'Why?'

'Don't you see? If I go there now, break a window or
something, and then calm her down . . .'

'No, I don't see.'

'There's probably no one trying to break in, right? Most
likely her imagination running overtime. After all she's
been through, she's unstable. So, I make her some tea to
quieten her, check the house over, grabbing the twenty
thousand from the safe in the process, then tell her that
the money's gone and blame Jackie. It's worth a try,

anyway. Stay here, with her, and don't unchain her –
whatever delights she offers you in return for her freedom, don't unchain her!'

Knowing that the temptation to taste the pleasures
between Jackie's thighs would be overwhelming should
she return to the den, Jane closed the book-shelving and
switched the TV on. Flopping onto the sofa, she made
herself comfortable before falling asleep.

She was woken by the incessant ringing of the doorbell.
Bleary-eyed, she dragged herself to the hall.

'Lost your key?' she asked, opening the front door.

'Police!' A balding man dressed in a dark suit was
brandishing his identity card. 'May we come in? We'd like
to ask you some questions.'

Stunned, Jane opened the door further to see another
man and a police woman lurking in the shadows.

'Yes, come in,' she said hesitantly, leading them into
the lounge and thanking God that she'd closed the book-
shelving.

'Who are you?' the first man asked as Jane motioned
for him to sit down.

'Jane – Jane Blackwell.'

'And David Blackwell is your brother?'

'Yes, yes. What's happened? He's all right, isn't he?'

'When did you last see him?'

'An hour or so ago, I think. Is he all right?'

'Did he say where he was going?'

'He went to see . . . Er . . .'

'Went to see who, Miss Blackwell?'

'A friend.'

'And the friend's name?'

'I can't remember.'

'I think you can.'

A thousand thoughts ran through Jane's head as she

looked in turn at all three police officers. She suddenly remembered Jackie, chained to the bed, and glanced at the book-shelving. They knew about the basement, she was sure, and she tried desperately to formulate a plan, an excuse, a reason for chaining Jackie to the bed, an explanation for the frame, the vibrators.

'The friend's name, Miss Blackwell?'

'Stockwell or something,' she blurted out.

'Lady Stockwell?'

'Yes, I think so. Is David all right?'

'Yes, he's all right. But she isn't – we've just arrested your brother for the murder of Lady Stockwell.'

Chapter Nine

Jackie was lying on the four-poster bed crying when Jane returned – eight hours later. She raised her head and stared into Jane's eyes, waiting to hear of her dreadful fate.

'Well?' she said. 'What have you two filthy perverts decided to do with me? Sell me into slavery? Kill me? Keep me here to use my body whenever it takes your fancy? Or have you . . .'

'Shut up! Just fucking well shut up, will you?'

'What's happened? Where have you been all this time? I've been chained up here for bloody hours!'

'Lady Stockwell has been murdered,' Jane announced coldly.

'Oh, that's a good one! I suppose you're going to arrange her timely death and then tell the police that I did it, is that the plan?'

'They've arrested David for her murder.'

'You do come out with them! What do you take me for, an idiot?'

'Everything's ruined. The business, everything . . .'

'You're serious, aren't you?'

'Of course I'm bloody serious!'

'But how . . . I mean, what happened?'

'David went to see Stockwell after she'd phoned him. He broke a window and climbed in, to make it look like a

161

burglary. She wasn't around so he took the keys from her bag and stuffed the twenty thousand from the safe into his pockets. Then he went downstairs – and found her dead in the lounge.'

'But the police can't prove . . .'

'They don't have to! David's footprints are in the snow and mud under the window, there are traces of mud up the stairs and on the carpet by the safe. He doesn't stand a chance!'

'But that doesn't prove that he killed her.'

'The idiot picked up the poker, the murder weapon, which was lying on the floor by her body. It seems that the burglar alarm is connected directly to the police station and, when they arrived, there was David – twenty grand in his pockets, fingerprints all over the safe, poker in his hand. That's it, isn't it? Case closed!'

'So, what happens to me now?' Jackie asked, knowing that without David, Jane would be completely lost.

'Fuck you! It's my brother I'm worried about!'

'Brother? You mean . . .'

'Yes, David's my brother.'

'But he's more than twice your age.'

'It's a long story, I don't want to talk about it now.'

'So, what about me?'

'You'll stay here, chained up. If it wasn't for you, none of this would have happened! You and your pathetic, bloody blackmail stunts – fucking everything up for us all. And to top it all, you've gone and written to the police! David was going to give you a thousand pounds a week. He'd paid the mortgage off on your flat for you when you moved in here. And look what you did in return!'

'But I didn't know! The police were after me and . . . Anyway, I didn't write to the police – I was bluffing. Thinking that I was leaving the country, I only posted my letter of resignation to the bank.'

'Well, that's something, at least. The police were never after you, either. David just said that to keep you here.'

'But the police called here. I heard . . .'

'David's good at changing his voice.'

'Why put me through all that?'

'Because I . . . Oh, it doesn't matter now. None of it matters any more – just shut up and leave me alone!'

Ignoring Jackie's pleas for her release, Jane left the room and climbed the stairs. Noticing David's leather bag lying on the floor, and knowing that he would have stuffed it with jewels and cash, Jackie decided that now was the time to escape.

She couldn't see how the chain was fixed to the leather collar. The other end was firmly clamped to the wooden bedpost with a large, steel band. There was no way she could remove it on her own. Pulling on the last link of the chain, she realised that it could only be sewn to the collar. 'You can't weld metal to leather,' she whispered, twisting and pulling the link from side to side. The more she twisted, the easier it became to move the link until, to her delight, it broke free. Grabbing the bag, she crept from the den and made her way up the stairs to the lounge. She knew that she'd be cold outside dressed in nothing other than a skimpy waistcoat and leather microskirt, but the safety and security of her flat were only minutes away – freedom so near now.

Reaching the front door, Jackie paused. The soft whimpers emanating from Jane's bedroom confused her. She cast her eyes up the stairs and then focused on the leather bag – the riches, her key to the future. Gripping the door knob in her hand, she hesitated.

'Shit! I can't leave her like this!' she cursed, dropping the bag to the floor as the telephone rang. Torn, she didn't know what to do. 'It might be about David,' she sighed, entering the lounge and grabbing the phone.

'Is that Jackie?' a woman's voice asked.

'Yes,' she blurted, wishing she'd said no.

'I warned you never to go to that house again and now you're living there – you never learn, do you?'

'Who is this? Who the hell are you?'

'An ex-client of David's – or, should I say, victim.'

'Victim?'

'Come on, you know what I mean.'

'I don't know what you're talking about! Who are you?'

'I lost my husband. It was no great loss as he had a filthy little mistress throughout our entire marriage. Anyway, he left me extremely well off. I went to David for a little sexual excitement, entertainment, I suppose, and he kindly relieved me of a large sum of money.'

'Why didn't you go to the police?'

'Someone in my position doesn't want the world to know . . . Well, let's just say that there was nothing I could do.'

'So what do you want now?'

'I murdered Lady Stockwell.'

Stunned, Jackie almost dropped the phone. She realised that she was out of her depth, too involved now to run. She could never live with her conscience. Her thoughts suddenly returned to Jane, sobbing for her brother, and then to her own future, the money, her freedom.

'Are you still there?' the woman asked.

'Yes, yes. Why are you telling me all this? I don't want to know.'

'Because you've ruined my plan. With David out of the way for fifteen years or so, I only had that young Jane to deal with. She'd have access to David's money and I'd

164

have had no problem getting it back. But now, it seems, you're in my way.'

'But I'm not involved! If anything, I was a victim, too!'

'Oh, but you are involved. You know far too much.'

'Well, I'm leaving so you can do what you like.'

'No, you're not leaving. I'm going to use you to my advantage.'

'You're not using me!'

'The old lady in the Grantham Wood post office would easily recognise you, and if the police knew that you'd been to Stockwell's house, well . . .'

'How do you know . . .'

'I want my money back – all five hundred thousand of it.'

'Half a million!'

'Yes. It's up to you, you either help me, or I'll make sure that you are arrested, not only in connection with the Stockwell murder, but Jane's, too.'

'But Jane isn't . . .'

'That could very easily be arranged.'

Stunned, Jackie listened to the dialling tone for several minutes before replacing the receiver. She suddenly felt responsible for Jane, she was no more than a child, left alone to fend for herself – to fend off a murderer. Jane's wailing filled the house as Jackie returned to the hall wondering what on Earth she could do. Picking up the bag, she opened the grandfather clock and dropped it into the hollow under the weights for safe keeping.

'What's the matter?' she called, rushing up the stairs and dashing into the bedroom. 'He'll be all right, pull yourself together! You've got to carry on!'

Jane pulled the quilt over her head and sobbed into her pillow. 'How can he be all right? He'll get life! And I can't carry on, not on my own.'

Jackie sighed and sat on the edge of the bed. She thought of her freedom again, the money, her own flat with no mortgage, no worries about the police. Then she looked at Jane, sobbing pathetically into her pillow, and thought of the phone call – the murder.

'Move over, you silly girl,' she whispered, slipping out of her clothes. 'You can carry on, you're not on your own – you've got me.'

'After all we've . . . After all I've put you through, you want to be with me?' Jane cried, lifting her tear-streaked face to look at Jackie.

'Yes, I want to be with you,' she whispered, gazing at the hurt in the young girl's eyes. 'I must be mad – either that or in love. Whichever it is, you've got me. Now move over, I'm getting cold.'

Jackie slipped under the quilt and kissed the soft curvature of Jane's warm stomach as she slid her hands between her legs and squeezed the spongy bulge in her palm. Jane responded by letting out an appreciative sigh and spreading her thighs, offering her intimacy to her lover. Running her fingers up and down the length of Jane's groove until her lips swelled and the wetness flowed, she moved her head down and began to kiss and taste and nibble the complexity of the sweet, pink folds.

Burying her face in the warm nest, she found an illicit love, a strange sense of security away from the cold world outside. Breathing in the inebriating scent, she pushed two fingers deep into the well to draw out more perfumed fluid from the source somewhere deep within. 'I do want my clitoris to be like yours,' she breathed, taking its length between her lips and flicking the tip with her hot tongue.

'It will be, soon,' Jane murmured as the beginnings of her orgasm began to rock her young body. Gripping Jackie's head with her hands, she arched her back and cried out as her elongated clitoris throbbed against Jackie's hot tongue, sending rapturous ripples of pleasure over her tingling flesh and through her mind. Jackie ran her open mouth up and down the creamy, swollen valley, covering her face with the delightful products of sexual euphoria before moving up to kiss Jane's full mouth.

'Lick your juice from my face,' she breathed as Jane's tongue gently touched against hers.

'I want to lick your juice from your pretty little hole,' she replied, pulling Jackie up and positioning her wetness over her face. Resting on her knees with her parted thighs either side of Jane's head, Jackie lowered the hot centre of her body to meet the waiting tongue. Gyrating her hips and rubbing the length of her warm slit over Jane's mouth, she poured her sticky fluid over her face until she began to pant and catch her breath. Reaching up, Jane squeezed Jackie's hard nipples between her fingers as she sucked on her bud, enticing an orgasm from the throbbing nodule. She was barely able to breathe as Jackie ground her cunt into her face and eventually collapsed in ecstasy.

Positioning herself over Jane, Jackie buried her face between her thighs once more, exposing the small, tight hole between her buttocks to her inquisitive tongue. Jane needed no cue: parting Jackie's pale crescents and running her tongue round the tiny hole, she tried to push it deep inside. Managing to press the tip of her tongue into the small brown hole, she delighted in the bitter taste and forced her tongue even further into the dark warmth. But Jackie's clitoris needed attention and she moved her hips back to position her slit over Jane's mouth as she took her clitoris between her lips.

The girls sucked and licked in unison until they both shuddered with delight. Their orgasms flowed round and round – lips to lips, lips to lips, closing the wondrous circle of sexual euphoria running through their bodies – bringing them together as one. Lapping the last of the cream from their spent holes, they breathed easily again, satisfied, calm, serene, and they finally fell asleep – entwined in love.

Opening her eyes to the sun streaming in through the window, the events of the night before suddenly came flooding back to Jane. A wave of adrenalin gushed through her veins, washing away the remnants of sleep as she leaped from the bed. Jackie stirred and lifted her head to admire Jane's glowing young body as she dashed into the bathroom.

'What a mess!' Jane called from the shower. 'David's gone and we've got a new client coming this morning. I don't know what I'm going to do!'

You don't know the half of it, Jackie thought as she joined her in the shower, you're on a bloody hit list!

Lathering Jane's young body to relax her, Jackie told her not to worry, that they'd work together, deal with the client together – all the clients. But Jane became despondent and began to cry. Dropping to her knees, Jackie buried her face between Jane's soft lips and gently kissed the wet folds. Jane responded by standing with her feet apart to allow Jackie better access to her drenched slit, her insatiable clitoris. The water flowed over her breasts and down over her stomach to cascade over Jackie's face as she sucked and mouthed at her lengthening bud. The tension-relieving orgasm shuddered through her body, washing away her fears, relaxing her mind as she slid down the tiled wall and rested in Jackie's arms. Touching, fondling, searching within the depths of each other's open holes, the girls sat beneath the hot, streaming water until they had gently drifted back to reality.

'I can't deal with this client, any client,' Jane sighed as they stepped from the shower and gently dried each other.

'Together, we can do anything,' Jackie assured. 'Now, take this damn collar off me and let's get dressed, have something to eat and make our plans. By the way, who is the doctor?'

'I can't tell you that, I'm afraid.'

'Why not? Look, if we are going to work together, I must know. Can't you see that? After all this so-called doctor has done to me, I must know who he is!'

'It doesn't matter what you say, I can't tell you.'

'Then I shall just have to find out for myself.'

Eating a hurried breakfast, Jackie pushed all thoughts of the doctor to the back of her mind and turned her attention to her situation – her ever-changing life. The security of owning her own flat pleased her, and she had plenty of money, if she could keep the bag a secret from Jane. She'd eventually ask where the money and jewels were, but she'd deal with that problem when it arose.

'I just can't think of anything other than David and what he's going through,' Jane said, nibbling on her toast.

'So what are we going to do about this client?' Jackie asked, not wanting to discuss David.

'Not me, you!' Jane announced, leaping up from the table. 'I'll tell you what to do, it's easy.'

'I can't do it on my own!'

'Of course you can. You'll like this one – it's a man.'

'A man! And he wants to be caned?'

'He's only young, nineteen I think David said. Anyway, he's a virgin and wants some initiation into the delights of sex. I don't think he'll want the cane – well, he might! Who knows?'

'But I thought that David only took on rich widows.'

'This one may not be a widow, but his parents are rich.

The idea is to find out when they are away, on holiday or whatever, and, using his keys, pop round to the house and borrow some cash.'

'God, is there no end to the lengths that you two will go to for money?'

'No – no end at all!'

The door bell rang just as Jane had finished giving her instructions. In a panic, Jackie made for the den as Jane dashed to the front door to welcome the client.

'This is Paul,' she smiled, showing the nervous young man into the den. 'Paul, meet Jackie – your teacher.'

Dressed in trainers, blue jeans and a polo-neck jumper, he looked like a naughty schoolboy who'd just been caught playing truant. His eyes darting around the room at the erotic paintings and then to the four-poster bed, he managed a smile.

'What do you want me to do?' he said nervously.

'Clothes off and get on the bed, we'll leave you to it, call when you're ready,' Jane instructed.

Waiting in the studio, Jackie watched Jane climb the stairs and close the book-shelving. Mulling over the hurriedly-given instructions, she wondered how she could fill a whole hour with her young male client. Once he's come, that's it, she thought, as he called out 'Ready' like a child playing hide and seek.

Jackie closed the door and eyed his fresh young body, spread across the bed, ready for her every whim. His penis was flaccid, the result of nerves, she supposed, fixing the leather straps round his wrists and ankles.

'I'm strapping you down because I don't want you to do anything. I do all the work while you just relax and enjoy yourself, okay?'

He nodded his head and closed his eyes in readiness for his initiation.

Heaving on the heavy rope, Jackie watched excitedly as his thighs spread wide, revealing the ample balls weighing down the hairy bag. Her clitoris throbbed slightly, the stranger within obviously delighting in the feast spread so invitingly before her, ready to be consumed. Taking the young, limp penis in her hand, she began to move the soft skin back and forth over the plum-like knob. Filling and opening her small hand, the shaft swelled until it stood rigid, no longer needing her gentle support. Lightly scratching his now tight balls with her finger nails, as Jane had instructed, she became aware of a trickle of warm fluid running down her inner thigh from her knickerless crotch.

The boy began to moan softly as she continued to move the skin over his hard, bulging knob – but he said nothing. He mustn't come yet, she thought, releasing her grip and climbing on the bed to sit astride the firm, tanned body.

'Have you ever seen what a woman has up her skirt?' she asked wickedly, rubbing her wetness over his hard stomach.

'Yes. Well, only in pictures,' he replied nervously.

'Do you want to see what I've got up my skirt?'

'Yes, but . . .'

'No buts,' she grinned, moving herself ever nearer to his face. Hovering only inches from his mouth, she looked down at the miniskirt covering her secret from his wide eyes.

'Say please, then,' she said impishly as she began to lift her skirt.

'But I don't want you to . . .'

'You do want to see it, don't you?'

'See it, yes, but I don't . . .'

'Ah, you don't want to taste it, is that it?' she asked, lifting her skirt up over her stomach to reveal her naked,

pouting lips. His eyes widened and his mouth fell open at
the sight of her hairless pussy hovering ominously over his
face. Parting her lips with her fingers, she moved a little
closer, delighting in exposing her intimacy to the young
virgin.

'Do you like it?' she asked, peeling her inner lips back
to expose her now very hard bud. He didn't answer.
Stunned, he could only gape as she slowly lowered herself
onto his warm mouth and gently slid her creamy wetness
back and forth over his lips.

'Put your tongue out and lick me,' she instructed,
pressing her open hole harder against his mouth. Folding
her lips over his face, she gasped as his searching tongue
eventually found its way inside and began to explore.
Near to orgasm now, she pulled away and pressed on the
soft flesh surrounding her swollen bud to pop it out.

'This is my clitoris,' she breathed, caressing the hard
little nodule with a finger. 'I want you to suck it and flick
your tongue over the tip as fast as you can. And don't stop
until I tell you to.' Without hesitating, he did as he was
told. Jackie tossed her hair back and looked up to the
ceiling, remembering the hidden camera and wondering if
Jane had the tape running. 'This is what's known as oral
sex,' she gasped as she felt her little bud swell and throb
slightly in the warmth of his mouth. 'Do it faster, get into
a rhythm, that's the secret of making a girl come with your
tongue,' she ordered authoritatively.

Glancing over her shoulder, she grinned to see the boy's
rigid penis twitching. 'You mustn't come! Not yet, you
naughty boy!' she yelled as she shuddered and flooded his
mouth with the hot, sticky fruits of her quim. Grinding the
centre of her body into his face, she arched her back and
spread her legs further as she cried out in euphoria.
Spluttering, he tried to turn his head to one side, but she

gripped his ears between her thighs until her climax gently abated and brought her down from her heaven. Only then did she smile down at his wet face and move her open fissure away, allowing him to gasp for air.

'And now it's your turn to come,' she said, turning around to face his virginal rod. Lowering her head, she pulled the skin back and took the hard knob into her mouth. He gasped and writhed, but said nothing as she moved her mouth up and down the fresh, rigid shaft, almost taking the full length down her throat. To add to his pleasure, and hers, she lifted her skirt and raised her hips to expose her small brown hole and inner lips to his gaze. Without warning, the shaft suddenly twitched and he filled her cheeks with his slimy sperm. Lowering her slit over his face, she sucked and ran her tongue round and round the pulsating plum to drain his body of every last drop of sperm.

Savouring his salty milk, she managed to rub her clitoris back and forth over his gasping mouth until, still sucking his knob, she shuddered and poured out her milk in exchange for his. 'Tongue out!' she ordered desperately as her orgasm began to erupt. He obliged and flicked the little nodule, causing her to scream and writhe in incredible sexual pleasure. Collapsing across his body, she relaxed.

'So, you now know all about oral sex,' she said.

'That was wonderful!' he gasped. 'I could do that all day long.'

After a few minutes, she sat up and turned around to face him.

'There's more to come besides that. This is what they call sexual intercourse,' she laughed, positioning her slit over his limp penis.

He said nothing as his young rod quickly stood to

173

Ray Gordon

attention again as Jackie rubbed her hot, open slit along its length. When he was ready, she introduced the knob to her entrance and gently lowered herself, easing the youthful penis into her body until her creamy lips settled neatly around its base. His eyes closed, he breathed heavily and moaned as Jackie tickled his balls with her nails and wiggled her hips.

'You're no longer a virgin,' she enlightened him as she gently moved up and down the length of his shaft. 'But to complete your initiation, you must come inside me.'

Gyrating her hips while bouncing up and down, she watched his face grimace and contort as he gasped. 'I'm coming, don't stop!'

'I won't stop, I promise you that. Can you feel my hot cunt around you? Can you feel my love muscles crushing you?'

'Yes, yes.'

'You're fucking me – you haven't fucked a girl before, have you?'

'No, I haven't.'

'You've actually got your hard cock deep inside my wet cunt – and you're fucking me!'

'Ah, yes, yes!'

'Now come, fill me with your sperm, come inside my wet cunt and then you can call yourself a fully fledged man.'

As if on cue, his body became rigid and he pumped out his second deluge of sperm, filling Jackie until it flowed down the glistening skin of his shaft and over her soft, naked lips. Suddenly, she burst into orgasm and screamed out her pleasure as her muscles crushed the young shaft.

'That's what I wanted!' he cried excitedly as Jackie writhed and convulsed. With a long groan, she shuddered violently and collapsed across his chest.

'I wanted to make *you* come! *Now* I am a fully fledged man!'

'You certainly are,' she panted, pulling her tight hole free from his shaft and climbing from his body. 'You certainly are!'

'I want to come again,' he announced confidently as Jackie regained her balance and loosened the leather straps.

'What? Three times in a row?'

'No, no, come here again – to see you.'

'Ah, Jane will make an appointment for you. Get dressed, I'll be waiting outside,' she said, moving towards the door with sperm trickling down her thighs.

Jackie found Jane lounging on the studio couch reading a magazine, waiting for her to emerge from the den.

'I did it,' she said, lifting her skirt to gaze at the creamy solution coursing its way down her leg.

'I know, I saw,' Jane grinned.

'You saw?'

'Yes, I watched you on the monitor, it's all on video tape. You did very well. Too well, in fact – I was quite jealous. Now, come here, you need cleaning up.'

Sitting upright, Jane pulled Jackie towards her and raised her skirt to examine her swollen lips. 'You're all wet, and it's running down your leg,' she said, and began to lap up the creamy juice from her leg. Working up her thigh, she eventually licked at her drenched lips, cleaning and drying them in turn with her tongue. Parting the lips, she pressed her mouth to Jackie's hole and sucked out the sperm before licking the full length of her valley. Gasping with the pleasure between her legs, Jackie was about to come when the door opened.

Jane leapt to her feet and took the young man's money as he wandered from the den, looking decidedly pleased

with himself. After making his next appointment, she
showed him out.

'Well, that's another two hundred,' Jane said as she
joined Jackie on the sofa in the lounge and lifted her skirt.

'I can't understand why these people pay so much.'

'Because they know that they're assured complete
confidentiality, they'll receive expert attention from an
attractive, clean, young girl, and get what they want,' she
said as she bent down to finish pleasuring Jackie. 'That's
what David says, anyway. Apart from the odd male client,
where can a woman go for whatever she fancies in the way
of sex? There's nowhere in the land, is there?'

'Are we going to rob him, then?' Jackie asked as her
clitoris neared its pinnacle.

'Yes, get him chatting next time and try to find out
about his parents' holiday plans,' she replied, bringing the
little bud to orgasm as Jackie writhed and gasped. Licking
the last of the fresh cream as it pumped from Jackie's
body, Jane sat up and smiled.

'Nice?' she said.

'God, yes,' Jackie panted, pulling her skirt down. 'I
needed that! Do you want me to do it to you?'

'Not now, later. I'm going to the police station to see
what's happening to poor David.'

'While you're out, can I look through the video tapes?'

'What for?'

'Er . . . So I can see what the clients want. If I'm going
to be working full-time here with you, I need to know the
ropes, so to speak.'

'Oh, right. You know where the machines are, don't
you? All the tapes are on the shelves. They're only
ordinary videos, just push them in and press play – the
monitors are switched on.'

The minute Jane closed the front door, Jackie went

down to David's work-room and scanned the rows of tapes. 'I don't even have a clue as to what she looks like,' she cursed, reading the coded labels. 'There must be a retrieval system, a way of identifying which tape belongs to which client.'

As she selected a tape at random, the telephone rang. Guided by the bell, she searched amongst the mess of vibrators and various pieces of electronic equipment on David's work bench and found the phone.

'Hello,' she whispered hesitantly.

'It's me again,' a woman's voice said coldly.

'And what do you want now?'

'I'm just ringing to make sure that you understood me. I want my money back.'

'Yes, I understand that, but you've overlooked one thing,' she replied, searching for an instant lie.

'And what's that?'

'I know your position, as you put it. I know everything about you – I know who you are.'

'So, who am I?'

'You are a lady who is about to lose everything – and I don't just mean money. You are about to lose your credibility, your station, your standing in society.'

'Full marks for trying, but your little bluff has failed.'

'You're a natural blonde, aren't you?'

'No, no – way off the mark! I'm as red as they come, so . . .'

'Thank you – thank you so much.'

Banging the phone down, Jackie returned to the rows of tapes to try and discover how David's system worked. A small drawer caught her eye and she opened it to find a small, hardbacked exercise book with 'Class One' neatly written on the front in red felt-tip. 'Class one,' she breathed. 'These must be the very rich clients.' There were only six names listed in the book against six tape numbers. 'I've got you now, you bitch!' she hissed, raising her eyes to the shelf.

Pulling out the six tapes, she pushed one into the machine and looked up to the monitor. A naked woman lay on her back on the frame, her nipples connected to the doctor's pulley arrangement and a small rubber pipe fixed over her clitoris. CDC, Jackie mused, remembering her own experience of the macabre deforming process. As the camera panned out, the woman's head came into view. She was middle aged, her contorted face fairly attractive and, to Jackie's disappointment, her long hair was auburn. 'One down, five to go,' she whispered, ramming another tape into the machine. 'That's not her!' she laughed, gazing at a young man's body being attended to by Jane. She watched for a while as Jane slid a rubber ring over his huge, erect penis and flicked a switch. The head bulged in response to the vibrating ring, but each time he was about to come, Jane flicked the switch and lightly stroked the twitching knob. Bringing the poor man near to orgasm a dozen times, she eventually ceased her torturing game and allowed him his relief. Jackie gazed at the massive purple knob as it ballooned and suddenly pumped its white liquid over his hairy stomach.

The fifth tape brought a smile to Jackie's face. 'You're the one!' she spat, staring at an extremely large red-haired woman lying across the frame with what appeared to be Jane's entire hand deep inside her stretched hole. Her massive body spilled over the edges of the frame as the rolls of fat wobbled in time with Jane's thrusting fist. Her colossal breasts hung either side of her trunk, the dark brown elongated nipples nestling in her hairy armpits.

'The diary!' Jackie shrieked, rushing into the studio. Rummaging around in the knee-hole desk amongst rags and paints, she found the leather-bound book. Flicking through the pages, she found what she was looking for. 'EX 27,' she said excitedly. 'Lady Forsythe-Byron – I've got you!' Clutching the diary, she wandered back into David's secret room and picked up the telephone. Gazing at the monitor while waiting for her call to be answered, she watched in disgust as Jane's fist pumped in and out of the cavernous hole while she held a vibrator at the top of her gaping slit. Her body shook violently, rocking the frame as her face reddened and her treble chin quivered uncontrollably.

'Hello.'

'Lady Forsythe-Byron?' Jackie asked, her eyes transfixed on the vulgar scene.

'Yes.'

'I'm watching you come, on television.'

'What? Who is this?'

'Jane has her fist inside you and she's using a vibrator on your clitoris. Wait, you're coming – yes, that's it, nearly there. Ah, wonderful! You could do with losing five or six stone, though – you nearly broke poor David's ingenious frame!'

'Is that you, Jackie?'

'Yes, sorry about that, I was engrossed.'

'So, you're not quite as stupid as I initially thought.'

'No, I'm not – but you are. David's insurance seems to have paid off, doesn't it?'

'Insurance?'

'The video tape – all his clients are on tape.'

'Can we meet? I need to talk to you.'

'Oh, yes. You want to come here so you can add two more people to your list of murders, is that it?'

'I need to talk to you. Perhaps we can work something out.'

'Be here tonight, at seven, but remember that I have several copies of this vile video tape so don't try anything stupid!'

Jackie hung up and glanced once more at the nauseating spectacle before ejecting the tape. I have it in my power to free David, she mused as she wandered upstairs to the lounge. But if he came back here, where would that leave me?

Chapter Ten

'How do things look for David?' Jackie asked as Jane wandered into the lounge, her face glum and lifeless.

'Not good, I'm afraid. In fact, decidedly bad! He didn't do it, obviously, but we need proof!'

Jackie bit her lip and sighed as she imagined David locked in a small cell. Her conscience pricking, she was about to tell Jane of Lady Forsythe-Byron but, suddenly, she became overwhelmed by a terrific sense of power. Money played on her mind, thousands of pounds – jewellery, cars, holidays abroad. 'There's nothing we can do,' she said agitatedly, desperately trying to rid herself of all thoughts of David and look to the future.

'I'll find a way,' Jane replied firmly. 'He didn't kill anyone, he couldn't! Whoever did it is lurking somewhere – nearby, I would imagine.'

'Nearby? What do you mean?';

'The culprit knows David, and me, I'm sure. And so it follows that we know him – or her. It's just a question of elimination. I'll get a private detective and . . .'

'You can't do that! You'll blow the whole operation! Imagine some man wandering around downstairs, looking at the video tapes and . . .'

'That's it! All the clients are on tape. It's got to be a client!'

Jackie's heart missed several beats as she remembered

the tape she'd left in the machine. 'Let's look through the tapes now,' she suggested, quickly moving towards the book-shelving and glancing at the mantelpiece clock. The time had passed so quickly, there was only a quarter of an hour before the culprit, as Jane had put it, was due to arrive.

Whether to lock Jane in the work-room or not, she wasn't sure, but she had to be rid of her for a while – just long enough to deal with the woman. Running down the stairs, closely followed by Jane, she ejected the tape and slipped it under some nearby papers.

'Look, I'll go and make us something to eat while you sort through the tapes – a sandwich, or something,' Jackie suggested. Jane nodded her answer as she selected the first tape and rammed it into the machine, her expression a mixture of determination and anxiety. Quietly locking the door from the outside, Jackie ran upstairs to the lounge as the doorbell rang. She panicked – the woman was early.

Slowly opening the front door, she found herself facing a fat, ugly, red-haired female. 'Come in,' she said, her heart thumping, her mind reeling with images of the woman pulling out a gun. But before reaching the lounge, Jackie had begun her ill-rehearsed speech.

'There is no money here, I've searched the house from top to bottom. If there is any money, then you can be sure that David has it stashed in a Swiss bank account, or somewhere where no-one can get at it!'

'There must be papers, a statement, something appertaining to the money's whereabouts?' the woman returned agitatedly.

'Nothing. I've searched everywhere, even under loose floor boards.'

'Then how do you envisage paying me back?'

'I don't! How do you envisage getting yourself out of

this mess? After all, you're a murderer! If I were you –
and thank God I'm not – I would go home and think
myself lucky that I'm not behind bars!'

'Are you suggesting that I forget about the money? Just
write off half a million pounds?'

'Do you have a better idea?'

'Yes, you can pay me back monthly, from the money
you receive from your clients.'

'There are no clients. With David in prison, the business is finished. Now, if you don't mind, I have things to
do.'

'At least give me the video tape!'

'Don't be ridiculous! That's my insurance! Just go, and
don't come back – unless you want to see the inside of a
prison!'

'I'm not leaving it like this. I'm not writing off half a
million pounds. I'll be back, I swear!'

Leaping down the stairs as the front door slammed shut,
Jackie joined Jane who was desperately ramming tape
after tape into the video machine. 'I'll bloody well find
her!' she hissed. 'If I have to sit here all night, I'll find her!
Did you make me a sandwich?'

'There's no bread. What if you don't find her?' Jackie
asked, in an effort to prepare her for disappointment.

'It's a client, I know it, and they are all on tape – every
single one of them.'

'I think not,' Jackie mused, wondering exactly what she
meant, and what she'd say next to put Jane off the scent.
'What sort of client would commit murder? You've met
them all – what are they like?'

'Pissed off by being robbed, for a start!'

'Yes, but what's that got to do with it?'

'Come on! They're not all thick. It wouldn't take much
to work out what's going on, would it?'

'Okay, so the murderer was a client who David has robbed.'

'Yes, exactly!'

'Then why kill another client?'

'To frame David!'

'But only you and I, and Lady Stockwell, of course, knew that David was going to her house. How could anyone have framed him?'

'They . . . Oh, I don't know – I'm confused!'

'It isn't a client, I'm sure. It doesn't add up.'

'So, what's your theory, then?'

'I reckon it was a burglar. Stockwell disturbed him and . . .'

'And he killed her and David just happened to turn up. It's too much of a coincidence.'

'Stockwell phoned him, didn't she? It's not coincidence, it was just lucky for the burglar – the murderer!'

'And unlucky for David!'

Jane threw a video tape onto the table and stormed upstairs, accepting, Jackie hoped, that she was wrong. Grabbing the tape of the fat woman, the murderer, from under the pile of papers, Jackie took it up to the entrance hall and hid it in the base of the grandfather clock along with David's leather bag. Glancing up the stairs to Jane's bedroom door, she slowly opened the bag and roughly counted out the money. 'Bloody hell, close on half a million!' she breathed, stuffing the notes back into the bag. 'I'm rich!'

The time had come, she knew, to make some real plans for the future. With David gone and Jane quickly losing faith in everything, there seemed little point in hanging around. Half a million will keep me comfortable for some time, she mused, closing the clock door. But another thought suddenly struck her. Why not stay on for a while longer and stuff a few more thousand pounds into the bag? Or another half-million?

Wandering into Jane's room, she put her roughly formulated plan into action. 'I've just taken two phone calls,' she began. Jane peeped over the quilt and frowned. 'Both from clients cancelling their appointments, I'm afraid.'

'Cancelling or postponing?'

'Cancelling. One said that, under the circumstances, she wouldn't be coming here again – and the other offered no explanation.'

'They must have heard about David. I knew it would be on the news before long.'

'You do realise, don't you, that we will probably lose all the clients?'

'I know. So, what do you propose?'

'How much money have you got?'

'God! That's a point. Where's David's bag?'

'What bag?'

'The one . . . Bloody hell! I haven't seen it since he went to Stockwell's! Didn't he leave it downstairs?'

'I haven't seen a bag. He must have taken it with him.'

'What, to the police station? Hardly!'

'What was in it?'

'Money – all David's money and jewellery!'

After helping Jane to search the house for an hour, Jackie added to her story of gloom by mentioning that she'd found the back door wide open after she'd freed herself from the chain and dog collar.

'It was definitely downstairs when David left,' Jane said as she wandered into the lounge and flopped into an armchair.

'Then someone must have come in and taken it,' Jackie returned.

'Great, so we've been robbed!'

'Poetic justice, is it not?'

'Call it what you like – I've had enough of the whole bloody thing!'

'What are you going to do?'

'I've no money to speak of, David's down for a good fifteen years, the clients will all shy away when they hear about him. What am I going to do? Sell up, that's what!'

For the first time, Jackie had a fleeting glimpse of her future – a good, financially secure future, but, it seemed, she'd be without Jane.

'I'll buy the house,' she said, stunning herself as well as Jane. Jane frowned and stared into her eyes.

'You haven't got any money.'

'I'll sell my flat and . . .'

'This place is worth four or five hundred thousand, if not more! What would you get for your flat – forty thousand?'

'My parents left me some money,' Jackie lied, realising that Jane would quickly put two and two together concerning David's missing bag.

'How much?'

'Enough.'

'You've got the bag, haven't you?'

'No, I know nothing about a bag.'

'I don't know why – but I believe you.'

'Good, then you'll sell me the house?'

'That's up to David, he owns it.'

'When you put it to him, tell him that I want the basement left exactly as it is – I intend to carry on with the business.'

'Without clients?'

'That's my problem. And a problem that I'll solve, somehow.'

While Jane was upstairs continuing her futile search for the bag, Jackie opened the diary and wrote 'Cancelled' by several clients' names before taking the opportunity to wander around the basement, imagining it all belonged to her.

Suddenly, she dashed from one room to the next, looking at the ceilings and walls. 'It doesn't fit,' she breathed. 'The house is more or less square, so there should be another room down here – under the hall.'

Tapping the wall under the stairs, she realised that the wooden panel was hollow. As she pressed around the edges, it suddenly swung open to reveal a secret room. She stepped into the darkness and fumbled for the switch. The light came on and she walked into a warm, cosy room, furnished as a lounge. A large table with a leather, padded top and leather straps fastened to each corner caught her eye. 'What the hell happens to people in here?' she whispered as she wandered, wide-eyed, across the thick carpet and opened the writing bureau. Thoughts of naked women tethered to the table quickly disappeared when she opened a large tin box in the bureau to find a fat bundle of fifty pound notes.

Movements upstairs sent her bounding from the room, clutching the notes in her hand. The panel closed, she dashed to the four-poster bed and stuffed the money under the pillow before lying down.

'What are you doing down here?' Jane asked.

'Thinking,' Jackie replied softly.

'About what?'

'Is there anywhere else in the house, or down here, where David might have hidden the bag?'

'No, there's nowhere.'

'No secret cupboards or anything?'

'Not that I know of, why?'

'Either he hid it, or someone came in and stole it. I just wondered if he had a hiding place somewhere.'

'No, no. Anyway, I've been thinking about it, too, and I agree with you, someone obviously wandered in through the open back door and took it.'

'A client, perhaps?'

'Maybe. It could be anyone, I suppose.'

'Has David ever dealt with a client down here and told you to keep away?'

'What do you mean?'

'Has he ever locked the book-shelving to keep you upstairs while he sees clients in private?'

'Yes, he has locked himself down here with a client, but what of it? What are you getting at?'

'I just wondered, that's all.'

'Well, I'm going to bed, I'm tired. Are you coming up?'

'Later. I'll stay down here for a while longer.'

Jackie waited fifteen minutes or so before creeping into the secret room and closing the panel behind her. Sitting at the bureau, she opened a bundle of letters addressed to David and signed 'Eileen.' As she read, she soon discovered, to her surprise, that the woman was David's wife. But more interesting was the fact that the letters had been posted from prison. '. . . and unless you tell Jane the truth, then I will have to', she read aloud. 'What truth?' she breathed as she picked up the next letter. '. . . you must not continue with your lies, David. Jane is our daughter and the day will come when she has to know of my existence'.

Having read through all the letters, Jackie was disappointed to find no further reference to Jane. But she did find Eileen's death certificate in the bureau. 'His late wife. But why lie to Jane?' she asked herself as she stuffed the certificate back in its place.

Climbing the stairs, Jackie became aware of her clitoris stiffening between her swollen lips and she was in two minds as whether to slip into bed with Jane or not. She became confused, her thoughts muddled. 'What have I become?' she whispered as she placed the money in the leather bag and crept upstairs.

Closing Jane's bedroom door behind her, she walked to the bed and smiled. Jane was sleeping with the quilt pushed down to her stomach. Her young breasts, firm and well rounded, seemed to beckon Jackie as she sat on the bed, admiring the young girl's body. Pulling the quilt down further, she gazed at her mound, her slit, youthful, hairless and tightly closed in sleep. Leaning over, she softly kissed the crack and ran her tongue over the soft, puffy skin. Jane moaned in her sleep and parted her legs as Jackie pushed her tongue into the groove to taste the delights within.

'You need a man,' Jackie breathed as she ran her tongue down to the warm, creamy hole. 'I can't give you what a man can, what a young girl needs.' Jane moaned again and parted her legs further as Jackie located her clitoris and hardened it with her tongue. 'I wonder if you'll come in your sleep?' she whispered. 'Perhaps you'll dream of a man as I lick you and make you come.'

Spreading Jane's lips, Jackie flicked the bud until it grew and Jane groaned and breathed uneasily. To her surprise, she did come in her sleep, writhing slightly as her bud throbbed with her orgasm and her nipples swelled. Caressing the bud as the orgasm subsided, Jackie was delighted to hear Jane breathe her name. 'I'm here,' she replied, closing the girl's inflamed lips over her clitoris to hide it and keep it safe, ready for another day. 'I'm here – now sleep, my angel, sleep.'

Rising before Jane was awake, Jackie quickly dressed

and made her way to the police station. She had it in her mind to confront David, to put her ultimatum to him before Jane got to him. Blackmail, she knew, was her only weapon, and she planned to use it to the full.

After explaining that she was a friend, the police officer led her downstairs and unlocked a cell. Ushering her inside, he told David that he had ten minutes, and no more. Jackie gazed at David, but said nothing until they were alone.

'Hello, David.'

'What are you doing here?'

'I've come to talk to you.'

'There's not much to talk about, I'm afraid. It looks as if I'm going down for a long time.'

'I've come to talk about Jane's future, my future – not yours.'

'Jane's all right, isn't she?'

'She's penniless, she no longer has you . . .'

'Penniless? But . . .'

'Yes, penniless, David. It seems that your leather bag has gone missing.'

'But . . . But it can't have. It's in the basement.'

'*Was* in the basement. It's gone.'

'Then who . . . You took it! You stole my money!'

'The clients' money, David – not yours.'

'What are you up to?'

'Nothing, I'm just trying to tell you that Jane's broke, lost without you – and she wants to sell up.'

'No, no. There's plenty more money. You've stolen the bag, I know, and I'll get it back. But there's more, a lot more.'

'Oh, yes, I was coming to that. I've put it in a safe place. Don't worry, no-one will ever find it – not Jane, not even you.'

'What are you talking about?'

'The money from your bureau, David.'

'But how . . .'

'I'm not stupid. Now, as I said, the money, *my* money, is in a safe place and Jane is penniless. I'd like to buy your house.'

'You bitch! You'll never get the house, it's mine – Jane's!'

'In that case, I suppose I'll just have to show Jane the letters. I mean, it's only fair to tell her that you're her father, not her brother. And if she knew that her mother had died in prison and, God knows why, you told her some cock and bull story about . . .'

'All right! You've said more than enough. Now, listen to me, young lady! Firstly, you're not having the house. Secondly, I think I'll tell the police that you visited Stockwell's place and . . .'

'And incriminate Jane? Is that what you want? For me to have to show the police your basement? Show them the video tapes? Or the Sunday tabloids! Imagine what a field day they'd have in your basement! Or it may be an idea to give the police the jewellery and some of the money, a few thousand, perhaps, and tell them that you stole it. There's not a judge in the land who'd give you less than twenty years!'

'I'm locked up and about to be tried for a murder I didn't commit. I've looked after you and . . .'

'You violated my body! As good as kidnapped me and . . .'

'I awoke your sexuality, brought out the woman in you!'

'You've woken a sleeping monster! Roused some base instinct that was lying dormant, as it should, and brought it to the surface. You've made me something I'm not!'

'You enjoy your body now, don't you? Of course you do, and I taught you how!'

'I'm a nymphomaniac! I had sexual feelings, the normal feelings of a normal woman. Now I've had vibrators, I've been caned, shown lesbianism at first hand, I've been tortured, and I've become a stranger to myself.'

'You've become your true self, the real you that was in hiding, oppressed, that's all, Jackie.'

'No, not my true self. Some *thing* within me has surfaced, yes. Something, possibly from a million years ago – when we were no more than animals! I was a woman – I'm now an animal!'

'You're talking rubbish!'

'Say what you like. You've changed me and yes, I love sex, orgasms, vibrators – Jane. I can't get enough – it controls me now!'

'You're exaggerating. Anyway, there's little time. So, about my house – we need to talk and that's not going to be easy in here, is it?'

'You agree in principle, then?'

'Do I have a choice?'

'No. That's settled, then. I'll be seeing you again, David.'

The pang of guilt that pricked Jackie's conscience as the police officer slammed and locked the cell door soon faded when she walked into the fresh air. The sun was shining, people were walking the streets, shopping with children, husbands – none knew or cared about David, locked in a cell awaiting his fate. Jackie didn't care – she tried not to care.

Returning to the house, she found Jane on the telephone in the lounge. 'See you in an hour, then, Miss Bradshaw,' she said before replacing the receiver. 'Well, that's one client who obviously hasn't heard about David yet.'

'An hour, did you say? That doesn't give us much time to prepare.'

'There's nothing to prepare, she's a regular client. David deals with her and, basically, she only comes here for masturbation. There's no caning or anything, just . . .'

'You can deal with her then?'

'No, you do it. I've got to go and see David. Before I go, I've been thinking. If you buy the house, you'll need clients. You won't be able to get wealthy clients, let alone rob them, as David did, so why not stick to giving men hand relief for twenty pounds a time – or sex, even, for fifty pounds? You'd soon build up a nice little business.'

'No, no, you don't understand. That's prostitution – that's not what David has built up here. This is a high class set-up catering for the monied – not a seedy massage parlour.'

The bank had given Jackie a head for figures, and David had given her an insight into the business. Jane was young, too young to see or begin to understand. 'Where will you go? What will you do?' Jackie asked, realising the extent of Jane's naivety.

'I'll work abroad somewhere. I can earn a fortune with my knowledge – and my body!'

Jackie suddenly noticed Jane's long nipples pressing through her tight T-shirt. Lowering her gaze, she admired her slender waist and shapely young legs and pictured her youthful, shaven slit. She knew that, working abroad as a prostitute, Jane would probably end up in trouble – or dead. But more, she became aware of a strange jealousy. The thought of men taking her beautiful, young body angered her. She wanted Jane for herself.

'Don't go and see David,' she whispered, moving

towards her and circling her nipples with her fingers. 'I want you here, with me. The client that rang – let's see her together. Let's really give her a good time, and perhaps she'll keep coming back for more, even when she finds out about David.'

'Okay, if that's what you want,' Jane replied, pressing her lips to Jackie's and exploring her hot mouth with her tongue.

Lifting Jane's skirt, Jackie pulled her panties aside and slipped a finger between her soft lips and into her wet hole. Jane writhed, pushing her tongue further into Jackie's mouth as they crumpled to the floor, their hands desperately groping each other's bodies. Soon, Jane's panties were discarded and Jackie began to lick at her slit, parting her lips with her fingers to gain her prize. Jane shuddered and raised her legs, pulling her ankles up either side of her head to expose her intimacy to Jackie's tongue.

Sinking two fingers into the two open holes, Jackie thrust them in and out, causing Jane to gasp and pant her appreciation. 'Harder!' she cried as her juices flowed and her muscles tightened. Jackie rammed her fingers, pounding the soft flesh within her bowels, her tightening cunt, until her clitoris pulsated and she screamed with pleasure.

'You wet me, you naughty girl!' Jackie laughed as she withdrew her sticky fingers. 'Bend over the back of the sofa and take your punishment!' Jane needed no coaxing. Leaping over the sofa, her skirt raised to reveal her pale buttocks, she waited. Jackie slapped each buttock in turn several times, reddening the flesh until it glowed and Jane was nearing her second orgasm, before kneeling and licking her crease. Parting the lips of Jane's young vagina with her thumbs, Jackie pushed her tongue inside to taste the thick, creamy fluid as it poured from her trembling body. 'You can come once more,' she said. 'And then we must prepare for the client.'

Jane moaned her answer and opened her legs, lifting her hips to allow Jackie's tongue access to her swollen clitoris. Jackie licked around its base, enlarging it even more until it throbbed and pumped its ecstasy over Jane's body and through her mind, causing her to cry with lust as she spurted hot come-juice over Jackie's face. Jackie lapped up the offering, licking the length of the crimson slit until it was dry and Jane fell limp.

'And now it's your turn,' Jane breathed wickedly as she climbed from the sofa, her face red and glowing with desire. Jackie smiled as her clitoris tingled and her cunt contracted expectantly. 'Are you wearing knickers?' Jane asked, feeling under Jackie's skirt as she knelt on the floor.

'Why don't you look and see?' Jackie replied as Jane lifted her skirt and kissed her inner thighs.

'You are!' she shrieked. 'And they're all wet, you bad girl! Now I'll have to wash you with my tongue.'

Pulling Jackie's knickers down to her knees, Jane pressed her face against her warm mound and ran her tongue up and down the tightly closed slit. The lips swelled and the groove opened slightly as she continued to lick and nibble the soft flesh. 'Feet apart,' Jane ordered, the skirt falling down to cover her head as she located the source of the sticky flow and inserted her tongue.

'Ah, I think I'm in love with you,' Jackie murmured as Jane moved up to her hard clitoris and began to suck.

'I *know* I'm in love with *you*,' Jane breathed, her tongue now flicking the pulsating tip of the hard bud.

Jackie's legs crumpled and she held on to Jane's head as her orgasm exploded and her body shook and emitted a warm flow of juice. Jane lapped up the nectarous cocktail until Jackie's second orgasm neared, shaking her body and weakening her legs even more until she collapsed to the floor, Jane's mouth still locked between her swollen lips, her tongue still teasing her bursting bud. 'I've come,' Jackie breathed. 'God, I've come in your beautiful mouth! Keep sucking . . . Keep sucking until . . . Until . . . Ah, that's it, that's it.'

Gazing into her glazed eyes, Jane pressed her wet, sticky mouth to Jackie's and rubbed the juice over her lips. Their tongues shared the sticky delight, licking, slurping, until the taste of sex had faded, diluted with their saliva. Lying entwined on the carpet, the girls kissed and fondled until their breathing had calmed and they had recovered.

'Who is the doctor?' Jackie asked.

'I can't tell you.'

'Please, things are different now, so you may as well tell me. The next time he comes, I'll see him anyway, so why not tell me?'

'The next time he comes here, I'll introduce you. But I can't say who he is now!'

The door bell sent Jane leaping from the floor to the hall mirror. 'God, she's early!' she exclaimed, adjusting her skirt and scrunching her hair.

'I'll go down and wait,' Jackie replied, sliding the book-shelving to one side.

'The frame, wait by the frame,' came Jane's loudly whispered instruction as she opened the front door.

Jackie listened as Jane showed the girl in and led her down the stairs to the studio. As they entered the surgery, her heart leaped and she dropped to her knees and opened a cupboard. 'This is Miss Bradshaw,' Jane announced.

'Hello,' Jackie replied, her head in the cupboard. 'I'll

be right with you, my name's Mary.'

Jane realised that something was very wrong, and helped the girl to undress and climb onto the frame as Jackie slipped into David's work-room.

'What is it?' Jane asked once she'd secured the girl to the frame and joined Jackie.

'I know her! I bloody well know her!'

'Where from?'

'She's a customer at the bank, for God's sake!'

'It's okay, she's got the blindfold on now. I'll call you Mary and she'll never know.'

Jackie wandered through the door to find Miss Bradshaw naked on the horizontal frame, her legs splayed to reveal the abnormally large, swollen lips of her hairless pussy. She stared in disbelief at the ballooning lips and then turned to Jane, her eyes wide with amazement.

'Mary will be with you this morning,' Jane said.

'Oh, someone new. That's good, I like surprises,' Miss Bradshaw replied with an expectant grin across her full-lipped mouth.

'I think you'll be pleasantly surprised,' Jackie said as she ran her fingers lightly over the girl's large, hard nipples.

'You must do whatever you like to me,' she instructed. 'Do anything you want – my body is yours for an hour.'

Jane grinned and stifled a laugh as she closed the door and left Jackie alone with the young nymphomaniac. Running a finger down over her smooth, flat stomach, Jackie drew a line between the huge lips to her hole and pressed her finger between the folds until they yielded and she was sucked inside.

'You're very hot and wet,' Jackie remarked.

'Oh, yes, that's good. Tell me everything you do to me. A running commentary,' came the reply.

'I'm pushing two fingers into your cunt, now,' Jackie said. 'And now three. Oh, you're even wetter, and you're so very hot. Now I think four – yes, that's it, four fingers!'

The girl moaned with pleasure as Jackie thrust her fingers in and out, inducing a hot flow of sticky juice. 'And now I'm going to look at your clitoris,' she said, pulling the huge lips up and apart. Growing to an inch in length, the hard, pink clitoris looked like a worm emerging from the ground, its head rounded and swollen, its shaft thin and moist. 'And now I think I'll suck it gently,' she said, moving her head down towards the now throbbing protrusion.

The girl breathed deeply and her body tightened as Jackie took the full length of her clitoris into her hot mouth and sucked. Within seconds, the shaft pumped and the girl's body quivered as her orgasm spilled from her clitoris to bathe her body and mind with euphoria.

Jackie rolled the shrinking shaft between her lips as the girl quivered and breathed heavily and her muscles contracted violently, crushing Jackie's fingers within her cavern. Suddenly, Jackie caught sight of the rubber hose, hanging ominously from the ceiling. CDC, she thought, a grin curling her lips as she unhooked the hose and placed the end over the spent clitoris.

Running her eyes along the hose to the machine, she reached out and flicked the switch. It hummed softly as the vacuum built up, sucking and vibrating the girl's clitoris in the hose. 'God, that's nice,' the girl breathed as she threw her head back.

'I thought you'd like it. Now, just relax and let the machine suck the orgasms from you while I attend your cunt.'

Opening and closing her mouth, Miss Bradshaw tossed her head from side to side as the machine gently sucked and pulled on her clitoris. Turning the control, Jackie stuffed four fingers into the wet, gaping hole and watched with bated breath as her body stiffened and her vaginal lips swelled like balloons and turned deep crimson. She cried out in pained ecstasy.

'That's enough! Ah, please, no more!' she pleaded as she trembled violently.

'I thought you liked surprises,' Jackie said as she turned the control a little higher.

'No, I can't take . . . No, no! My God, I'm coming again!'

Taking a nipple in her mouth, Jackie sucked hard as she pushed her fingers deeper into the hot cavern, stretching the tightening flesh until the girl pleaded again for mercy. 'How many times can you come?' Jackie asked as she took the other hard nipple between her lips and sucked.

'No more! I can't . . . Ah, ah . . .'

'A little more suction, I think,' Jackie whispered as she reached for the control again.

'God, no! I'm coming again . . . Ah, ah!'

Dripping with perspiration, the girl's body convulsed again. Her nipples were ready to burst, her bulging pussy lips hard and full and red as her last orgasm ripped through her. Screaming with sexual gratification, she gyrated her hips and thrashed her head until the sexual intensity subsided, leaving her semiconscious, her breasts heaving with every gasp for air.

Turning the machine off, Jackie removed the hose and examined the girl's clitoris. Long, hard and red, it throbbed and twitched as the sensations faded until, finally, it retreated under its pink hood to rest. 'That was nice, yes?' Jackie asked, her own clitoris tingling slightly.

'I thought I was dying,' the girl replied shakily. 'I've never come so much in all my life!'

'Do you want to come again?'

'No, please, not again, I couldn't!'

'Oh, I think you can – just one more time,' Jackie coaxed as she slipped her hand under her skirt and between her hot lips to appease her own now very hard bud.

'I can't. Please, take the blindfold off – I've had enough!'

'But we've barely started the session . . .'

'No, that's enough!'

Turning the handle, Jackie tilted her body until her legs were high in the air and her head low. 'I'm going to rub myself over your mouth to heighten your pleasure,' she said, standing with the girl's head between her legs. Before she could reply, Jackie had lowered herself over her face and begun to rub her wet slit back and forth over her mouth. The girl licked and drank from Jackie's hole until her juice flowed and her clitoris was near to bursting point. 'Now!' Jackie cried, pressing her clitoris into the girl's mouth as it exploded. 'Suck it, suck it! Ah, yes, I'm coming! Ah, that's nice, don't stop, don't stop! Suck me, suck my clit!'

Jane appeared as Jackie staggered back and almost collapsed on the floor. Quickly ushering her from the room before she could reach for the hose and torture the girl further, she closed the door and brought Miss Bradshaw back to the horizontal position and freed her.

After booking another appointment and showing the girl out, Jane put her head round the door to find Jackie resting on the four-poster bed. 'You enjoyed yourself, then?' she asked. Jackie smiled and nodded.

'And so did she,' she said. 'I made her come and come with the CDC hose!'

'Well, you must have done a good job because she's booked to come again tomorrow morning.'

'Then come again, she will!'

'I'm popping out, see you later,' Jane said and ran upstairs before Jackie could question her.

The front door slammed as Jackie reached the lounge. 'Damn, she's gone to see David!' she cursed, wishing she'd not told him that she wanted to buy the house. She knew that David would turn Jane against her, tell her about the money and the secret room. And probably fill her head with lies so that when she returned she'd hate her. But all she could do was pace the floor and wait for the inevitable. Her plan would backfire, she was sure – and she'd lose Jane for good.

Chapter Eleven

As Jackie waited for Jane to return, she sat in front of the dressing table mirror and applied her makeup. David would never agree to selling the house, she knew, and feeling sure that he would destroy her relationship with Jane, she decided to prepare for the worst and, if necessary, leave with the money.

Brushing her hair, she smiled. Her complexion was fresh, vibrant, younger somehow – her eyes, wide and full of life. 'A million dollars!' she laughed, admiring herself in the mirror as she turned her head and tossed her hair. 'No matter what David says to Jane, no matter what happens, I'm rich!'

After an hour, bored and frustrated, she decided to visit the pub and talk business with Tim and Rosita, and discover, at long last, their connection with David. Tim would come clean now that David was behind bars, she was sure. He has nothing to lose, she mused as she wandered down the steps and across the road.

'Jackie!' Tim cried as she walked to the bar. 'My God, how you've changed!'

'That I have,' she replied coolly, her short skirt showing her stocking tops as she sat on a bar stool. 'I'll have a gin and tonic to start with, and then you will answer some questions for me, Tim.'

Tim frowned as he poured her drink. 'Questions?' he

said. 'What have I done? You make it sound as if I'm in trouble.'

'*You* tell *me* what it is that you've done – Doctor?'

'Doctor? Sorry, I'm not with you, love.'

'You went to David's house the other day.'

'Oh, yes. Poor David, I suppose you've heard.'

'Yes, I have. Now, tell me all you know about him.'

'Well, he's an artist, he lives over the road – and that's about it, I'm afraid. He doesn't come in here very often. What's this all about, anyway?'

'Why did you go to his house – Doctor?'

'To buy a painting. What is all this 'doctor' business?'

'You don't know?'

'No, I've no idea. Anyway, some time ago I asked David to do a painting from a photograph, and I went to see how he was getting on with it. It's as simple and as innocent as that!'

'You're not a doctor, then?'

'What are you on about? Of course I'm not a doctor!'

Wandering through the other bar, Tim left Jackie confused. She felt that she ought to believe him, although she wasn't sure why. She supposed he looked innocent, but there again, she knew he would. David would only employ professional people, and Tim would have been paid as a visiting doctor, which would explain his apparent wealth. But, she concluded, his excuse for visiting David was good enough. And Rosita? She wasn't in the pub. But, Jackie decided, she was probably innocent, too. Although, thinking of the girl's dark skin and huge breasts, she still thought of strapping her to the frame and tasting her body – punishing her, lovingly, with the cane. One day, she promised herself – one day.

Jackie had missed Tim, the pub, and displaying her panties and nipples to strangers. And the excitement was still there, only more so now that her transformation was almost complete. She would visit the pub that evening, she decided, with Jane, perhaps, and enjoy a few hours of exhibiting her curvaceous body. Without saying goodbye to Tim, she finished her drink and made for the house, wondering if Jane had returned and, if she had, what mood she was in.

Jane was sitting in the lounge when Jackie arrived. She appeared forlorn, sad, and barely managed a smile. 'Seen David?' Jackie asked.

'Yes, I've seen David. His trial is tomorrow.'

'That was quick!'

'Well, it's not really a trial, is it? They've got it all sewn up! It's not a question of whether he did it or not, they're just going through the motions, it's a farce.'

'What did he have to say?'

'He asked after you – and my plans.'

'Did you mention the house?'

'Yes, he's going to get the necessary papers drawn up and sign it over to you – on receipt of the cash, of course.'

Jackie's stomach somersaulted at the prospect of owning the house. She could barely believe it. 'How much? And what about the furniture?' she asked as she poured herself a drink.

'Five hundred thousand – half of which I am to have. There are one or two antiques that he'd like to keep, but apart from that, it's all yours. I don't know what's got into him. Depression, I suppose. He loved this house – we both did.'

'What will you do?'

'I don't know, go abroad, perhaps?'

'We'll go to the pub tonight and celebrate!' Jackie said triumphantly.

Ray Gordon

'Celebrate what? Me losing my home? David's imprisonment? No, I don't think so – you go, you're the one with something to celebrate, not me.'

Biting her lips, Jackie sighed. She couldn't live without Jane, she knew. To lose her would be devastating – she might as well lose everything if her plan meant losing Jane. 'Stay here, with me,' she said. 'We can work together, be together, and when David is released . . .'

'Then what? Where will he go?'

'I don't know, we'll see. Look, live here with me and . . .'

'In *your* house?'

'Yes, but what does it matter who owns it? We'll be together, don't you want that?'

'You know I do!'

'That's settled, then! Now, will you come to the pub tonight?'

'I suppose so. Oh, I nearly forgot, David gave me this letter for you.'

Leaving Jane on the sofa, Jackie wandered down to the studio and opened the letter.

Dear Jackie,
I'm sorry that things have turned out the way they have but there is nothing I can do about it now. Mind you, you have done very well for yourself. Nicely set-up, aren't you? I've been thinking about what you said. You have changed, yes, and I brought about the change. You will thank me for it, one day, I am sure. Once you become used to being a real woman, you'll thank me. My trial is tomorrow and all I can do is hope for the best. The day will arrive, of course, when I am able to come home. Home? What am I saying? I don't have a home! Anyway, look after Jane for me. You won't believe this,

but I miss you very much. Don't come to the trial and keep Jane away, too. I couldn't bear to see my girls standing together, watching me.

Love, David

A tear fell from Jackie's eye as she folded the letter and slipped it inside the envelope. She began to realise exactly what it was that she was doing. She held the key to David's freedom, but she couldn't use it. The stranger within only seemed to laugh. A voice, chuckling in her head, goaded her to forget David and think only of her success, her wealth – her body. 'I own this house!' she laughed, bounding into the surgery. Running her fingertips over the frame, she smiled. 'You are going to earn me a fortune,' she whispered. 'And bring me a lot of fun!'

Jane called from the lounge. Jackie ran up the stairs, hoping to discuss the future, but Jane's only news was that a new client had booked for that evening. 'We're going out!' Jackie said. 'We can't have a client tonight!'

'He's booked for six, it will only take an hour.'

'He?'

'Yes, apparently, he's a friend of that young man that you dealt with. What was his name?'

'Paul.'

'Yes, that's the one. He said that he has heard all about you and . . .'

'Has he got any money?'

'Presumably.'

'But we don't know him! We can't have strangers coming here!'

'He's a friend of . . .'

'How do we know that? He could be an undercover cop.'

'Don't be ridiculous!'

'This isn't at all professional. What would David have done?'

'I don't know.'

'I'll deal with it – leave him to me.'

'Oh, of course, it's all *yours* now, isn't it?' Jane returned sarcastically.

'Don't be silly!'

'Well, it is, isn't it? You're in charge now.'

'Yes, I am running the business, but nothing else has changed. Not between us, anyway.'

Realising that she would have a problem with Jane if she didn't play her cards right, Jackie smiled and kissed her. 'It's our business,' she consoled. 'Don't fill your head with these silly notions. I love you, I want you.' Jane smiled and returned the kiss, stroking Jackie's thighs and running her fingers up to her panties.

'Later,' Jackie breathed, pulling away. 'I . . . We've got to prepare for this so-called client.'

The time had passed so quickly that Jackie had barely given any thought as to what to do with the client when the door bell rang. Taking him straight to the den would not, she decided, be a good idea. A drink in the lounge, perhaps? That way, she would be able to gauge his motives.

'Come in,' she said with a welcoming smile, opening the front door to a young, dark-haired man in his early twenties. From a Sunday tabloid, she mused. Eyeing his tight blue jeans, she showed him into the lounge and asked him to take a seat. 'Your first time, is it?' she enquired. He smiled uneasily and nodded. 'Don't worry,' she said confidently. 'There's a first time for everyone. What do you do for a living?'

'I work in an office,' he replied, relaxing a little as she poured him a drink.

'A newspaper office?' she asked, passing him the glass.

'No, no. I'm an estate agent.'

'Then, how can you afford to come here? If you don't mind me asking, that is.'

'I buy and sell houses – executor sales, that sort of thing. It's very lucrative.'

'It must be,' Jackie smiled. 'Shall we go through to my den?'

Following her down the stairs, the young man mentioned that the house must be worth around half a million. Jackie smiled and agreed that it was, indeed, worth at least that amount, if not more. 'Now, as it's your first time, I think we'll start you off in here,' she said, leading him to the four-poster bed, knowing full well that Jane would be in the work-room in readiness to record the event. 'I'll be with you in a moment, just take your clothes off and lie on the bed,' she instructed as she left the room.

'I thought we'd agreed to take him to the frame?' Jane said agitatedly as Jackie wandered through the surgery.

'I know, but it's his first time and . . . Anyway, you can still record it, can't you?'

'Yes, I suppose so.'

'Good. He should be about ready – see you later.'

Returning to the four-poster bed, Jackie smiled to see the young man's slim, naked body in readiness for her attentive hands. 'I'll just strap you down,' she said, quickly binding his ankles.

'No, no, that won't be necessary,' he returned nervously, but she had already moved up and strapped his wrists. Pulling on the rope, she watched as his limbs stretched out and his long, thin penis grew in expectation.

'There, that's better, isn't it?' she smiled, taking his penis in her hand and running her finger over the hard knob. 'Tell me, how long have you known David?'

'Only about . . . David? Who . . .'

'The man who sent you here, silly, that's who!'

'I don't know what you mean. Now, let me go, I've changed my mind.'

'But *I* haven't. Now, what am I going to do with you? We have a nice selection of canes in the other room!'

'All right, I do know David. He sent me here to . . . I needed the money . . .'

'We all need money. Are you really an estate agent?'

'No, no. Look, all he told me to do was break in and get some letters. Let me go and I'll just disappear, I don't want to get involved in all this!'

'But you are involved! So, why didn't you just do as he asked?'

'I thought that I'd . . .'

'Enjoy yourself first, is that it?'

'Yes, yes. But . . .'

'Oh, you *are* going to enjoy yourself – for a while, anyway!'

Jackie left the young man pleading for his freedom as she fetched Jane. 'We have a problem,' she said, leading her towards the bed. 'This young man has come here to expose us. He's from a newspaper.'

'Oh, my God!' Jane cried.

'It's all right, he's not going anywhere. Not until . . . Well, don't worry about that now.'

'I'm not from a newspaper! I'm . . .'

'Jane, get a gag or something from the surgery, we don't want him talking too much, do we?'

Returning with a large piece of sticky tape, Jane fixed it over his mouth while Jackie held his head steady. 'There, now we have some peace and quiet,' Jackie laughed. 'What shall we do with him?'

'We can't keep him here!' Jane cried.

'Of course we can't! We'll have some fun with him, and then . . . Well, we'll see. Now, let's go upstairs for a drink, shall we?'

In the lounge, Jane broke down and cried. 'You see!' Jackie stormed. 'This is what happens when you take calls from strangers. Without David, you don't know what you're doing, you can't cope. I'm dealing with the business now, so let me do things *my* way – accept that I'm in charge, as you put it, and we'll be all right!'

'But what about that man?'

'Don't worry, I'll work something out.'

'Don't kill him!'

'Of course I won't kill him!'

'Then what?'

'I'm not sure yet. Just stay calm, and it will be all right. Trust me! Now, we're going out, aren't we? So let's get ready.'

'But you can't leave him . . .'

'He'll be all right! He isn't going anywhere in a hurry – he'll still be here when we get back! Now, you go and get ready while I take the plaster off his mouth – we don't want him suffocating, do we? Not yet, anyway!'

Creeping into the studio, Jackie spied through the crack in the door at the young man. He appeared to be asleep as she wandered in, but he opened his eyes and stared hard at her. Pulling off the sticky tape, she smiled. 'We're going out for a drink. Don't go away, will you?'

'When I do get out of here, I'll . . .'

'Now, now, no silly threats. Is there anyone you want us to contact to say that you're safe? Not that you are safe, of course. Your wife, perhaps? Is she expecting you?'

'She . . . I'm not married!'

Searching through his coat pockets, Jackie pulled out his wallet and found his name and address. 'Ah, Mick

Johnstone. Right, Mick, you see that little round object above the bed? That's a video camera. The tape was running earlier when I played with your stiff penis. It might be a good idea if I drop the tape round to your wife. She'll be able to see for herself that you're safe, won't she?'

'What do you want from me?'

'Ah, that comes later, when we get back from the pub. Now, you just have a nice rest and wait for us.'

Dressed in a red pigskin miniskirt and tight top, Jane met Jackie in the hall and twirled her young body round. 'What do you think?' she asked, excitedly.

'I think you're much happier now, and you look very sexy!' Jackie replied. 'Are you wearing panties?'

'Yes – and hold-up stockings,' Jane laughed, lifting her skirt to reveal the alluring red silk covering her bulge.

'Take your panties off, you won't be needing them,' Jackie grinned.

'What do you mean?'

'Just take them off, you'll find out,' she laughed, lifting her own miniskirt to expose her smooth slit. 'Shall we go?'

There were only a few people in the pub when the girls arrived. Three men in their early thirties sitting at a table caught Jackie's eye. 'They'll be on their way home from the office,' she whispered. 'Let's sit on a stool and have some fun.'

'What are we going to do?' Jane asked.

'I love your naivety! Just watch me,' Jackie replied, grinning wickedly as she sat on a bar stool.

The men gazed at Jackie's thighs as she parted them slightly to reveal her naked slit. 'What would you like to drink?' Rosita asked grumpily.

'Allow me,' one of the men said, leaping to his feet. Wearing a dark, well cut suit, he walked towards the girls and smiled to show a perfect row of white teeth.

'Gin and tonic for me, please,' Jackie said. 'And you, Jane?'

'The same, please,' she replied, slipping onto a stool next to Jackie.

'My name's Bill. Why don't you come and join us?' he asked, his eyes transfixed between Jane's legs as she parted them.

'Our boyfriends will be here soon, but thanks, anyway,' Jackie returned.

With a pained look, he paid for the drinks and, much to the delight of his friends, returned dejectedly to the table and took his seat. 'Well, that's one free drink,' Jackie whispered, opening her legs a little further and smiling at the man as if by way of payment.

'You've done this before, haven't you?' Jane laughed.

'Oh, yes! Haven't you?'

'No, David rarely let me go out. I've never been here before.'

'You live opposite and you've never been here?'

'He liked me to stay in most of the time. We went out for the odd meal together, but that's about all.'

Jackie was in two minds as whether to question Jane about her parents or not. David obviously didn't want his daughter out and about dressed in miniskirts and skimpy tops, but what were his long term plans for her? she wondered. Why the fantastic lie? Not wishing to spoil the evening by upsetting Jane, she decided against asking too many questions, but did ask her how long she'd lived at the house.

'We moved down here when I was twelve,' Jane said sadly. 'Our parents died in a car crash when I was three, so I don't remember them. David has looked after me ever since.'

'There's quite an age gap between you and David, isn't there?'

'Yes, he said that I turned up out of the blue – Mum and Dad hadn't planned me. Anyway, there's a man coming in, are you going to surprise him or shall I?'

The grey-haired man, in his sixties, approached the bar with his eyes glued to Jane's slim legs. Parting her thighs as she twisted round on her stool, she smiled and allowed him a glimpse of her young pussy lips. 'May I buy you two ladies a drink?' he offered, his eyes fixed on her opening groove.

'We'll both have a gin and tonic, please,' Jane replied as she closed her legs.

'And I'll have a pint of bitter, please,' he said, turning to Rosita who had been watching the proceedings. 'Now, ladies, are you waiting for someone? Or are you both spending the evening on your own?' he asked as he paid Rosita.

'We're waiting for our boyfriends,' Jackie replied.

'Then they are two very lucky young men, I hope they appreciate you.'

'Oh, they do,' Jane said. 'They look after us very well. And your wife, does she appreciate you?'

'Yes, she does. But she's not well, I'm afraid, so we don't have . . . She's in hospital at the moment and . . . Well, it's a long story and I don't intend to bore two lovely young ladies such as yourselves with it.'

Picking up his drink, he found himself a small table in a corner and sat down. 'Poor man,' Jackie observed. 'He needs some company.'

'And the rest. I'll bet he hasn't had a woman in years.'

'Are you thinking what I'm thinking?'

'Yes, I suppose I am, but we're not prostitutes. Besides, you said that we should be professional! And we couldn't take him back to the house, anyway.'

'You're right, we're not prostitutes – we're humanitarians. I'll get his address – we can visit him.'

Jane watched the man's face light up as Jackie leaned over his table and took his address. The three businessmen gazed at Jackie's rounded buttocks as she leaned further over the table to whisper in the man's ear.

'I expect they're wondering how he's pulled and they didn't,' Rosita remarked sarcastically.

'He didn't pull, as you put it! He's a friend of ours!' Jane snapped.

'He may be a friend now, but it's the way you make friends and get free drinks that worries me!'

'Then take your knickers off and show those three men your cunt and, if you're lucky, they may allow you to buy them a drink!'

'What's going on?' Jackie asked as she approached the bar.

'She's accusing us of being prostitutes,' Jane said.

'I didn't say that,' Rosita returned.

'Then what did you say?' Jackie asked.

'Just that . . . Oh, what does it matter, anyway? I suppose I'm just fed-up with working here every night for a pittance when people like you . . .'

'Then why not change your job?' Jackie asked, gazing at the girl's nipples pressing hard against the tight material of her blouse.

'And do what you do?'

'Why not?'

'I wouldn't know . . .'

'You don't know exactly what it is that we do yet. What time do you finish here tonight?'

'About twelve.'

'Then come over to our house afterwards. Opposite the pub, number twelve.'

'I don't know . . .'

'Go on – change your life!'

'I might, I'll think about it.'

As Rosita wandered into the small bar, Jane turned to Jackie and asked if she thought that leaving a man tied to the bed and pulling an old man and the barmaid in the pub could be considered professional behaviour.

'I have great plans,' Jackie returned. 'Plans that, as yet, aren't quite formulated, but they are coming together nicely.'

'What sort of plan is it that involves a prisoner, an old man and a barmaid?'

'We will need help to run the business. Two of us can't cope.'

'But the clients are dropping away like flies!'

'No, no, they'll be back, you'll see.'

'You're the boss, I suppose. So, are you going to pull the girl who's just walked in? Or do you think we've enough on our hands for now?'

Jackie turned to look at the girl. In her teens with long blonde hair and the body of a model, she strutted to the bar as if she was on the catwalk. 'No, she's too stuck-up for my liking,' she whispered. 'Anyway, I think we ought to be getting back, the time's getting on and we've a lot to do before Rosita arrives.'

'Yes, we've got to deal with the little problem on the bed, for a start! Anyway, how do you know the barmaid's name?' Jane asked, allowing the businessmen one last look at her slit before she slipped off her stool.

'I've met her in here before,' Jackie replied. The men grinned as they watched the girls leave the bar and one asked if they'd be there again. 'You never know your luck!' Jackie called as she opened the door and walked out into the cold night air.

Her thoughts turned to Mucky Meg as she crossed the road. She remembered her sordid little stories every morning and smiled, knowing that Meg's exploits were nothing but innocent fun compared to hers.

In the warmth of the lounge, Jackie flicked through the phone book and found Mick Johnstone's number. 'I'm just going to chat with our young man's wife,' she told Jane, dialling the number.

'What for?' Jane asked with some surprise.

'Hello, is that Mrs Johnstone?'

'Yes, it is.'

'I'm just calling to say that your husband will be a little late – he's been tied up, I'm afraid.'

'Who is this?'

'A friend, he asked me to call . . .'

'But he's supposed to be at his mother's.'

'Yes, I know. He'll explain when he gets home – 'bye.'

'Right, Jane, let's go and see our prisoner!' Jackie said excitedly as she bounded down the stairs. Jane followed, not quite knowing what to expect next from Jackie who seemed to be several jumps ahead of her.

'Mick, how are you?' Jackie asked as she approached the bed.

'Not very happy!' he stormed.

'Then let's see if we can cheer you up a little,' she replied, running her fingertips over his large balls. 'Jane, run the video, will you? We'll need two tapes, of course, one for us and one for Mick's wife. I want her to enjoy this as much as he does. She can watch it when there's nothing much on T.V.'

Confused, Jane said nothing as she left the room and wandered to the video machines. Jackie waited a couple of minutes before taking Mick's limp penis in her hand and massaging it gently. 'It won't work,' he said coldly. 'She will see quite clearly that I'm not enjoying it!'

'There's no sound track, so feel free to chat. And if you think that you have greater control over your penis than I have, then you're wrong,' she returned, pulling the loose skin back to expose the purple knob. 'And now I'm going to suck some life into the poor little thing,' she teased as she took it into her mouth.

He breathed deeply at first, but managed not to allow himself any pleasure. Jackie ran her tongue round the purple knob but after some minutes he was still sadly limp and she called for Jane's assistance. Sitting astride his face and pulling her young groove open, Jane masturbated as Jackie resumed her sucking. Quickly, his penis grew to a good eight inches and began to throb slightly against her hot tongue. Moving her head to one side, Jackie sucked and licked on the bulging knob in full view of the camera until he began to moan and his body became rigid. 'Now you're going to come,' she whispered, licking his shaft from the bottom to the top where it twitched with every stroke.

Jane ground her clitoris into his mouth and gasped with delight as her juices flowed and she neared her orgasm. Looking up to the camera, she licked her lips before moving away to reveal the obvious pleasure on his wet face. 'Ah, my cunt!' she cried, stroking her clitoris as her climax erupted. 'Ah, suck my cunt!' Thrusting her hips forward again, she pressed herself over his mouth as her cream gushed from her body and ran down his throat. 'You certainly know how to use your tongue on a girl, don't you!' she gasped.

'God, yes!' he mumbled through her wet folds, licking her opening dry.

Now his knob bulged and twitched in Jackie's hot mouth and she pulled away just in time for the camera to catch the white liquid as it pumped and spurted through the air to land in a pool on his stomach. He gasped and writhed against the leather bonds as she squeezed the last drop from the ballooning head and lightly licked it clean.

'That was nice, wasn't it?' she asked, stroking his balls as he fell limp.

'Nice, it was heaven!' he breathed.

'I've wet his face!' Jane laughed. 'Did you like me coming in your mouth? Did I make enough juice for you?'

'Yes, yes, more than enough! You two know how to please a man, don't you?'

'We do, indeed!' Jackie agreed. 'And now that I'm really wet, it's my turn to come in your mouth.'

Taking Jane's place, she opened her wet slit and rubbed her hard clitoris against his lips, pouring out her sticky juices as she rocked to and fro. Jane had moved down the bed and taken his growing penis in her mouth, sucking fervently on the pulsating head to bring up her share of his sperm.

He came quickly, much to Jane's surprise, filling her cheeks with his bitter-sweet fruits as Jackie reached her orgasm and filled his mouth with her cream. Gasping and writhing, all three eventually fell limp, but Jane had a surprise for Jackie. Opening her mouth, she kissed her, transferring the hot sperm to share her spoils with her lover. They licked each other's tongues, sucked on each other's lips, and kissed passionately, lubricated all the time with the white, creamy sperm. Gulping down the cocktail of sperm and saliva, they turned to Mick who had been watching the lesbian scene intently. His penis was hard again, twitching and awaiting more attention. The girls opened their mouths and kissed each other again, but this time with the bulging head of his penis between their full lips. Their darting tongues, soft lips and hot saliva quickly brought up his third offering of sperm which pumped from the head and oozed between their lips to dribble down their chins as they sucked and lapped up the fruits. Gasping and pleading for the girls to stop, he eventually relaxed, his knob crimson, his shaft flaccid.

'I enjoyed that,' Jackie whispered as she kissed Jane.

'God, so did I!' Mick panted. 'We must do this again, some time.'

'We will,' Jackie said. 'But now I think you'd better go home to your loving wife. I rang her and told her that you'd be a little late, but I expect she's still worried about you.'

'You rang her!'

'Yes, I said that you were tied up and that you'd explain when you got home.'

'Oh, God! What a mess!'

'It's all right, I'm sure you'll come up with some lie or other. Now, before we release you, I'll just go and hide our copy of the video tape in case you get any funny ideas. Oh, by the way, talking of lies, I'm afraid I told one. There is a sound track, so it's pretty obvious that you enjoyed our game as much as we did. Your wife's going to love the tape! What was it you said? You two know how to please a man – yes, that was it.'

Jane ran after Jackie and asked that she be allowed to have ten minutes alone with Mick before they let him go. Jackie frowned and a pang of jealousy churned her stomach, but Jane reassured her that it was in their best interests. Jackie agreed and took the tapes upstairs to hide them.

Watching the lounge clock, she paced the floor, wondering what on Earth Jane was up to. When the time was up, she returned to the four-poster bed and burst out laughing. 'It's not bloody funny!' Mick yelled as Jane released him.

'I think it rather suits you!' Jackie giggled, gazing at his hairless stomach and balls. 'You look like a little boy! You'll have a job explaining that one to your wife! Well done, Jane!'

Cursing the girls and begging that they never show his wife the tape, he quickly dressed. 'Now, should you do anything to upset us, anything at all, your wife will be given a copy of the tape,' Jackie warned. 'Do you understand?'

'All too well!' he replied as he left the room and climbed the stairs, followed by the girls. 'All too bloody well!'

'All in all, it's been a good day,' Jackie commented as she closed the front door.

'It's not over yet,' Jane said. 'Or had you forgotten the barmaid?'

'Oh no! I was having so much fun that I . . . I'm going to have a shower – we've got a couple of hours yet.'

'I'll make something to eat while you're upstairs. I hope you know what you're doing, what with poor Mick, that old man, and now the bloody barmaid!'

'I'm not sure if I know what I'm doing – but something inside me does, I'm sure of that,' Jackie said, leaving Jane more confused than ever as she wandered upstairs.

Chapter Twelve

After the girls had showered and eaten, they settled in the lounge to wait for Rosita. 'I've been thinking,' Jackie began as she poured the drinks. 'It seems to me that, as the business caters mainly for women, shouldn't we employ a male to entertain them? I mean, they're not all lesbians, surely?'

'With David gone, yes, that's a good idea. But there are no clients left, to speak of.'

'There will be – plenty of them, I can promise you that!'

'You seem to have everything planned. I just hope it doesn't all go wrong. What will you do, for example, if David happens to be released?'

Jackie had given David a great deal of thought since Mick Johnstone's arrival on the scene. She knew that, until the house was legally hers, he presented a problem. Jane seemed to have accepted the new set-up but, Jackie thought, that was just because she had little or no choice. But Jane's feelings for her had changed from what had simply been a lesbian crush to something far deeper. Love, although Jane was probably far too young to understand the difference between love and infatuation, had grown between them, binding them, uniting them in a way that even Jackie couldn't comprehend.

'If David happens to get off – and don't get me wrong, I hope he does,' Jackie began, praying that she'd have time to secure the house before anything of the sort happened. 'Then, obviously, I . . . we will have to rethink the situation. I mean, he will have to live here, I suppose, with us.'

'He wouldn't accept you as the boss, I know him too well.'

'Then he'll just have to buy his own house, he can afford it easily, can't he?'

'And me?'

'I hope that you'll choose me – if you ever have to choose, that is.'

The door bell rang, halting what was fast becoming a difficult situation for Jackie. She wanted to keep Jane happy but, on the other hand, she had to be realistic. She was now in business, and the business had to come first – no matter what.

'It's your friend,' Jane said, showing Rosita into the lounge.

'Rosita, I'm glad you decided to come – drink?' Jackie said warmly. 'This, by the way, is Jane, my . . . my friend.'

'I haven't decided to change my job,' Rosita said as she flashed a smile at Jane and sat down. 'I've only come to see what it is, exactly, that you are offering me.'

'Before I tell you that, I want to know a little more about you, Rosita,' Jackie said. 'Let's have a brief run down of your life first, shall we?'

Rosita took the glass from Jane and explained that she'd moved from her native Greece to England five years previously. Her boyfriend had left her and she'd decided that England would have more to offer in the way of work and men. She was wrong, she said, on both counts, and had ended up in a lonely bedsit with bar work as about the only job on offer.

She had little in the way of money and was about to be forced to sell the jewellery that her father had left her, to pay her rent arrears. Jackie smiled, knowing, at long last, the story behind Rosita's gold.

'And that's about it,' Rosita said sadly. 'The sum total of my life of twenty-two years is a bedsit and a bar job. How can you change it for me? Without sending me to work on the streets, of course.'

Jackie painstakingly explained the business, being careful not to say exactly what the clients received for their money. She mentioned massage, and added the business centred on sensual massage for wealthy clients, and that Rosita would be required to assist. Noticing the girl's nipples, hard beneath her tight blouse, as she had done several times before, Jackie began to lose control to the stranger within and raced ahead, suggesting that Rosita take a look at the surgery.

'It's a bit soon for that, isn't it?' Jane said wearily. 'I mean, I thought it was just to be the two of us, not . . .'

'I've already explained that we will need extra help, and no, I don't think it's too soon,' Jackie returned. 'Tell me, Rosita, do you masturbate?'

The girl's stunned face turned red and she began to stutter.

'Well, er, yes, I . . . I suppose so – why?'

'Have you ever had any lesbian experiences?'

'Well, no. No, of course not!'

'Are you sure?'

'When I was younger, there was a girl at my school. She was my best friend and we . . . We used to visit each other after school and . . .'

'All right, you don't have to go into the details. Now, I am going to ask you to do something for us. This is necessary, I'm afraid, but it will be well worth it for you, financially, if you pass my little test.'

Jane gazed at Jackie and then at Rosita who was rolling her glass between her palms and looking decidedly anxious. 'Do you want to take the test or not?' Jackie asked a little impatiently as her clitoris stirred and her juices trickled over her warm, swelling quim lips.

'Yes, I suppose so,' Rosita replied, having some idea, Jackie surmised, of what the test would involve.

'Good! Now, remember that there is a very secure job at the end of this with more money than you've ever seen in your life – if you decide to take it, of course. So, if you're ready, take all your clothes off.'

Placing her glass on the coffee table, Rosita stood up and unbuttoned her blouse with her shaking fingers. The girls watched with open mouths as she tossed her long, dark hair back and slipped her blouse off her shoulders to reveal her bra, straining to contain her ample breasts. Unzipping her skirt, she let it fall to the floor and kicked it aside, almost, Jackie mused, as if she was deriving some sexual pleasure from her disrobing. Her panties, framed by a black, silk suspender belt, bulged with secret delights and Jackie could barely restrain herself as she watched the girl move her hands behind her back to unclip her bra.

'How am I doing?' Rosita asked as she lifted her bra away to expose her full, rounded breasts topped with large, almost black areolae, and the longest cigar-shaped nipples the girls had ever seen.

'Very well,' Jackie breathed and added softly, 'keep going.'

Removing her suspender belt, Rosita kicked off her shoes and rolled her stockings down her slim legs before standing upright to face her audience. Her smooth, unblemished skin, dark and alluring, shone in the light which captured her fine curves, accentuating her femininity. Her tiny waist was out of all proportion to her breasts and hips, and Jackie licked her lips as she waited for Rosita's final move. Slipping her panties down, she kicked them aside and stood, legs slightly apart, to display her full, naked glory. Her jet-black bush was thick on her mound, but cropped short below, doing very little to cover her intimacy from the girls' gaze. Her ballooning pussy lips, doing nothing to conceal her huge, pink inner labia that protruded like the petals of a flower, swelled to twice their original size as a globule of milk oozed from the complex tangle of flesh and dripped to the floor.

'So far so good,' Jackie said appreciatively, glancing at Jane who was obviously sulking.

'What now?' Rosita asked hesitantly.

'What indeed? You tell me,' Jackie coaxed.

'I don't know what you want me to do,' Rosita replied shakily.

'Oh, surely you can think of something? I know, lie on the floor and we'll show you – if you want to continue with the test, of course.'

Lying full length on the hearth rug, Rosita relaxed and closed her eyes. Jackie sat by her side and indicated to Jane to sit the other side of the girl's young, fresh body. Jane raised her eyes to the ceiling, joined Jackie and followed suit by running her fingertips over Rosita's now quivering skin. Breathing deeply, she arched her back and parted her legs slightly as if to offer herself completely to the girls.

'You can tell me about your school friend now, if you want to,' Jackie whispered as she circled the girl's hardening nipples with her fingertips.

'My friend and I used to visit each other after school,' Rosita breathed. 'Her name was Nicky and we used to play with each other – touch each other.'

milk that it ran down her cheeks, her neck and over her dark hair.

Before Rosita had caught her breath, Jane had taken Jackie's place and begun to rub her clitoris over her hot, wet mouth. Pushing her tongue out Rosita licked Jane's dripping valley and drank from her hole until Jane emptied her womb into her mouth in way of a reward. Shaking violently, Jane threw her head back and suddenly froze as her clitoris pulsated again and her cunt squeezed out its last drop of nectar. Collapsing to the floor, Jane writhed and twitched until her clitoris retreated under its pink hood, leaving her calm and satisfied.

'Have I passed the test?' Rosita gasped as she ran her fingers between her bulging lips to explore her new-found pleasure centre.

'You have passed with flying colours!' Jackie cried. 'What do you think, Jane?'

'Definitely. Ten out of ten,' she murmured, generous in the wake of her climax.

As Rosita dressed, Jackie poured another three drinks and beckoned Jane to join her on the sofa. Jane's face lit up as she sat next to Jackie and placed her hand on her thigh, as if to lay claim to her should Rosita have any ideas. Tossing her hair over her shoulder, Rosita picked up her glass and sat in the armchair. 'I must be going or I'll never get up in the morning,' she said, quickly finishing her drink. 'It's been quite an experience, but I really must be going.'

'We'll see you again, of course?' Jackie asked.

'Oh yes, you can be sure of that!'

'Leave your job and come here tomorrow evening so we can discuss everything,' Jackie suggested.

'I still don't know what the work entails. Well, I've a pretty good idea, I suppose, but . . .'

'A pretty good idea is enough for now. We'll go into the details tomorrow,' Jackie said, following Rosita to the front door.

The time approaching two a.m., the girls made their way up to bed. Although she hadn't a clue what Jackie was up to, Jane had to admit that things had certainly brightened up since she'd been in charge – but she didn't like the idea of sharing her with Rosita.

David's trial the following morning played on Jane's mind but, with Jackie's carefully chosen words of encouragement, she was becoming used to the idea that he might not be around for some time. The trial also played on Jackie's mind, more so, in fact, than on Jane's, for everything depended on David being locked up, at least until the house had been signed over.

'You won't go off with her, will you?' Jane asked as they huddled their warm, naked bodies together in the bed.

'Who? Rosita?'

'Yes, you seem to like her quite a lot, and I . . .'

'Don't be so silly! We're together, you and me, and that's the way it's going to stay! Now, let's sleep, we've a busy time ahead of us.'

Jackie woke at ten the following morning to find Jane had gone. Making her way downstairs in her dressing gown, she guessed that Jane had gone to court to watch David's trial. Tuning in to the local radio station, she made some coffee and sat at the table, picturing David standing alone in the dock.

Her heart leaped when the front door bell rang. Imagining it was the police, she gingerly inched the door open. 'Aren't you going to let me in?' Mick asked. 'It's freezing out here!'

'What the hell are you doing here?' she demanded, opening the door further.

'I came to talk to you – any chance of a coffee?'

Following Jackie through to the kitchen, he slipped his coat off and threw it over the back of a chair before sitting at the table. Jackie passed him a cup of coffee and leaned against the wall, gazing at him. 'If it's the tapes you're after, they're no longer here,' she said cautiously.

'I'd like the tapes, yes, but that's not why I'm here. You see, David is a powerful man, in my book, anyway, and I'm worried. I don't know what to say to him. I'm supposed to take him the letters and, well, I haven't got them, have I?'

'Tell him that you couldn't find them. They're not in the house, anyway. And besides, no-one will be able to talk to David for a while – he's in court.'

Mick gazed at Jackie's partially open dressing gown and smiled. 'You look nice without make-up,' he said.

'I look better with it! Now, I have things to do so . . .'

'I enjoyed last night. You see, my wife, Helen, is a bit of a prude and . . . Well, this may sound silly, but I wondered if you had any tips. You know, how to turn her on.'

'How to bring out the woman in her, you mean?'

'Yes, that's exactly what I mean. She's got a great body, but she doesn't seem to want to use it.'

'Is she busy this evening?'

'No, we've nothing planned . . . What will happen to her?'

'I'll bring out the woman in her, if that's really what you want.'

'Oh, it is!'

'All right, leave it to me. I'll ring her and get her to come here tonight. Ring me tomorrow and we'll talk again. Now, I've things to do so off you go. Oh, by the way, what excuse did you come up with when you got home?'

'I told her that I'd been to a meeting and . . .'

'And you haven't shown her your haircut?'

'No, I haven't! It bloody well itches, I can tell you!'

'Keep it shaved and it won't itch,' she advised, showing him the door.

After seeing Mick out, Jackie dressed, wondering what on earth she was doing by involving so many people in the business. For a moment, she felt that she'd lost control and considered not ringing Mick's wife, cancelling Rosita and forgetting about the old man. Taking a deep breath, she composed herself and wandered downstairs to the lounge to flop onto the sofa.

Waiting for news from Jane, news that could change her entire life, minutes seemed like hours. Pacing the floor won't help, she thought, and eventually decided to go out for a walk. Grabbing her coat and bag, she slammed the front door shut and wandered out into the cold street.

The pub appeared inviting with its welcoming coloured lights and Jackie's thoughts turned to Rosita. Confused, she began to wonder if she'd ever settle down to a normal life – a normal relationship. But, there again, she wasn't sure if that was what she wanted. Rosita, Jane, Mick, David even, all were attractive in their own way and had many different things to offer – but which one, if any, should she choose?

Turning away from the pub, she walked up the street, contemplating the old man's situation, and remembering her days of sitting in her flat with nothing more than a book and the television to keep her company. Pulling his address from her bag, she walked briskly round the corner and headed for his house two blocks away.

The small, cottage-style bungalow with smoke curling

from the chimney appeared homely. Somehow too homely, Jackie mused as she rang the door bell – to invade the couple's home with cold sex. But, she convinced herself, she was only being humanitarian and bringing a little pleasure to a lonely old man.

As he opened the door, his eyes lit up like a child's. 'Come in, come in,' he said eagerly, 'I really didn't think I'd ever see you again. Oh, I'm sorry, I don't even know your name.'

'Jackie, and yours?'

'Eric. I can't believe that you're here!'

'I told you that I'd call in on you,' Jackie smiled, slipping her coat off as they entered the lounge. 'How is your wife?'

'About the same,' he replied sadly. 'She'll never really get better, of course, but she's comfortable.'

Sitting on the sofa in the small but comfortable room, Jackie felt sorry for the old man and decided against anything other than a friendly chat. But as she waited for him to make the tea, she imagined herself as an unorthodox home help and suddenly realised that he needed far more than company.

'There we are,' he said, placing the tray on the table. Sitting in the armchair opposite Jackie, he admired her slim legs and told her that he'd not had the pleasure of anyone's company who wasn't under the age of sixty for many years.

'No grandchildren, then?' she asked.

'No, no children, in fact! We, my wife, never wanted any.'

Listening to the sad story of his marriage to a virtually celibate woman, Jackie allowed her legs to fall apart to at least bring him some memories of his youth.

'You're a fine young lady,' he sighed. 'I haven't seen

anything like . . . Well, it's been thirty years since . . .'

'Thirty years? Good God! Put your tea down and come over here,' she whispered, opening her legs wide and moving her hips forward to present her gaping slit to his hungry eyes.

Standing between her splayed legs, he fell to his knees and began to lap at her wet valley like a dog. 'Is it nice?' she asked as her clitoris responded and her juices began to flow.

'God, it's wonderful!' he breathed, stretching her lips wide apart and pushing his tongue into her creamy hole.

'My clitoris,' she whispered. 'Lick my clitoris and I'll come in your mouth.'

Following her instructions, he licked around her hard bud until she began to writhe and moan, a little more than usual. As she became aware of an approaching orgasm, she gasped and her bud pulsated with delight. On and on her climax coursed its way through her shuddering body until she could stand no more. Pumping out her sticky fluid, she begged him to lick her open hole and drink her nectar. As her climax subsided, he pushed two fingers into her warmth and explored inside her young body until she pulled him away.

'Come nearer,' she ordered, unzipping his trousers as he walked on his knees towards her open body. Pulling out his flaccid penis, she moved the skin back and forth until the shaft grew in length and the head bulged in her tiny hand. 'We'll bring back some pleasant memories for you,' she smiled as she introduced the purple knob to her entrance. Gasping with delight as she pulled him towards her, he slipped effortlessly into her creamy hole and rested there, savouring her tightening muscles. 'A little further,' she said, pulling him nearer until he was in to the root. 'Look,' she whispered. 'See how you've got it all into my hot cunt?'

'Yes, yes,' he breathed, gazing at her wet, stretched lips tightly encompassing his bulging shaft.

'Now you can fuck me – nice and hard – and come inside me,' she said, opening her blouse to reveal her firm breasts and erect milk buds.

After only a few thrusts, the old man cried out and crumpled over her heaving stomach. Sucking fervently on her erect nipples, he ran his hands all over her body, reminding himself of the female form he once knew so well. 'God, that was nice!' he breathed as he looked up to her young face. 'I wish I could do it again!'

'Sit on the sofa,' she instructed, pulling his long, dripping penis from her body. The old man sat down, his trousers around his ankles, and watched as Jackie settled between his legs. Taking his limp shaft in her hand, she pulled the soft skin back as far as she could and took the head in her mouth. Running her tongue round and round the hardening knob, she watched his eyes roll with euphoria.

'I can't do it again, I'm sure!' he gasped. Jackie didn't answer, continuing to work on the head with her hot tongue and running her hand up and down his shaft while kneading his large balls. Several times he grimaced but couldn't quite make it until, suddenly, his body shook and he filled her flushed cheeks with more sperm than she'd thought possible. Gripping the root of his throbbing penis, she took the full length to the back of her throat, using her mouth as she would her pussy until he fell limp and his penis flopped between her lips.

'You are naughty,' Jackie said as she stood up. 'I thought you said that you couldn't do it again?' He only smiled as he zipped up his trousers and pulled out his wallet.

'I haven't got much, but what do I owe you for the most wonderful experience of my life?'

'Nothing! Don't be so silly! I liked it too, so how much do I owe you?'

'You are an angel!' he cried. 'Please come and see me again.'

'I'm no angel, but yes, I will see you again. And now I really must be going.'

'But, when?' he asked as she neared the front door.

'I don't know, but I promise you that I'll come back. And I may even bring a friend.'

'The one you were in the pub with?'

'No, not her. But a lovely dark-haired girl – and she's very good. In fact, between us, we'll make you very, very happy!'

Closing the front gate, Jackie waved to the old man and quickly walked home. She was happy that she'd been able to make someone else happy, and she wondered just how many men were lonely and in need of a young girl's company. 'God, keep it under control,' she laughed as she opened the front door. 'I'm not running a pensioners' sex club!'

The house was empty and she contemplated phoning the court to see how things were going. 'They probably wouldn't tell me, anyway,' she mused as she ran upstairs. Dumping her coat on the bed, she decided to take the opportunity to look over the house and wandered in and out of each room until she came to David's bedroom. It was large, decorated in shades of blues and greens, and expensively furnished.

'Fuck it!' she cried as she sat on his bed. 'I can't live with myself knowing that he's innocent!' Flopping on her back, she gazed at the ceiling and decided to tell the truth, or at least make it known to the police, once she was the legal owner of the house. 'It's only fair,' she breathed as she ran a finger down her sticky groove and contemplated toying with one of the vibrators.

Running down to the studio, she suddenly remembered the CDC equipment, and thought it a good idea to while away the time relaxing on the frame. Switching the machine on, she grabbed the rubber hose and lay down on the soft velvet. Parting her puffy lips, she ran her finger from her wet hole up her valley to lubricate the little bud. Placing the hose over her now hard clitoris, she closed her eyes and relaxed as the sensations reverberated through her body and began to calm her troubled mind.

Rather than an orgasm, sleep came quickly, and Jackie drifted away to dream that her clitoris was six inches long and she was able to masturbate like a man and even make love to women with her penis-like protrusion. Her dream brought her mansions with servants and money and vivid images of making love with Jane, Rosita and many beautiful girls. But also images of David, hanging from a rope as she looked on and laughed.

'What are you doing?' a distant voice echoed in her ears. 'Jackie, Jackie! Look what you've done!' Slowly opening her eyes, she focused on Jane and raised her head to look down to her clitoris. The crimson, swollen bud protruded a good inch from her puffed lips. Her thighs were covered with a lavish slick of love cream. 'You've had the ultimate wet dream!' Jane laughed, helping her from the frame. Her legs unsteady, Jackie wandered to the sofa and sat down, examining her clitoris and asking how long she'd been asleep.

'For several hours by the look of your clit!' Jane laughed.

'I came down here about mid-day, what's the time now?'

'God! It's six o'clock – you've had six hours on the

Ray Gordon

machine! David always said never to have more than one hour a day.'

'Oh well, I suppose I've had a crash course,' Jackie mused, trying in vain to fold her lips over her long clitoris. 'Oh, you've been to court, haven't you?'

'Yes, the trial continues tomorrow. All they did was go over the facts, as they call them, and listen to all the statements. We won't know anything for a day or two, I'm afraid. Anyway, what have you been up to, apart from lengthening your clit and wetting yourself in your sleep, that is?'

Jackie decided not to mention the old man, but she did tell Jane about Mick and his prudish wife. 'She's not a bank clerk, is she?' Jane laughed. 'Only they *can* be rather prudish until they come here!'

'I don't know what she is, but I'm supposed to ring her and get her to come here so I can bring out the woman in her, as I put it to Mick.'

'What will you say to her?' Jane asked as they wandered up to the lounge.

'I'll think of something.'

'Tell her that she's won a holiday abroad and she must come here to pick up the tickets!'

'Okay, I'll try it,' Jackie grinned as she flicked through the phone book.

As she was dialling, the front door bell rang. 'Oh, Rosita,' Jane said disappointedly as she opened the door. 'Jackie's on the phone, she won't be a minute. Have you left your job?'

'Yes, I have. And I hope I've done the right thing!'

'I hope Jackie's doing the right thing! You'd better come into the lounge, I suppose.'

'It worked!' Jackie yelled as Jane entered the room. 'Hi, Rosita, left your job?'

'Yes, yes, I have.'

'That's good, welcome aboard. It worked, Jane! She'll be here in an hour!'

'What's going on?' Rosita asked.

'You've come just at the right time – your first client's on her way,' Jane quipped.

Barely able to believe her eyes, Rosita gazed in amazement as Jackie slid the book-shelving back to reveal the stairway to the studio. Following the girls, she gasped several times and didn't stop asking questions until she found herself confronted with the frame. Standing open-mouthed, she looked to Jackie for an explanation.

'Right,' Jackie said, turning the handle. 'Vertical, horizontal, and, by turning this one, we can bend the victim, I mean, client, over. Ingenious, as its inventor put it, don't you think?' Still, Rosita said nothing. 'And these clamps are for pinning the . . . the client down while we work on her, or him, as the case may be.'

'Bloody hell!' Rosita eventually exclaimed.

'Bloody hell, indeed!' Jane breathed.

'Yes, well, we haven't got much time so I'll show you around quickly. You'll see everything in operation later, when she gets here,' Jackie said.

'And these?' Rosita asked, pulling out a cane.

'Self-explanatory, I think,' Jane said sarcastically.

Taking Jackie to one side as Rosita examined the vibrators, Jane asked how she thought Mick's wife would react to being raped. What would they do if she went to the police when they eventually released her. 'The video tape,' Jackie whispered. 'That's the very reason that I couldn't go to the police when I first came here, isn't it?'

'Yes, but that was different. David lured you down here. We're going to have to drag her!'

'No, no, we won't. I have a little plan in mind,' Jackie replied, covering the frame with David's white coat. 'Now, put your nurse's uniform on and I'll go up and wait for her while you show Rosita the ropes, so to speak!'

When the door bell eventually rang, Jackie's heart leaped and she wished that she'd never offered to assist Mick in his quest for a real woman. But it was too late, and she opened the door with a big smile and welcomed Helen in.

In her early twenties, blonde and extremely attractive, Helen was an ideal candidate – the perfect woman to have her sexuality woken, Jackie reflected, remembering her own initiation as her clitoris tingled slightly.

Following Jackie into the lounge, she slipped her coat off and sat down. She was slim, too slim, Jackie thought as she eyed her small breasts. But, slim or not, she would have a lovely little clitoris that was, no doubt, in dire need of attention. Her big brown eyes darted around the room as she waited for Jackie to reveal the holiday of a lifetime that she'd won. Jackie smiled and poured her a glass of wine, eyeing her long skirt as she passed her the drink, wondering how tight her hole was, how long her clitoris.

Divulging that the holiday was for two in America, and that she really should have brought her husband along, Jackie explained that a quick medical check-up was necessary for insurance purposes and the company had its own doctor and surgery downstairs.

Although somewhat mystified and hesitant, Helen finished her wine and followed Jackie down to the studio and through to the surgery. Rosita and Jane were nowhere to be seen and Jackie could only hope that they were hiding somewhere nearby in readiness.

'Nurse, Mrs Johnstone is ready for you!' Jackie called. Jane wandered into the room looking every bit like a real

240

nurse, except for the fact that her uniform was so short that her naked slit could be seen smiling between her young thighs. 'I'll leave you to it, nurse,' Jackie said, motioning for Jane to disrobe the woman as she closed the door.

Watching on the T.V. monitor, Jackie waited for Rosita as the woman undressed, assisted by nurse Jane, for the examination. When she was naked, but for her bra and panties, and standing with her back to the frame, Jackie returned to the surgery and removed the white coat. Before Helen realised what was going on, the girls had gently moved her back a step and deftly clamped her ankles and wrists.

'What is this?' she screamed as Jackie cut off her bra and gazed longingly at her small but very hard breasts. 'Let me go! I'll go to the police!'

'I've heard it all before,' Jane laughed, glancing at Jackie who was now on her knees gazing at Helen's bulging panties.

'No-one's going to hurt you. We're just going to show you what your body is for, how to get the most out of it,' Jackie reassured as she rose to her feet and turned the handle to tilt her onto her back.

'You have a wonderful body, Helen,' Jane remarked, stroking her tight panties. 'We are going to show you how to have wondrous orgasms – it'll make your marriage, your sex-life, all the better!'

Helen stopped her wriggling and screamed when Jackie threatened to gag her and cane her unless she shut up. No longer struggling, she lay her head back and closed her eyes and allowed the girls to fondle her breasts. Slipping a finger under her panties, Jane located her groove and gently pushed her way between the soft folds. 'Shall we take your panties off?' she asked quietly, pushing her finger further into the hot, tight hole.

'No, please, no!' came the sobbed reply.

'Hasn't anyone ever seen you naked before?'

'No, no, not even my husband, please . . .'

'Oh, your poor husband!' Jackie cried. 'How long have you been married?'

'Two years, and . . .'

'And he's never seen your pussy?'

'No, no, I'm not like that!'

'Not normal, you mean? You soon will be.'

'No, no!'

'Has he ever licked you there?' Jane asked, wiggling her finger further into the dark wetness.

'Never! Certainly not! That's disgusting!'

Jane carefully cut her panties off to reveal her little downy bush. 'That's nice. You shouldn't hide it away – especially from your husband!' Jane admonished as she caressed the tight little groove without so much as a word of protest from Helen. Rosita slipped into the room and joined in the stroking and caressing as if she were an old hand at it. Helen soon became aroused and, much to everyone's surprise, began to writhe slightly and breathe deeply in response to the six caressing hands.

Grabbing a vibrator from the trolley, Jackie switched it on and parting Helen's lips she pressed it to her little bud. 'God, that's nice!' Helen gasped and raised her hips to push her clitoris harder against the buzzing intruder. Taking another vibrator, Jackie eased its length slowly into her now very wet hole and clamped it in place. Jane and Rosita sucked on her nipples and caressed her twitching stomach as Jackie worked with the vibrator, running it round and round the base of her hardening bud until it suddenly grew and flowered. Throbbing with orgasm, it sent its powerful waves of ecstasy over Helen's trembling body, causing her to pant with pleasure. At the height of her climax, Jackie stretched Helen's pussy lips wide apart and engulfed the little bud in her mouth and sucked and licked until Helen gasped her appreciation. 'God! I like that! Oh, what are you doing to me? Ah, ah, I've never . . . never . . . Ah!'

'Never come so much in all your life?' Rosita prompted, running her tongue round the hard milk bud.

'I've never come in my life before!' came the gasped reply.

'What!' Jane cried in disbelief as she looked up from the nipple she'd been working on and gazed at the swollen lips encompassing Jackie's mouth. 'Never in your life?'

'No, never, never! Ah, ah, that's nice . . .'

As Helen relaxed, Jackie motioned for the girls to leave. 'We're going to let you rest for a while,' she said. 'And then we'll come back and show you something else that I think you'll find most pleasurable. After that, you can go home – a new woman.'

Dashing to the phone, Jackie called Mick and asked him to come to the house as soon as he could. Jane frowned but was offered no explanation as Jackie sat down. Rosita was becoming decidedly aroused and, Jackie noticed, had secretly slipped her hand between her legs. Nudging Jane, Jackie nodded in Rosita's direction. Jane managed half a smile to see her with eyes closed and her hand moving quickly beneath her skirt. Suddenly, she gasped and, lifting her skirt clear, openly masturbated her knickerless pussy to a wonderful climax.

'Well, *you're* enjoying the evening!' Jackie laughed.

'God! I needed that!' Rosita panted, still caressing her clitoris as she lay back in the chair. 'I don't know what's happening to me. I've never masturbated so much before!'

'There'll be plenty more to come, now that, apparently, you're working with us,' Jane sighed as the door bell rang.

Sending the girls down to blindfold Helen, Jackie let Mick in and explained her plan. Creeping into the surgery, his eyes opened wide with amazement to see his young wife strapped to the frame, her body wet and open, a smile across her face. Tugging on his trousers, Jackie pulled them down and positioned him between Helen's legs.

'Now, Helen, I promised you something pleasurable, and here it is,' Jackie whispered, taking Mick's hard, long penis and butting the knob between Helen's gaping lips. Slowly, he pushed it in, his eyes rolling, his mouth hanging open.

'No, no!' Helen screamed. 'Not a man! It's adultery! Please, no! Mick will . . . Ah, ah. He will . . . Ah!'

Ramming for all he was worth, Mick took his wife as never before as the girls sucked on her milk buds and vibrated her clitoris until the happy couple cried out in pained pleasure. Filling her body with his sperm, Mick breathed out heavily, but daren't speak. Helen, though, cried out as she gripped his shaft and allowed her true self to surface.

'Ah, fuck me! Fuck my cunt! God, if only Mick would do it to me like this!'

'Have you ever let him?' Jackie asked as the couple relaxed and Mick withdrew his satisfied rod.

'No, no, I suppose not. But I will!'

'And now I have one more thing to show you,' Jackie whispered, indicating for Mick to move towards her head and the girls to her hot, dribbling hole.

Gently turning Helen's head as the girls licked at her crack, Jackie waited until she began to gasp with her third climax before pushing Mick's purple knob into her open mouth. She choked and cursed but soon started to suck on the wet, bulging head. Mick gazed in disbelief at Helen, his wife, the prude that he'd thought to be totally sexless, slurping at his penis, begging for his sperm. Closing his eyes, he pumped out his liquid, filling her hungry mouth until the juices spilled over her lips and ran down her cheek. Near-senseless with pleasure, she suckled until the last drop had gone and her prize withdrew. Swallowing hard and licking her lips, she asked to see the man with whom she'd committed adultery – and reached heaven.

Quickly ushering Mick and the girls out, Jackie removed the blindfold and released Helen's quivering but satisfied body. Rubbing her eyes and her mouth as she climbed from the frame, she looked at Jackie and smiled. 'Thank you,' she whispered. 'But who was the man?'

'Don't thank me,' Jackie replied, passing her clothes. 'The identity of the man who brought you womanhood must remain a secret, I'm afraid. But the day may well come when you discover who it was. Now, go home to your husband and enjoy your body, his body – enjoy your life! Oh, and take this,' she added, passing her a vibrator. 'It will add that little bit of extra fun to what should now be the perfect marriage.'

Having shown Helen out, Jackie found Rosita and Jane asleep on top of the four-poster bed. Settling down beside them, she closed her eyes, contemplating her new rôle as marriage guidance counsellor and old people's dream-maker, as she, too, fell asleep.

Chapter Thirteen

A ring at the front door interrupted breakfast. Jackie left the table and closed the kitchen door behind her, fearing that it might be Lady Forsythe-Byron come to seek revenge. Opening the door, it occurred to her that she had too many dark secrets – the letters, the leather bag containing the money and jewellery, the old man, David's innocence and the identity of the real murderer. The time had come to free herself if she was to concentrate solely on running the business.

An official looking man carrying a briefcase was standing on the doorstep. 'Miss Jackie Wilson?' he enquired.

'Yes, what is it?' she replied shakily.

'My name's Clarke, I'm a solicitor. I represent Mr David Blackwell. He's asked me to call on you to sign some papers concerning the sale of this property – may I come in?'

'Yes, yes. Come into the lounge.'

Sitting on the sofa, he opened his briefcase and spread some papers on the coffee table. Frowning around the door, Jackie motioned Jane to go away.

'Now, Miss Wilson, there's the question of payment for the property. Er . . . five hundred thousand, I believe, half of which is to go to Miss Jane Blackwell and the other half to be held by my firm for Mr David Blackwell. How do you intend to pay?'

'Cash,' Jackie said, wondering how she was going to explain how she had that amount of money lying around the house.

'That's rather difficult. Er . . . where is the money now?'

'In the house,' she whispered, praying that Jane wasn't listening behind the door.

'I can't really accept that amount in cash, Miss Wilson. Can't you pay by cheque?'

'No, no, I'm afraid not.'

'Then I'll have to ask that you come into my office so that we can have a witness at the transaction.'

'Yes, yes. When, now?'

'No, no, at your convenience.'

'This afternoon?'

'All right, shall we say three o'clock?'

'Yes, three o'clock.'

Closing the front door, Jackie breathed a sigh of relief and wandered back into the kitchen. The girls had finished their breakfast and were discussing Rosita's bedsit.

'There's room here for you,' Jackie said as she sat down.

'Who was that?' Jane asked.

'It was about the house – you know . . .'

'Oh, right. I don't think there is room, Jackie. I mean . . .'

'Of course there is, it's a massive house. We can't have Rosita living in some squalid bedsit!' Jackie said firmly, passing Rosita the spare front door key.

'Well, I suppose you're in charge,' Jane said sulkily.

'Great! I'll go and get my things now, then,' Rosita replied eagerly, leaving the room.

No sooner had she left the house than the door bell rang. 'A bloody busy morning – and it's going to be a

bloody busy house with her moving in!' Jane complained
as she walked through the hall. 'Oh, Mrs Blythe-Smith!'

'Good morning, Jane. Presumably my appointment is
still on. I mean, with David . . . Well . . .'

'Yes, yes. Er . . . Come in, come in.'

Frowning at Jackie, Jane led the woman to the surgery
and asked her to undress for her session. Jackie dashed
downstairs and met Jane in the studio. 'Who's that?' she
asked.

'A client,' Jane whispered. 'We haven't done her yet.'

'What do you mean?'

'Her house. David had set it all up for this morning, I'd
forgotten. There's her bag, you'll have to do it.'

'What? Rob her house?'

'Yes, it's your business now so . . .'

'God! I'm not ready for this sort of thing!'

'You'll have to be. Get her keys, her address is in the
diary. It's all right, David has been planning this one for
ages, her house will be empty.'

Closing the surgery door behind her, Jane left Jackie
gazing at the handbag lying on the couch. Opening it, she
picked up a bunch of keys and walked to the knee-hole
desk and flicked through the diary. 'God!' she whispered.
'She only lives up the bloody road!'

The sound of the swishing cane sent Jackie bounding up
the stairs. Grabbing her coat, she slipped her gloves and
scarf on and walked the short distance to the woman's
address – a huge, detached house set well back from the
road. Creeping up the drive, she pulled her coat collar up
and pushed a key into the oak front door. As it opened, a
buzzer sounded loudly. Frantically searching for the
source of the noise, she opened a cupboard to see a red
flashing light on the control box. 'A small key!' she
breathed, eyeing the little lock. 'It must be a small key!'

The only small key on the ring fitted the lock and she quickly turned it – the buzzer stopped. 'God!' she gasped. 'What the hell am I doing?'

Being careful not to disturb anything, she crept around the house in search of the safe. Moving a picture aside in the dining room, she grinned. 'And now a big key,' she whispered, pushing the only large key on the ring into the lock. It clicked and the door swung open to reveal two bundles of notes. Without looking further, she grabbed the money and closed the door. As she was about to leave the house, she remembered the alarm. 'Shit! How do I set the bloody thing?'

Turning the small key, the red light flashed. Gazing at two buttons marked 'Activate' and 'Test,' she hesitated. In a panic, she pressed the button marked 'Activate'. She slammed the cupboard door closed before running from the house and out into the safety of the street.

Cold and shaking, Jackie ran home and banged the front door shut behind her. Leaning against the wall, she broke down and cried as she pulled the money from her coat pocket. 'I've done it!' she sobbed. 'I've bloody done it!' Composing herself, she crept downstairs, dropped the keys into the handbag and collapsed onto the four-poster bed.

'Twenty thousand!' she cried as she counted the last few notes and stuffed them under the pillow. Howling emanating from the surgery drew her to take a look through the keyhole. The woman was standing against the frame, her buttocks red-raw, and yet still Jane was thrashing her with the cane, taking no notice of her pleas for mercy. Thinking that she'd lost control of her senses, Jackie opened the door and grabbed her arm.

'Don't stop now!' the woman yelled. 'I'm nearly there!' Releasing Jane's arm, Jackie watched in amazement as she landed blow after blow across the woman's buttocks, causing her to cry out as her body shook violently. 'Now!' she yelled. '*Now!*' Dropping the cane, Jane thrust a vibrator into her gaping slit and massaged her clitoris with her fingers for all she was worth. 'Ah, yes, yes! More, more!' she cried as Jackie grabbed another vibrator and eased it into the smaller hole. The girls thrust the vibrators in and out in unison as Jane brought the woman's clitoris to bursting point.

Howling like a dog, the woman convulsed in an orgasmic ecstasy. Her long black hair, drenched with perspiration, showered the girls as she thrashed her head from side to side. 'That's it! No more!' she screamed. Quickly relinquishing the vibrators, the girls stood back and gazed at the weals across the flesh of her trembling buttocks. 'That was the best yet!' she cried. 'How many hands have you got?'

With that, Jackie slipped from the room, leaving Jane to answer the impossible question. Lying on the four-poster bed, she contemplated her new life as not only a wealthy business woman – but a thief. The excitement of the robbery had left her elated, but also fearful. She began to imagine that she'd been seen and followed home. 'Fingerprints!' she suddenly gasped, but breathed easier when she remembered that she'd worn her gloves. 'My scarf!'

'It's here,' Jane whispered as she opened the door. 'On the couch. Are you all right. You've turned very pale.'

'Oh, God! Has she gone?'

'She's dressing. Did you get the money?'

'Yes, yes. Get rid of her!'

Jane eventually wandered back into the room. 'Did it turn you on?'

'What, the robbery?'

251

'Of course – what else?'

'Yes, in a way – the danger, the excitement turned me on. Anyway, I'd better go and have a shower.'

'Right, I'm off to the court to watch them slaughter poor David. I'll see you later.'

Rosita returned to the house lugging a huge suitcase and met Jane at the front door. 'I don't know which room you're having,' Jane remarked rudely, letting her in. 'You'd better ask Jackie – she's the boss!'

'I don't know, either,' Jackie said as she walked from the lounge. 'Leave the case there for now, we'll sort it out later.' Waiting until Jane had closed the front door, Jackie took Rosita's arm and led her into the lounge. 'Fancy some fun?' she asked with a wicked glint in her eye.

'What sort of fun?'

'Well, don't tell Jane, but I have an elderly gentleman friend who I bring a smile to sometimes. As you're to be working with the clients, and some of them are male, I wondered if you'd like a little practice?'

'An old man! Argh! Horrible!'

'Don't be silly! You've got to learn to deal with all sorts. Now, leave your coat on and come with me – it's only around the corner.'

Eric opened the front door and grinned. 'Come in, girls,' he said cheerfully. 'And who's this little beauty?'

'Rosita,' Jackie replied as they wandered through to the lounge.

'Ah, Rosita! And where do you originate from?'

'Greece,' she replied, frowning her disapproval at Jackie as they sat on the sofa.

'Now, I have an appointment at three, so we don't have a great deal of time,' Jackie began. 'Rosita, Eric hasn't had much of a sex life, so I think it would be rather nice if you were to undress and remind him what a young beauty, as he puts it, looks like.'

Rising to her feet, Rosita slipped her coat off and unbuttoned her blouse as the old man eagerly looked on. Pursing her lips, she glared at Jackie, who was smiling sweetly and nodding her head by way of encouragement. Raising her eyes to the ceiling, Rosita unclipped her bra and released her huge breasts. 'May I?' he whispered, standing before her young body and taking one breast in each hand. Rosita said nothing as he weighed them and lowered his head to take a nipple in his mouth. 'God, they're lovely specimens!' he breathed as he sucked on her hardening nipple.

Eagerly tugging at her skirt, he dropped to his knees and managed to pull it down to her ankles. 'Ah, yes,' he breathed, gazing at her neat crack. 'You shave, too, I see.'

'When did you do that?' Jackie asked.

'Earlier. I thought that, as you and Jane . . .'

'It's beautiful!' the old man cried, parting her groove to explore the secrets within.

Standing with her feet apart, Rosita pulled her lips wide apart and allowed him to lick her open slit from the bottom to the top. 'Make some juice,' he begged. 'I love drinking juice!'

'That's your job,' Jackie giggled. 'The more you lick, the wetter she'll get.'

Clutching her buttocks, he licked fervently, stiffening her rosebud clitoris until it protruded enough for him to squeeze it between his lips. 'Ah, that's nice,' Rosita breathed. 'Keep doing that and you'll get your juice.'

'God, I can't get enough of you – you're beautiful!' he gulped, burying his face between her stretched, pink folds.

Leaning back and pushing her hips forward, Rosita

presented her hole to his tongue and poured out her cream as he slurped and sucked her wet folds. Gazing down at his grey hair, she became aroused as never before and pulled her lips open wider. 'Oh, that's good,' she gasped. 'God, that's good! Now my clitoris, my clitoris – I'm coming!'

Engulfing her hard bud, he flicked the tip with his tongue until she shuddered and cried with pleasure and pumped more cream from her now gaping hole. Guzzling up the last few drops of his reward, the old man sat back on the floor and gazed at the spent slit, crimson, glistening, sagging open before him.

'Now that you've prepared her so well, I think you should fuck her,' Jackie suggested as Rosita lay back on the carpet with her legs splayed and her hairless crack open. Pulling his trousers off, the old man proudly took his huge, erect penis in his hand and asked Rosita what she thought of it.

'God, it's big, isn't it!' she gasped, gazing at the full eight inches hovering ominously over her smooth belly.

'All the better to fuck you with!' Jackie laughed.

Presenting the swollen head to her pink lips, he slowly pushed the entire length of his shaft into her hot cunt and rested it there, savouring her twitching muscles. Slowly pulling away until her lips caressed the head, he slipped it in again, pushing her across the carpet with every thrust. Violently, he rammed her young body, slowly moving her towards the sofa where Jackie sat with her fingers stroking her own wet slit. Her breasts heaving and bouncing, Rosita gasped her appreciation and begged him to come in her mouth.

His body becoming rigid, he pulled the pulsating head from her hole and quickly moved up to her face and pushed it into her open mouth. Closing her red lips over the purple knob, she ran her tongue round and round and sucked hard as she cupped his huge balls in her tiny hands. Jackie moved between Rosita's thighs and licked the length of her milky valley and round her hardening clitoris as the old man's knob bulged even more and suddenly exploded, pumping her cheeks full of his hot, creamy liquid as she arched her back and ground her clitoris into Jackie's mouth.

Falling to the floor, the old man lay on his back, gasping for air and thanking the girls for allowing him the pleasure of their young bodies. Taking the opportunity to indulge herself, Jackie sat astride his face and rubbed her wet groove back and forth over his mouth as Rosita sat on his flaccid penis and tried to stuff it into her body. Soon, it rose and she lowered her body, gently impaling herself on the eight-inch rod until her puffy lips encompassed the root. Pressing hard against her cervix, the knob swelled within her tube, stretching and filling her body as she gyrated her hips and leaned forward to rub her clitoris against his pubic bone.

All three came together, gasping, writhing in the magical union, pumping their fruits into each other's quivering bodies until they collapsed and rested, side by side on the floor.

'Ah, I've never enjoyed myself so much in all my life,' the old man panted, licking Jackie's juices from his lips.

'There's more to come,' Rosita giggled wickedly, moving her dripping hole over his face. 'I'm full of your sperm and, to save it from running down my legs as I walk home, you can suck it from me and drink it.'

Peeling her lips open and pressing her entrance to his mouth, she tightened her muscles, squeezing his sperm from her tube as he sucked and drank the bitter cocktail until she was empty. Licking his penis clean, Jackie stroked his large balls and kissed the purple head before rising to her feet. 'We must be going,' she said solemnly, helping Rosita to her feet. 'But we'll be back.'

'Oh, yes, do come back – you've given an old man renewed life! I can't thank you enough.'

'I'll definitely be back,' Rosita assured, bending down and kissing him. 'Don't get up, we'll see ourselves out.'

Once out in the street, Jackie asked Rosita if she'd enjoyed herself. 'Very much!' she grinned. 'In fact, it was strange – I felt somehow at one with him.'

'God, you're not in love, are you?'

'No, no, of course not! I don't know what it is, I just feel good, relaxed, being with him.'

'I thought you were different somehow,' Jackie smiled as they climbed the steps to the house. 'I could see that you totally lost yourself when you were coming. I felt like that once with David. He . . . Well, it doesn't matter – perhaps it is love!'

Closing the front door, Jackie led Rosita upstairs and found her a nice large room with a double bed. 'This must be a spare room,' she mumbled, opening the wardrobe.

'It's your house, don't you know which room is which?'

'Oh, take no notice of me, I'm just thinking aloud. So, is it all right for you?'

'It's great! I'll go and get my things.'

Following Rosita down to the hall, Jackie waited until she'd lugged her case up to her room before pulling the leather bag from the clock base and carrying it to the secret room. Closing the wooden panel, she pulled out several wads of notes and carefully counted out five hundred thousand pounds. 'God, it's like being back at the bank,' she reflected as she bundled the notes together and stuffed them into her handbag.

Quietly closing the panel, she bounded upstairs and

called out to Rosita that she was going out for a while. Happy to be left arranging her room, Rosita yelled goodbye as Jackie closed the front door and, clutching her bag tightly, walked into town.

The warmth of the solicitor's office welcomed her in from the cold as she approached the receptionist and asked for Mr Clarke. Appearing in a doorway, he invited her in and offered her a seat.

'Do you have the money?' he asked, opening a file.

'Yes, but a receipt. I'll . . .'

'Don't worry, you'll have the title deeds to the property in your name, and a receipt – and the whole affair will be witnessed.'

After half an hour, Jackie emerged from his office as the legal owner of the house and its contents – apart from the grandfather clock and a couple of small pieces of furniture. Returning home, she couldn't stop grinning. Even if David is acquitted, it's my house, she mused as she opened the front door and called Rosita.

'She's gone out,' Jane said sullenly. 'Having installed herself in the spare room, she's buggered off out.'

'How's David?' Jackie asked, ignoring her mood.

'It doesn't look good – the trial should be over tomorrow. Anyway, what did you get up to while I was out?'

'Nothing much, why?'

'When I got in, Rosita called down the stairs, thinking that it was you, and asked when you were both going to visit the old man again as she'd really enjoyed it. Have a nice time, did you – wanking off some old man?'

'Yes, I mean, no. I only went to see him as I promised him I would.'

'Let him fuck you, did you?'

'Well . . .'

'Did he fuck you both? Did he watch while you licked

your new girlfriend? Did he come in your mouth?'

'What's the matter with you?'

'I'm fed up with that Rosita! Now she's moved in here, I suppose you'll be sleeping with her? Prefer her Greek cunt to mine, do you?'

'Don't be silly, Jane. You know it's you I . . .'

'No, I don't know that! The way you carry on behind my back, how can I know that?'

'Look, I can't handle neurotic, bloody teenage girls! We're trying to run a business – you're just jealous! It's ridiculous!'

'Yes, of course I'm jealous! I thought we had something special between us!'

'We have! All I did was . . .'

'It's her or me – you'd better choose!'

'The house is legally mine now, so you'd better choose – do it my way, or leave!'

'Then I'll leave!' Jane sobbed as she ran up to her room and slammed her door shut.

'Oh, God!' Jackie breathed as she walked into the lounge and sat on the sofa. 'It's one bloody problem after another with her!'

Spending the rest of the afternoon in her room, Jane wouldn't come down for the evening meal Jackie had cooked. Rosita arrived home at seven and wandered into the kitchen to find Jackie eating alone. 'Jane's upset,' Jackie said, taking Rosita's food from the oven.

'I know. I called out, thinking it was you and . . .'

'Never mind, she'll be all right – she's young, that's all.'

Joining Jackie at the table, Rosita asked about David. She knew very little about him but had read the newspaper reports. Jackie explained as much as she thought necessary and was about to change the subject when Rosita saved her the trouble.

'There was a robbery,' she began. 'I heard it on the radio. Twenty grand was taken from a house up the road belonging to a Lady someone or other.'

'What else did they say?' Jackie asked cautiously.

'Nothing much. Oh, yes, the police reckon whoever did it had a key.'

'Were there any witnesses? Was anyone seen?'

'Don't know. I didn't take that much notice, really.'

'Look, as Jane's upset and I've got one or two things to do, why don't you go over to the pub and have a drink when you've finished your meal?' Jackie suggested, passing Rosita a twenty-pound note.

'Why don't you join me later? We can chat about the business.'

'All right, I'll sort Jane out and come over later.'

When Rosita had gone, Jackie wandered upstairs to try and console Jane. Lying in her bed, the girl pretended to be sleeping. 'Jane,' Jackie whispered. 'I want you, I love you. Wake up and kiss me – I want to kiss you.'

'Go away!'

'Oh, come on, this is getting silly.'

'Go and kiss your new girlfriend!'

'She's not my new girlfriend! Look, she's over the road, in the pub. Get dressed and we'll go and join her – have a drink and show off our pussies.'

'Why don't you go and play your pussy game with her?'

'I will, unless you stop being so silly and get out of bed!'

'I'm staying here!'

'Have it your way, then. But don't expect me to put up with this for long – it's stupid and I've got better things to do!'

Sauntering into the pub in her short skirt, Jackie smiled to see Rosita sitting at the bar chatting with Tim. But the thought suddenly struck her that she might well be telling him all about her new job. 'Hi!' she called, quickly approaching the bar.

'Hi, Jackie!' Tim replied, reaching for a glass. 'The usual, is it?'

'Please – so, what are you two talking about?'

'Nothing much,' Rosita said, eyeing Jackie's knickerless pussy as she slid onto a bar stool. 'I see you're dressed to impress!'

'Yes, are you?'

'I thought I'd give it a try – look,' she whispered, lifting her skirt as Tim turned his back to reach for a bottle of tonic.

'You look good.'

'Thanks, but there's no-one in here to see, is there?'

'It's early, yet – give it time and it will fill up.'

'How's Jane?'

'Being silly – she won't get out of bed.'

'That's on the house,' Tim smiled, passing Jackie her drink before going through to the small bar.

'It's all my fault, isn't it?' Rosita reflected.

'No, no. Jane's young, that's all.'

'I'll go and talk to her – get her to come out for a drink,' Rosita said, grabbing her bag. 'See you in a minute.'

She found Jane tidying up in the surgery. Putting her arm round her, she kissed her mouth. Jane responded by pushing her tongue into Rosita's mouth and reaching down to lift her skirt. 'Why are you so unhappy?' Rosita asked, closing her eyes as Jane located her hole and pressed her fingers inside the warmth.

'Everything's gone wrong for me. David's gone, I thought Jackie and I . . . Well, she wants you now, it seems.'

'No, she doesn't. You've got it all wrong.'

'Will you allow me to put you on the frame and make

love to you? I need someone to . . . I just need . . .'

'Yes, of course I will. I just want you to be happy, I mean, if we're all to live and work together, we should all be happy,' Rosita explained as she slipped her clothes off.

'You've shaved!' Jane gasped. 'Did she do that for you?'

'No, no, I did because you both shave.'

Climbing onto the frame, Rosita lay on her back. 'No, no, turn over,' Jane whispered. 'I want to love you properly.' Once on her stomach, Rosita allowed Jane to clamp her wrists and ankles. Her dark young body shone in the light, her rounded buttocks swelling either side of her dark crease. 'You have a lovely body. No wonder Jackie fancies you,' Jane whispered, running her finger-tips from her back and down her crease to her soft lips. 'I'm just going to bring the frame up so that you're standing,' she added, turning the handle.

With her legs wide apart and her arms stretched, Rosita closed her eyes as Jane knelt behind her and licked the length of her crease. She gasped and quivered every time Jane's tongue ran over her small, brown hole. Rising to her feet, Jane took a cane and tapped Rosita's buttocks, grinning wickedly as the girl turned her head and opened her eyes wide.

'You've spoilt everything,' Jane said, tapping a little harder.

'I haven't! Don't cane me, please!'

'Pleading won't get you anywhere – we're all alone in the house, there's no-one to save you!'

The first swish of the cane caused Rosita to scream out, more in fear than pain. The second cut across her dark buttocks, tightening them and leaving a thin weal. 'For God's sake! Let me go, please!'

'Why should I?' Jane asked, and she thrashed the girl

until she sobbed for mercy. 'Don't you like it?' Jane eventually panted, landing blow after stinging blow across the dark, crimson moons. 'I'm not going to stop! On and on I'll beat you for what you've done!'

Finally running out of energy, Jane dropped the cane and gazed into Rosita's streaming eyes. 'Enough, for the moment, I think,' she breathed. 'Until I get my strength back, I'll amuse myself with this.' Taking a large vibrator, she dipped the tip in the jar of vaseline and parted the girl's inflamed buttocks.

'No, God, no!' Rosita screamed as the cold, hard shaft sank into her bowels.

'Yes, God, yes!' Jane replied, laughing as she switched the device on and rammed it further home. 'Wait there a minute, I'm going to get one of David's latest inventions – you'll just love it!'

Returning from the work-room, Jane waved a long, slim, metal object under Rosita's nose. 'This is David's version of a vaginal speculum,' she laughed as she moved behind the girl and pushed it into her vacant cavern. Pressing the cold steel against her cervix, she slowly twisted the end.

'What are you doing?' Rosita asked fearfully.

'Turning the end expands it. It's similar to the ones gynaecologists use – only this one expands to about eight inches in diameter! Bigger and bigger it will get, stretching your hole open so wide that I'll be able to see right up it!'

As the object grew in girth, Rosita squeezed her eyes shut and grimaced. Wider and wider the soft, pink walls of her tube were stretched until she thought she was going to split open. 'Stop, please – stop! Argh! No!'

'Ah, it's lovely!' Jane cried. 'I can see your cervix! It's round, pink, and very wet. I've never seen a cervix before, David told me never to use this thing as it's so dangerous.

'Your cunt is about three inches across now – let's see if we can open you up a bit more.'

'God, no! Please, Jane – let me go, I'll leave the house, if that's what you want – please!'

Turning the device again, Jane gazed in amazement as Rosita's tube opened even wider, stretching the pink skin further and further. 'Please, please, it hurts!' Rosita yelled. 'You'll kill me!'

'No, no, it won't kill you. Mind you, something will have to give before long – the skin can't stretch much more without tearing.'

Grabbing the cane again, Jane left David's device in place and thrashed Rosita's buttocks a dozen times, filling the house with her screams, flinging the cane down again to examine her work. 'I think another turn or two will open you up just enough for me to get my fist inside.'

'Oh, no, no!' Rosita cried hysterically as Jane turned the device. 'Don't kill me!'

'Oh, look! It's about five inches across now! I can see right up your cunt! Anyway, I'm going now. You won't be seeing me again, I'm leaving. Enjoy yourself with Jackie – if you've got a cunt left to enjoy, that is!'

Having endured David's horrendous device for half-an-hour, Rosita gasped a cry of relief when Jackie arrived. 'God, what's she done to you?' Jackie asked, pulling out the vibrator before trying to remove the device.

'No, no, don't pull on it! Turn the end to make it smaller!' Rosita yelled. 'Quickly, turn it!'

As it decreased in girth, Jackie slipped the speculum from Rosita's inflamed hole and threw it to the floor in disgust. Her pussy lips sagged wide open, leaving her hole gaping and stretched, the soft walls wet and sore.

'You'll be all right,' Jackie assured, helping Rosita from the frame.

'Where's Jane?'

'Gone, for good, I hope!'

'Left the house?'

'She said that we won't be seeing her again, thank God.'

Leading Rosita to the four-poster bed, Jackie told her to rest, and covered her with the quilt. 'Stay there until the morning. You'll be all right, don't worry.'

'I hope so. She said she'd stretched me to about five inches.'

'No, no, she hadn't – she wouldn't do that. It was only about three inches – there's no damage done. Rest now, and I'll see you in the morning.'

Opening Jane's wardrobe, Jackie shook her head in despair to find most of her clothes had gone. 'Stupid girl,' she breathed as she slipped out of her clothes and climbed into the bed. Closing her eyes, she wondered where the girl had gone – and if she'd ever return. And she wondered about David, alone in his cell.

Chapter Fourteen

There was a note for Jackie on the four-poster bed when she went down to check Rosita in the morning.

Sorry, but all this isn't for me. I have learned a lot, of course – too much, in fact! Something inside me has stirred, I've changed. I feel as if I'm a real woman now that I understand my body and the pleasures it can bring me – and others. So I've gone to live with Eric. From what he told me this morning when I put the idea to him, I don't suppose his wife will ever come out of hospital. I know you will laugh, but I feel something for him, I don't know what. I can make him happy and, I believe, he will make me happy. I'll keep in touch. Take care – and thanks for everything.

Love, Rosita

Flopping onto the bed, Jackie crumpled the letter in her hand and cried. Empty, lost, lonely, she wondered at the change. She'd become a real woman, as Rosita had put it, and she needed a relationship, someone to share her life, her body with – male or female, she wasn't sure, it didn't matter.

Walking into the lounge, she glanced at the clock. Ten-thirty, she'd overslept. Wandering into the kitchen, she put the kettle on. The house was quiet, empty, lifeless. Gazing out of the window into the garden, she smiled to see the snow falling heavily. 'Ah, well,' she sighed. 'Look on the bright side, I suppose. Money, big house, no boring job.'

Pouring her coffee, she became aware of her clitoris, calling her from the warmth of her tightly closed groove. 'Sorry,' she whispered, lifting her skirt and parting her lips. 'There's no-one here to play with you. There's only me, and it's not the same, is it? I can't kiss you, lick you.'

The telephone rang. She dashed into the lounge.

'Is that Jane Blackwell?' the male voice asked.

'Yes,' she replied, wondering if it was news of David.

'Bill Godley here, from the Gazette. Any chance of popping round for an interview?'

'What for?'

'Don't you know? The jury's just gone out and . . .'

Banging the phone down, Jackie shot down to the studio. Gazing at David's knee-hole desk, she smiled, remembering when she'd crept in and stolen the jewellery. Opening the diary, she stared at the blank page. 'No bookings for today, thank goodness,' she breathed. 'And not many for the rest of the week. I haven't got a clue how to get any new clients.'

The phone rang again as she climbed the stairs.

'I'd like to make an appointment,' said a harshly spoken woman.

'Oh, right. Er . . . what name is it?'

'Lady Bridlington, I've been several times before – is that Jane?'

'No, no. My name's Jackie – I run the business now.'

'Oh, isn't David there any more?'

'No, he's gone away for a while. When would you like to come?' Jackie asked, grinning at her choice of words.

'This evening, if that's possible.'

'Yes, yes – about seven?'

'Fine, I'll be there. It's still two hundred, is it?'

'Yes, it's still two hundred.'

'Good. Thank you very much.'

Feeling a little chilly, Jackie searched for the central heating control. She found it in the hall and turned it up. 'At least I don't have to worry about the bills,' she mused as she descended the stairs to the studio, remembering her cold flat. Walking into David's work-room, she cast her eyes over the various plastic objects and grinned. 'I can't make tailor-made sex-aids!' she laughed as she turned her attention to David's special electric trolley on wheels. 'God, he put me on that!'

Again, her clitoris stirred between her swelling lips. 'I can't keep masturbating,' she breathed, trying to ignore the enticing voice within. Tingling between her soft lips, her clitoris still called for attention and her juices began to flow. 'What have I done to myself?' she asked, wandering back into the surgery. 'I *need* to come!'

Switching the equipment on, she slipped out of her clothes and lay on the frame, placing the hose over her now hard clitoris. Warm sensations immediately began to flood her mind as she closed her eyes and pictured Jane and Rosita, naked, kneeling over her mouth. 'Oh, Jane – come back,' she whispered as a tear rolled down her cheek. 'I do want you.'

Taking a vibrator from the trolley, she pushed it into her body and relaxed. Ripples of pleasure ran through her pelvis and deep into her womb as she breathed heavily and squeezed her nipples. Her orgasm rose slowly from the floor of her pelvis – up and up through the shaft of her clitoris as her muscles gripped the buzzing phallus and her cream oozed. Gasping now, she threw her head back as the throbbing sensations neared the hard tip of her bud, swelling her lips as the small, pink hood receded to expose the full length of her pulsating glans. 'That's it, that's it!' she cried as her bud burst and her body shook uncontrollably. 'Ah, yes, yes, that's nice! Oh, oh! Ah, God!'

Resting in the wake of her climax, she opened her eyes and gazed up at the clips hanging from the low ceiling. Adjusting the suction in the rubber tube, she smiled. 'CDC!' she laughed. 'I may as well put myself on the clitoral development course – and the nipple development course!'

The clips biting her nipples, she reached out and hung two weights on the cord hanging from the pulley system. Her breasts were pulled into cones, pointed, hard and erect. 'Quite nice,' she whispered, adding another weight and turning the suction control up. Feeling for the trolley, she grabbed another vibrator and pushed it gently into her smaller hole. In a dream-state, she gasped as the sensations mingled within her body, soothing, massaging, caressing her very soul.

Turning the control up even more, she added yet another weight. Her body trembled, her breasts stretched to distortion, her nipples hurting, her clitoris aching. 'Oh, wonderful! God, how I love my body!' she gasped as her womb gave birth to her second orgasm. Rising quickly from the depths of her cunt and up the shaft of her clitoris, it erupted and rippled over her perspiring body, reaching out to caress every tingling nerve ending to touch the innermost core of her being.

Recovered, she unhooked the equipment and climbed off the frame, her legs trembling as she walked slowly to the door. Satisfied as her body was, something remained unfulfilled. Something was missing, she knew, as she climbed the stairs, naked, to answer the phone.

It was another booking. I'm going to be bloody busy – and it's all down to me! she thought. Her mind began to reel as she thought of running the business without David. Fifteen years is a long time, she reflected, remembering the fat, ugly Lady Forsythe-Byron.

Fetching the diary from the studio, she looked up her number. 'Come on, come on, answer the bloody phone!' she hissed impatiently.

'Hello.'

'Forsythe-Byron?'

'Lady – Forsythe-Byron speaking.'

'It's me, Jackie. Are you really going to let David go down for a murder he didn't commit?'

'Yes, I have no choice in the matter!'

'But you did it!'

'You know that, I know that, but . . .'

'I've never met such a cold, callous cow as you in my life!'

Banging the receiver down, Jackie ran upstairs and dressed in jeans and a jumper. Grabbing her bag, she slammed the front door shut and walked around the corner to her car. Gazing at her dark, empty flat as she tried to start the engine, she smiled. It seemed like years since she had lived there – but it hadn't been her, had it? That had been the old Jackie – someone who no longer existed. As if in response to her thoughts, the engine burst into life. Jamming it into gear, she drove off.

She arrived at the court as the jury were coming in. Seating herself at the back, she gazed at the row of newspaper reporters. David stood in the dock, staring at her with glazed eyes. She smiled as the judge droned on and the spokesman for the jury stood up.

'Has the jury reached a unanimous decision?'

'Yes, my lord.'

'And what is that decision?'

'Guilty, my lord.'

Life! David's head fell and Jackie cried out as the judge passed his sentence. The court room bustled and reporters ran out clutching pens and pads as David was led away. 'Bastards!' Jackie hissed, pushing her way past the crowd to leave the building.

'That's it, then, my girl!' she told herself as she started her car. 'You're on your bloody own now!'

Depressed, she pulled up outside the house and ran across the road to the pub. Tim was behind the bar. 'He's got life,' she said tonelessly, flopping onto a stool and dumping her handbag on the floor.

'David?'

'Who do you think? Oh, Tim, I'm sorry. I didn't mean to . . .'

'Come on, it's all right, love. Here, have one on the house,' he smiled, pouring a quadruple gin and tonic.

'Thanks, Tim. I don't know what I'd do without you. I've got no-one else!'

'You've got that young blonde girl.'

'Jane? No, she's gone.'

'Roz, then?'

'Who?'

'Rosita – she's with you, isn't she?'

'No, no, she buggered off with . . . There's no-one, Tim.'

'Well, I'm here.'

'Yes, but I need . . . Oh, Tim, why do you have to be gay? Oh, I'm sorry, I shouldn't have said that.'

'It's all right, I understand. Now, drink up and I'll refill your glass.'

Chatting with Tim, Jackie relaxed. 'I've bought David's house,' she blurted out.

'Where on earth did you find that sort of money?'

'My parents,' she replied, aware that, of late, her lies were coming all too easily.

'They're not alive now, then?' he asked.

'No, no. Dad went some time ago, and Mum last year, I'm afraid. So, you see, Tim, I really am alone in the world.'

'You'll be all right. A good-looking girl like you with a nice house – there'll be dozens of men after you!'

'I'm not even sure that it's a man that I want!'

'You're not . . .'

'You tell me. I don't know!'

'Don't worry, have another drink.'

'No, no. It's no good getting drunk. I'll get back home, I think. Thanks anyway – I might see you this evening.'

The phone was ringing as she opened the front door and dumped her bag on the floor. Taking the woman's name, she made the appointment for the following day, wondering whether she should give up the business and do something else. During the afternoon, she took three more bookings. Why the hell are they all ringing now? she wondered. An omen?

The time approaching seven, she tidied the surgery and dressed in Jane's nurse's uniform. 'Very sexy!' she breathed, twirling before the hall mirror and eyeing her smooth slit peeping out from under the short skirt. Aware of her insatiable clitoris stirring yet again, she sighed. Perhaps this client would give her little spot some attention?

Answering the doorbell, she was surprised to confront a plain woman in her early thirties wearing a scruffy overcoat and carrying a large leather bag.

'Lady Bridlington?' she enquired doubtfully.

'Yes, excuse my appearance, only I don't want to be

recognised. And do call me Fiona.'

'Oh, right. Come in, please.'

No sooner had the woman walked into the studio than she threw her coat across the sofa. Jackie gazed open-mouthed at Lady Bridlington – naked, except for heavy leather bondage straps, a studded collar and leather bra with cutouts for her very long nipples.

'Shall we get started, then?' she demanded, adjusting the tight straps running either side of her bulging lips.

'Yes, yes. What is it that you normally . . . I mean, what did David . . .'

'Ah, allow me to show you what it is I like,' she grinned, opening her bag. 'I don't like the cane, I can tell you that! What I want is for you to chain me up.'

Pulling several heavy chains from the bag, the woman flourished them triumphantly. Covering her surprise, Jackie grinned. 'What do I chain you to? I mean, to the wall, or what?'

'David's little room, as he calls it. Through the secret panel. Come on, I'll show you.'

Opening the panel, she walked through into the secret room and dumped her bag on the floor. 'Now, I get on the table and you chain my arms and legs to the four straps so that my legs hang over the end of the table, effectively exposing my pussy for your attention,' she explained. Following her instructions, Jackie bound the toned limbs with the chains, manoeuvring her client until she lay, lips splayed, her buttocks over the edge of the table.

'What now?' Jackie enquired, wondering how Fiona could endure the pain of the heavy chains cutting into her flesh.

'Open my bag and you'll find some knickers,' she ordered. 'As David isn't here, you'll just have to do your best with those.'

Lifting a pair of thick leather knickers from the bag, Jackie could barely stifle a laugh as she gazed at the eight-inch, hard rubber phallus protruding from the crotch, complete with soft balls hanging neatly under the shaft. 'Put them on then, girl!'

Slipping her skirt off, Jackie pulled the contraption up her legs and realised that there was another phallus on the inside. 'What do I do with the other one?' she asked.

'What do you think?' came the agitated reply.

Smiling nervously, Jackie pulled up the knickers and, with some difficulty, manoeuvred the inner phallus into her creamy hole. Wiggling her hips and pulling the knickers higher, the solid rubber length filled her cavern and she was able to fasten the belt firmly around her waist.

The long, hard shaft protruded menacingly, wavering from side to side in readiness for penetration as she approached Fiona's gaping hole. Stroking the dark growth of pubic hair, she stabbed between the wet lips before succeeding in pushing the phallus home. Slowly, at first, she began to thrust in and out. 'Ah, that's good!' Fiona cried. 'Better than the real thing as it won't fall limp!'

'That's wonderful!' Jackie agreed, aware of her own cunt gripping the shaft as she thrust harder, causing her clitoris to rub against a hard nodule within the strange contraption.

The chains clanking and the leather straps binding her body, the captive was soon gasping her delight and thrashing her head from side to side. 'I'm coming – do it harder, faster!' she cried as Jackie quickly accustomed herself to the male role, ramming the rubber penis deep between Fiona's stretched lips. She, too, was nearing her orgasm as the inner rod moved around the hot wetness deep inside her body, massaging the soft walls of her canal as her clitoris stiffened against the nodule.

Shuddering, Fiona cried out and gripped the rod hard within her cunt. So strong were her muscles that Jackie had some trouble keeping the thing in motion. But she managed to continue until Fiona was begging for her to stop. 'In a minute!' Jackie cried as her climax exploded within the heat of her knickers, causing a stream of come-juice to fill the tight leather pouch under her crotch.

'And now put the other pair on,' Fiona ordered. Stepping out of the wet knickers, Jackie pulled another pair from the bag and slipped them on.

'What's this?' she asked, gazing at the two hard rods.

'One for each hole,' Fiona chuckled. 'Come on, I'm paying you well for this, so get started!'

Easing the two hard rubber lengths into Fiona's body, Jackie began her thrusting movements, observing in awe the pained pleasure on her client's face. 'Ah, yes, that's it!' Fiona gasped. 'Do it harder and pull on my hairs!' Jackie tugged on the little black curls as she rammed the two rods further into the used body. 'Harder!' Fiona cried. Almost tearing out the curls, Jackie complied, opening the lips wide to expose her clitoris. 'That's it, harder, faster! Ah, ah, yes, yes!' Gritting her teeth, her body rigid and face scarlet, Lady Bridlington breathed quickly and deeply. 'Ah, I've come, I've come . . . That was good, very good! I am more than pleased with you.'

Slipping the rods out, Jackie stepped back and released the belt. 'Is that all?' she asked as she dropped the soiled knickers into the bag.

'One more thing, just one more thing. You are such a pretty little thing and . . . Kneel over my face, I want to lick you while you lick me.'

Only too willing to comply, Jackie leaped onto the table and hurriedly pressed her wet slit over Fiona's open

road, wondering what on Earth to do next. Opening her
front door and flinging her handbag and coat on the floor,
she sighed. The house seemed bigger, somehow – silent
and empty. In the lounge, her depression returned. The
effects of the drink, her naughty game with the strange
man, had been short-lived. She contemplated ringing
Mick Johnstone to ask him round for company, but
decided against it. Her loneliness, she knew, was something she would somehow have to overcome herself.

'I can't stand the T.V. or books any more,' she complained inwardly, curling up on the sofa and closing her
eyes, remembering the long winter evenings at her flat
when she'd been only too pleased to be left alone with her
own company.

Stretching her arms, Jackie opened her eyes and focused
on the clock – ten a.m. 'God, I've been here all night,' she
groaned, climbing off the sofa and rubbing her aching
back. 'And now it's time for bloody breakfast, I suppose.'

The front door bell rang as she poured her coffee.
Dashing through the hall, she was sure it was Jane, come
home at long last. 'Jane!' she shrieked, opening the door.
Her heart leaped as she saw David standing forlorn on the
doorstep. 'My God! What are you . . . Have you
escaped?'

'No, no,' he smiled. 'If you'll allow me to come in, I'll
explain.'

'Of course you can come in – haven't you got your key?'

'Yes, but it's your house now, isn't it?'

'I suppose so. Come in, come in!'

Flinging her arms around his neck, she was really glad
that he was home. Gazing around the lounge, David
smiled. 'It seems like years since I was last here,' he said
sadly. 'Where's Jane?'

'Gone – she ran off somewhere.'

'Oh, she's always doing that – she'll be back. So what's been going on? How's the . . . your business?'

'It's okay. What I want to know is, what are you doing here?'

'That woman, Lady Forsythe-Byron, gave herself up. I'm only out on bail, of course, but now that she's confessed, I'll soon be a free man.'

'God! I don't believe it!'

'Well, it's true. Apparently, Stockwell had been having an affair with Forsythe-Byron's husband for years, right up until his death, in fact. Having lost half a million, Forsythe-Byron went to Stockwell for money and, I don't know if she was blackmailing her or not, but a fight broke out and . . . Well, you know the rest.'

Suddenly fearful of David's motives, his plans for the future, Jackie poured him a drink and began to question him. 'If Jane is your daughter, then how can you exploit her body? I mean, it's not really the way to bring up a child, is it?'

'I don't, and I never have. You see, she joined me in the business last year, after she'd discovered exactly what it was that I did for a living.'

'What, the clients, you mean?'

'Yes, she hid in the studio one day and saw what was going on. Since then, well, she's helped me out.'

'You've never done anything to her, then?'

'No, no!' he laughed. 'Good God, she's my daughter! I'm rather sorry that she's a lesbian, but there's nothing I can do about that, is there? I only want her to be happy.'

'Why tell her that you're her brother?'

'She thought I was her brother when she was young. As she grew older and began to confide in me about mastur-bation, sex and all that, I decided that I'd make a better brother than a father. Brothers are somehow more approachable, I think. And my wife? Well, she and I never really got on and when she was convicted of murder, I was happy to be rid of her. Ironic, really isn't it?'

'Murder?'

'Her poor old mother came to live with us and, having had enough of nursing her and running around twenty-four hours a day, she bumped her off one night.'

There was only one question left unanswered – but David wouldn't reveal the identity of the doctor. 'When he next comes here, I'll introduce you to him,' he smiled.

'That's what Jane said! Am I never to know who he is?' Laughing, David changed the subject and asked if she still owned her flat.

'Yes, I do – why?'

'Do you want to sell it? Only I've got nowhere to live.'

'Live here, with me!'

'You want me here? After all . . .'

'Yes, on one condition. Well, several, actually.'

'Go on.'

'Firstly, you can only live here as my husband.'

'Marriage! Marry you?'

'Yes – you don't know how much I've missed you. I didn't really know myself until today. They call it love, I think.'

Stunned, David took her in his arms and kissed her full lips. Moving to the sofa, she unbuttoned his shirt, kissing and licking his chest, his stomach, before releasing his belt and tugging his trousers down to claim her long-awaited prize. The stranger within, the real Jackie, had surfaced again. But now the change was permanent, the stranger no longer a stranger.

'I've been dreaming of this,' she breathed, taking his

long, thick penis between her lips.

'So have I!' he gasped as she pulled the loose skin back and ran her tongue round the swollen knob, moving her head up and down the full length of his shaft as she cupped his balls in her hands. All too soon he was shuddering and pumping his sperm into her throat as he groped under her skirt for her soft lips. Sucking and mouthing as a babe at the breasts, she brought out every last drop of his fruits before lying back and opening her wet groove to his appreciative and very hungry gaze.

'God, you're very wet!' he exclaimed, kneeling between her open legs. 'And still shaved!' Licking up her cream, he located her clitoris and expertly stiffened it, breathing his love for her as he sucked out its full length. She gasped, delirious with the pleasure between her swollen lips, the sensations deep within her hot cunt. Wrapping her legs around his head, she gasped again and poured her juices out as her orgasm exploded within his mouth and coursed its way through her trembling body.

Without wasting a second, he pulled her naked lips apart with his thumbs to present his purple knob to her portal. 'I've been dreaming of this, too,' he murmured as he drove the head inside her hot body until it touched the end of her tightening tube. 'This is something that Jane can't give you.'

Placing his hands beneath her knees, he lifted her legs high in the air to expose her full lips, so tightly encompassing his glistening shaft as it slid in and out. 'God, that's nice!' she cried as her whole body quivered in response to his every pounding thrust. Reaching under her legs, she supported his swinging balls in her warm hand and closed her eyes. Drifting into a swirling pool of sexual ecstasy, she let out a long, low moan of gratitude as her sheath tightened around the bulging shaft and her clitoris engorged.

Ramming the depths of her body, her being, the knob burst and filled her womb with its hot liquid as her own orgasm erupted. Throwing her head from side to side, she cried out again, losing herself, her senses, as she left her body and reached her heaven. Gasping, heaving, satisfied as the swell subsided, they finally lay still, their mouths locked, his penis deep in her vagina.

'What are the other conditions?' David asked as he withdrew his shaft and rested his head on her warm mound.

'I run the business, no more robberies, and you'll only cane me when I ask for it – and not too hard.'

'I do believe you're asking for it now,' he laughed, taking her hand and pulling her from the sofa. 'Come on, *Mrs Blackwell*, downstairs to meet the doctor!'

'Like this?' Jane whispered, her mood swinging as she ran her fingers up and down the girl's opening valley.

'Yes, yes. Ah, ah, that's nice. It brings back fond memories of Nicky. She used to push her fingers inside me and wiggle them.'

'Like this?' Jane asked, pushing three fingers into the hot wetness between her dark, swollen lips.

'Ah, yes, yes. And she would pinch my little breast buds and rub my spot until . . . Until . . . Ah, that's it, that's it!' she cried as Jane massaged her long, hard clitoris and Jackie sucked on each erect nipple in turn.

Bringing her close to her climax, Jane moved between her legs and kissed her inner thighs while Jackie kissed her smooth stomach. 'Did Nicky ever do this to you?' Jackie asked, placing Rosita's thighs either side of Jane's head to expose her wet valley to Jane's rolling eyes.

'No, no, she didn't,' she gasped.

'Did she do this?' Jane asked, running her tongue up the length of her creamy slit to her full rosebud clitoris.

'God, no! Ah, no, never!'

'Or this?' Jackie whispered, pulling apart her own pussy lips and lowering her open body over the girl's gasping mouth.

Rosita could only writhe and moan as the girls took her to ecstasy. Her juices flooded Jane's mouth as she licked and drank while Jackie poured her milky cream into Rosita's thirsty mouth as they shuddered and reached their goals in unison. Gasping and choking, Rosita brought her knees up to put an end to the orgasm of her life, but Jane continued to lick and caress the long protrusion until it exploded again, pumping its euphoria into the depths of the girl's womb, her soul. Jackie pressed her bud into her mouth again as she came for the second time, and then moved up to fill her with so much sticky mouth. Bending forward, she buried her own mouth in the hairy bush and lapped between the swollen lips. Their clitorises hard, they licked until their cream pumped from their holes and they erupted into a euphoric sexual ecstasy. Chewing on Jackie's inner lips, Fiona rolled and sucked the flaps deep into her mouth, tasting, savouring the creamy wetness until she lay her head back in exhaustion. Gently caressing each other's shrinking buds with their tongues, they lay satisfied and relaxed until their drained bodies had recovered.

Releasing Fiona, Jackie became despondent. She would soon be left alone again in the house with no-one to talk to, no-one to love. Watching the woman pack her bag and don her scruffy coat, she asked when she would like her next appointment. 'I'll ring you,' she said, pulling two hundred pounds from her bag. 'Thanks for the session, I really enjoyed it.'

Alone again, Jackie flopped onto the lounge sofa and thought about Rosita and Eric and how they were probably entwined in lust. Then she remembered Jane and wondered where she was – and if she'd ever come home. Mick Johnstone and his wife, Helen, too. They were probably naked in bed, licking and sucking between each other's legs, drifting, yet again, into the warm ecstasy of orgasm. Loneliness could now strike her down within seconds, quickly followed by deep despair.

'Shit!' she cried, leaping to her feet and pacing the floor. 'I'm not used to my own company any more.' Moving to the window, she pulled the curtain aside and gazed out onto the cold street. A few cars were crawling along the snow-covered road. A young couple, hand in hand, wandered into the pub and Jackie smiled. It seemed to entice her as she stared at the brightly coloured lights hanging around the windows, the doorway. Feeling low, discontented, her clitoris calling and her cunt yearning, she changed into her short skirt and ventured across the road.

Tim was still behind the bar and she wondered if he ever went home, or if he had a home to go to. Perceiving her mood, he smiled and poured her usual gin and tonic. 'I'm not sure I want a drink,' she sighed. 'It will probably make me feel worse.'

'It's up to you,' he replied, placing the glass on the bar before turning to serve the happy young couple. Jackie gazed at the man and then the girl, wondering how often they made love and in which position. Opening her thighs for a reaction from the man, she wondered, too, if they indulged in oral sex and pictured his hard, throbbing penis filling her small mouth with sperm.

Feasting on Jackie's naked lips from the corner of his eye, the man quickly turned his back to the girl. She was busy rummaging in her bag; he was safe, and he looked again, not sure whether to believe what he was seeing. Jackie smiled and let her thighs fall open further, revealing the full length of her tight, wet slit, resting comfortably on the padded stool. Catching her eye, he returned her smile before glancing back to the girl.

Choosing a table where he'd have a good view, the man made sure his girlfriend sat with her back to his treat. Enjoying the game, Jackie crossed her legs for a few minutes, allowing his tension to build. Then, as he looked on in anticipation, she opened them fully. Before going home, she decided to give him something to remember and, when Tim's back was turned, stretching her legs to the hilt, she peeled her lips apart. Choking on his beer, the man stared at her wet, pink folds. But the show was over and slipping from her stool Jackie made for the door.

'I could earn a fortune,' she laughed as she crossed the

Sadistic Impulse
by Jack Spender

Professor Jack Spender is hired to teach a group of amoral sorority honeys in the French Riviera, but must also regiment their heedless sexual frolics under the brooding, lustful shadow of the Marquis de Sade. More devastating yet, Spender knows that beneath the surface glitz and fleshly opulence of the Azure Coast lies older traditions of Greek orgiastic rites. Continuing his passion for the beautiful Mlle. Kore, he finds a "yearning libidinal welcome rooted in the very earth itself."

Eveline II
by Anonymous

Eveline II continues the delightfully erotic tale of a defiant aristocratic young English woman who throws off the mantle of respectability in order to revel in life's sexual pleasures. After returning to her paternal home in London in order to escape the boredom of marriage, she plunges with total abandon into self-indulgence and begins to "convert" other young ladies to her wanton ways.

Elaine Cox
by Richard Manton

Elaine Cox is an adolescent tomboy of short skirts, bare thighs and snub-nosed insolence. Her misconduct puts her under the command of her middle-aged admirer, and as punishment and seduction alternate, a dark romance begins in the soundless vaults and tiled discipline rooms. Soon Elaine is a tomboy well-chastised, the recipient of passionate punishments.

Slaves of the Hypnotist
by Anonymous

Harry, son of a well-to-do English country family, has set out to "conquer" all the females within his immediate reach. But no sooner does he begin his exploits than he encounters the imperious beauty, Davina, who enslaves him through her remarkable power of hypnotism. Thus entranced, Harry indulges in every aspect of eroticism known to man or woman.

The Sensualists
by Frank Mace

Who are these young, beautiful women who willingly display themselves in the most degrading and defenseless position for their sex? And who is this man who provides them with prolonged spasms of ecstasy, leaving them whimpering, limp and grateful things? They are otherwise ordinary people, but share the same relentless need to reach the heights of sensual pleasure by submitting to the lowest of degradations. Marc Merlin can unleash their erupting sexuality—but by appointment only.

Yakuza Perfume
by Akahige Namban

While still recovering from their ordeal in the Kiso Mountains of Central Japan, Japanese American brothers Jim and Andy are surprised by a female agent of the Clouds and Rain Company who seeks refuge with them. After she leaves they are accused of having stolen the secret of the sexually intoxicating pheromone perfume that is the basis for the company's power. They set out to find the real thieves and prove their innocence, while embarking on lustful adventures along the way.

Rough Caress
by James Holmes

This erotic collection tells of the strange seduction of Isabel Seaton, who keeps her passion corked like fine champagne, under the mistaken notion that it, too, will improve with time. But writhing in the caresses of her abductors, her illusion is shattered as she succumbs to quivering bliss. There are also Miss Clarke and Miss Franks, two young maids who inventively satisfy each other's rampant lust—as well as the pubescent passions of squealing schoolgirls, to whom they apply the birch.

Mistress of the East
by Dean Barrett

Captured by Taiping women warriors in China, a young lieutenant, Thomas Rowley, is flagellated into a docile and obedient slave. As he becomes immersed in the exotic world of the Taiping warriors, he witnesses the carnal needs of these fiercely powerful women. He becomes enraptured with the beautiful and indomitable Sweet Little Sister, and is introduced to new realms of erotic pleasure.

Available now

Images of Ironwood
by Don Winslow

Ironwood. The very name of that unique institution remains strongly evocative, even to this day. In this, the third volume of the famous Ironwood trilogy, the reader is once again invited to share in the Ironwood experience. *Images of Ironwood* presents selected scenes of unrelenting sensuality, of erotic longing, and occasionally, of those bizarre proclivities which touch the outer fringe of human sexuality.

In these pages we renew our acquaintance with James, the lusty entrepreneur who now directs the Ironwood enterprise; with his bevy of young female students being trained in the many ways of love; and with Cora Blasingdale, the cold remote mistress of discipline. The images presented here capture the essence of the Ironwood experience.

Available Now

Ironwood
by Don Winslow

The harsh reality of disinheritance and poverty vanish from the world of our young narrator, James, when he discovers he's in line for a choice position at an exclusive and very strict school for girls. Ironwood becomes for him a fantastic dream world where discipline knows few boundaries, and where his role as master affords him free reign with the willing, well-trained and submissive young beauties in his charge. As overseer of Ironwood, Cora Blasingdale is well-equipped to keep her charges in line. Under her guidance the saucy girls are put through their paces and tamed. And for James, it seems, life has just begun.

Order These Selected Blue Moon Titles

Souvenirs From a Boarding School	$7.95	Shades of Singapore	$7.95
The Captive	$7.95	Images of Ironwood	$7.95
Ironwood Revisited	$7.95	What Love	$7.95
Sundancer	$7.95	Sabine	$7.95
Julia	$7.95	An English Education	$7.95
The Captive II	$7.95	The Encounter	$7.95
Shadow Lane	$7.95	Tutor's Bride	$7.95
Belle Sauvage	$7.95	A Brief Education	$7.95
Shadow Lane III	$7.95	Love Lessons	$7.95
My Secret Life	$9.95	Shogun's Agent	$7.95
Our Scene	$7.95	The Sign of the Scorpion	$7.95
Chrysanthemum, Rose & the Samurai	$7.95	Women of Gion	$7.95
Captive V	$7.95	Mariska I	$7.95
Bombay Bound	$7.95	Secret Talents	$7.95
Sadopaideia	$7.95	Beatrice	$7.95
The New Story of O	$7.95	S&M: The Last Taboo	$8.95
Shadow Lane IV	$7.95	"Frank" & I	$7.95
Beauty in the Birch	$7.95	Lament	$7.95
Laura	$7.95	The Boudoir	$7.95
The Reckoning	$7.95	The Bitch Witch	$7.95
Ironwood Continued	$7.95	Story of O	$5.95
In a Mist	$7.95	Romance of Lust	$9.95
The Prussian Girls	$7.95	Ironwood	$7.95
Blue Velvet	$7.95	Virtue's Rewards	$5.95
Shadow Lane V	$7.95	The Correct Sadist	$7.95
Deep South	$7.95	The New Olympia Reader	$15.95

Visit our website at www.bluemoonbooks.com

ORDER FORM
Attach a separate sheet for additional titles.

Title	Quantity	Price
_____	____	_____
_____	____	_____
_____	____	_____
_____	____	_____

Shipping and Handling (see charges below) _____

Sales tax (in CA and NY) _____

Total _____

Name _____

Address _____

City _____ State _____ Zip _____

Daytime telephone number _____

❏ Check   ❏ Money Order   (US dollars only. No COD orders accepted.)

Credit Card # _____ Exp. Date _____

❏ MC   ❏ VISA   ❏ AMEX

Signature _____

(if paying with a credit card you must sign this form.)

Shipping and Handling charges:*

Domestic: $4 for 1st book, $.75 each additional book. International: $5 for 1st book, $1 each additional book
*rates in effect at time of publication. Subject to Change.

Mail order to Publishers Group West, Attention: Order Dept., 1700 Fourth St., Berkeley, CA 94710,
or fax to (510) 528-3444.

PLEASE ALLOW 4-6 WEEKS FOR DELIVERY. ALL ORDERS SHIP VIA 4TH CLASS MAIL.

Look for Blue Moon Books at your favorite local bookseller
or from your favorite online bookseller.